Through  and $T H \perp N$

A Cat Leigh and Marci Welles Crime Novel

by Donna M. Carbone

Through Thick and Thin is a work of fiction. Names, characters, businesses, organizations, events and incidents either are the product of the author's imagination or are used fictitiously. Any references to historical events, real people, living or dead, or real locales are used fictitiously.

Acknowledgements

Many thanks to my family and friends and all of the people who have been forced to read and re-read chapters whether out of loyalty or fear, especially Kathy Banfield—a Jersey girl par excellence—and Takis Pepe, a very talented writer with a bright future. Their unfailing encouragement, editorial guidance, proof reading and copyediting skills kept my language from being bothersome and boring.

Special thanks to my husband, Mike, and our children, Michael and Jessica, who put up with my long absences while locked away in my office and who encouraged me to "keep writing" even while they wondered if they would ever see me again. I also want to thank Jessica and Mary Bedwell Bain, a daughter of my heart if not of my loins, for allowing me to use them and their lives as inspiration for this story. You are two of the bravest women I know—my personal heroes—and I'm proud to introduce you both to the world. I know that my readers will love you the way I love you—with all my heart and soul.

PROLOGUE

October 2006

"I hate death. I especially hate the people who make death their life's work."

Cat Leigh, 30, but looking like a fresh-faced college cheerleader, sat on her living room sofa muttering while sifting through a stack of 8x10 glossies. Her long blonde hair hung down around her face like a curtain, hiding the piercing blue eyes that stared hard at the images of death before her. If appearances are deceiving, then Cat was the ultimate chameleon. Dressed in navy blue Capri pants, navy and white stripped short-sleeve cotton sweater and red low-heeled sandals, she appeared ready for a day of boating not one spent examining corpses and interviewing murder suspects.

One by one she held a magnifying glass to the photos and looked for something—anything—that would put an end to the reign of terror that had taken hold in Palm Beach County and, in particular, her hometown of Palm Beach Gardens, Florida and the neighboring town of Jupiter. Larger and more heavily populated West Palm Beach, a city to the south, was also caught in the grip of this diabolical crime spree.

The Kalendar Killer, christened by a local reporter with degrees in both English Literature and Theology, had left his victims displayed like gifts wrapped in banners celebrating the holiday of the month. The reporter, not content to merely slap the madman with a media worthy nickname, chose to use the ecclesiastic spelling... a not-so-subtle message that God had been missing in action when the crimes were committed.

So far, there had been five murders: Janice Handera, 47, married, stabbed through the throat with a nine-inch steel florist's pick on Mother's Day; Wallace Lanier, 60, a deadbeat dad, buried up to his neck and "stoned" to death with baseballs on Father's Day; PFC

Timothy Varde, 23, bayoneted on July 4th; Peter Colangelo, 63, retired president of the local Electrical Workers Union, hung with a heavy duty extension cord from a Gumbo Limbo tree on Labor Day; and Amber Culp, 28, a palm reader with one of the smaller traveling circuses that made their way up and down the east coast, suffocated with tarot cards shoved down her throat on Halloween.

No connections had been found between the victims, no usable evidence was uncovered at the scenes and other than Lanier's history of non-support for his three children, the victims appeared to be decent people. The holiday banners in which the victims were wrapped were a dime a dozen in every party store in the country and on the internet. None of the local stores had surveillance video and, since hundreds of people had bought the banners... well, to quote one store owner, "You think I can remember every person who bought decorations over the past year. Think again!" If there was anything to be thankful for, it was that no murders occurred in August—a month with no recognized holidays.

Located at the north end of Palm Beach County, Palm Beach Gardens and Jupiter, the formerly quaint fishing villages on growth hormones, had zip codes that were popular winter destinations for wealthy retirees who called the northeast home only during the spring and summer. Come November, thousands of snowbirds, as they were less than affectionately called by the locals, arranged for their BMWs and Mercedes to be shipped to their temporary residences in the Sunshine State via auto transport. They booked first class tickets on not-so-first-class airlines and flew south before a single flake of white marred their manicured lawns; firm believers that it was better to sweat than to shiver.

For those fanatics who carried a golf club bag like a dowager's hump, Palm Beach Gardens was heaven on earth. There were 12 USGA rated courses within the city limits and the Professional Golfers Association of America was headquartered on the Avenue of Champions inside PGA National Resort and Spa, one of two sites which annually hosted the Honda Classic; the other being the Country Club at Mirasol.

Both Palm Beach Gardens and Jupiter were home to some very famous people in show business and the sports world, and Jupiter also had the distinction of being rated the Ninth Happiest Seaside Town in

America by Coastal Living. With the potential for more murders hanging heavy in the air, there were no waits to tee off, the driving ranges and putting greens were empty, and the smiles of North County residents had turned into grimaces of fear.

Even the citizens of West Palm Beach, for whom the sound of sirens was a nightly occurrence, were behaving less apathetically than usual. Many were spending their evenings at home, which was putting a crimp in revenues at popular nightclubs and bars on trendy Clematis Street and at restaurants in upscale City Place. With each murder, the economy was becoming as big a concern for local government as crime statistics.

Headlines on the front page of the Palm Beach Post, the forever shrinking newspaper which was little more than a directory of new and used automobiles for sale, fairly shouted demands for answers. In every edition, the mayors and councils of every city in the county were quoted hurling verbal assaults on Sheriff Mike Brickshaw and some were threatening to drop the Palm Beach County Sheriff's Office from their payrolls.

Brickshaw's constant assurances that PBSO homicide detectives were working overtime to discover the identity of the Kalendar Killer had done little to assuage their concerns. The Sheriff himself had been issuing a few threats, telling his staff if he heard any of them using the made-for-tv sobriquet he would fire them.

Among local law enforcement and across the country, a deep dislike for crime shows such as the popular Las Vegas based CSI had been intensifying over the past few years. The public's belief that the technology seen on these shows actually existed had put an added burden on already overworked staff to solve crimes quickly.

Although the FBI's Integrated Automated Fingerprint Identification System could provide results in as little as 27 minutes, DNA processing could take weeks to months and sometimes years. When you considered that an estimated 400,000 rape kits were waiting to be processed nationwide, crime solving took on a whole new perspective.

Sheriff Brickshaw was often heard to state in his *I dare you to contradict me* voice, "Wouldn't it be wonderful if crimes could be solved in the time between commercials for urinary incontinence and erectile dysfunction."

Unselfconsciously, Cat spoke aloud to Kneesaa, the little black and white Shih Tzu perched beside her. Despite the dog's powder puff appearance, she was more protective of Cat than any ten-times-her-size Rottweiler and, judging by the attentive look in her eyes, Kneesaa understood every word her mistress was saying.

"We need a miracle, NeeNee," Cat whispered to Kneesaa, using her nickname for the dog. "What if we don't find this guy before Thanksgiving?"

The simple act of communication seemed to have a calming effect on Cat, who cradled the dog in her arms and buried her face in the scruff of her neck. A few seconds later, the dog squirmed away and Cat once again began to scowl. She returned to looking at the photos, frustration obvious in the Frisbee-like way she tossed each one to the floor.

The carpeting around Cat's feet was littered with throw-aways—those pictures that documented the depravity of mankind while providing nothing new in the way of hope. Newspapers from weeks past, highlighted in yellow and circled in black, were stacked on the cushion next to her. So intent was she on looking for clues that the banging of the apartment complex maintenance man installing a new air conditioner in the kitchen was like a cotton ball bouncing on concrete.

So many people had tried to fix the rusting parts that Cat had grown immune to the sound of wrenches and saws hacking away at the old plumbing running through the walls of her second floor unit. Weekly complaints over the last three months had finally gotten her the result she wanted—a new a/c with the power to keep her apartment and her temper cool even on the hottest of days.

Only the ringing of the maintenance man's cell phone, which played an offensive rap tune with each incoming call, got Cat's attention. With irritation, she mumbled aloud, "Why that song?"

The droning sounds of the morning news anchors coming from the television were mere white noise until the voice of one of Cat's favorite "shiny girls" broke through her concentration. Shiny girls—that was what Cat called the overly sunny personalities of the local female weather forecasters who were more annoying than informative. Usually this was the point at which she turned off the news, but on this morning Cat reached for the remote and amped up the volume as the map of south Florida filled the screen.

"For a few days, our normally cool October weather will be replaced with the sweltering heat of summer so dress accordingly," bubbled the early morning Miss Shiny, who was clad in a too tight, low cut dress left over from some long forgotten holiday party.

"Wardrobe advice from a wannabe actress. I guess she doesn't own a mirror, NeeNee. That outfit is better suited to New Year's Eve at a strip club than morning television."

Cat picked up Kneesaa's rubber chew toy from the floor and threw it at the widescreen across the room. She shook her head in wry amazement and reached again for Kneesaa. "Well, NeeNee, shall we take bets on how Marci will be dressed today?"

The look in Kneesaa's eyes seemed to say, "You have to ask?"

Cat clicked off the television and returned to looking at the photographs, effectively blocking out the world around her. Deeply engrossed, she failed to hear the maintenance man announce his pending departure.

"Miss."

The tall, muscular black man in his early twenties adjusted the Bluetooth in his ear and pulled the brim of his baseball cap low on his face as he called to Cat from the hallway between the kitchen and living room. When she did not answer, he raised his voice slightly and tried again. "Miss, I'm leaving. If you have any more problems, please call the office."

Again Cat didn't acknowledge his presence and, again, he raised his voice. Kneesaa growled in response to its aggressive tone. Cat looked at NeeNee, who was staring into the hallway. Following the dog's gaze, she saw but didn't make eye contact with the repairman as she offered a response. His back was now towards her as he prepared to exit the apartment. "Did you say something?"

The maintenance man spoke over his shoulder. "I'm leaving. If you have any problems, call the office."

Cat, who had already turned back to studying the crime scene photos, waved a hand in acknowledgement as the maintenance man opened the front door. "Thanks."

The next thing Cat heard was a scream, which barely caused her to flinch.

"Yikes!" Cat's partner, Marci Welles, yelped as she stood in the doorway, blocking the maintenance man's exit.

Cat looked at Kneesaa and rolled her eyes. With photographs still in hand, she called to her dearest friend to enter. "Nice of you to wake the neighborhood, Marci. Come on in."

Short and pleasingly plump Marci was dressed in a man-tailored, long-sleeve shirt, suit jacket and heavy rubber soled tie shoes. Her boyish haircut was softened by long bangs which framed mischievous dark eyes and a pert little nose. Freckles were scattered over her cheeks like soot that had drifted on the wind. Her raspy voice held a tinge of suppressed laughter. "You scared the crap out of me," Marci joked with the repairman who, with head lowered, side stepped around her. Mumbling, "Sorry," he moved quickly down the stairs. "No problem. Now, at least, I have an excuse for the grey streaks in my hair."

The maintenance man didn't respond. Marci shrugged her shoulders at his rudeness and moved into the apartment, closing the door behind her.

"Are you ready?" Marci called to Cat as she strode into the living room. "They're waiting for us."

"Yeah, I'm just going over the shots from the Blowing Rocks murder."

Marci threw a manila envelope onto the coffee table. "Here. Look at these. I guarantee they won't make you cringe."

As Cat opened the envelope, Marci picked up Kneesaa and rubbed her belly. She directed her comments to the dog but the intended recipient was well within earshot. "NeeNee, your mommy needs to get a life."

Cat stuck her tongue out at Marci as she withdrew another stack of photos from the envelope. A huge smile crossed her face. "Oh, Marci, these are precious."

"Yup. Your goddaughter is one cute kid even if I do say so myself."

"You and Ian are so lucky."

"You'll have one of your own before long."

"Maybe."

"Definitely," Marci assured her with a punch to the shoulder. "But right now we've got a hot one waiting for us downtown." Marci gave Kneesaa a final rub on the belly and laid her back on the sofa.

Rising from the sofa, Cat gave Marci's outfit the once over. "Hot being the definitive word, Marci. You do know that it's 96 degrees outside, don't you?"

"Your point?"

"You're dressed for winter—in Vermont."

"I look professional."

"I'll remind you of that statement in an hour when you're struggling to breathe and dripping like a melting icicle." Cat turned and headed for the front door. Kneesaa followed her. "Sorry, sweet pea. No time for a walk now. Be a good girl while I'm gone."

In the small alcove off the entranceway, Cat opened the drawer of an antique credenza. She removed a holstered gun and a gold detective's shield on a lanyard. She took the gun from the holster, snapped in a clip and slid the gun back into the holster before dropping it into her satchel, which was hanging on a nearby coat rack. She slipped the lanyard around her neck and tucked the badge inside her shirt. Marci, anxious to get on the road, already had her hand on the door. Cat stopped her as she was about to step onto the porch.

"Are you sure you don't want to change into something cooler?"

"I'm fine. This is my signature look."

"Whatever you say, Nanook. Lead the way."

CHAPTER ONE

September 2007

Detective Marcassy Welles—Marci to her friends, and Detective Jessica Leigh— affectionately called Cat—had been a big part of each other's lives long before they became partners in the Homicide Division of the Palm Beach County Sheriff's Office. Best friends since freshman year at Wellington High School, the differences in their physical appearance were often fodder for jokes cruel and kind perpetrated by their classmates. From the beginning, they had watched each other's backs at all times. Pity the poor fool who tried to hurt either one of them be it with a gun, a knife or sweet words that broke a trusting heart.

Known for being quick on the comeback, brunette Marci was round and short—4'11" but adamant that she was five feet tall. Her turned-up nose and laughing hazel eyes gave her an impish appearance, which many a criminal had learned had nothing to do with her unswerving dedication to upholding the law. Her relentless pursuit of those who didn't share her penchant for order and justice was legendary.

The more serious Cat was a statuesque 5'10" with nearly waist length blonde hair and big blue oval-shaped eyes. Those eyes were the reason for the nickname her Aunt Annie had bestowed upon her when just a toddler. "Jessicat" had been shortened to "Cat" as the lithe little girl grew into a lovely young woman.

Cat, like Marci, saw the world in black and white. What was wrong was wrong and what was right was right. There was no grey area where excuses justified hurting another human being except in self-defense. Both women were resolute in their pursuit of those who thumbed their noses at the justice system, rarely finding a reason to cut an offender any slack.

Eighteen months earlier, Marci, 31, and her husband, Ian, had adopted a beautiful baby girl, Sonora Leslie. Having waited a long time for the fulfillment of this dream, their lives were now complete.

Cat, whose beauty had intimidated many men, was finally in a serious relationship that appeared to be heading for the marriage aisle. Having recently crossed into the third decade of her life, she had struggled to find Mr. Right and feared that her sudden good fortune was just a nasty bit of teasing on the part of fate. The two couples spent most of their downtime together and had forged a bond that was titanium strong.

In spite of all the ugliness the women saw daily, they had refused to let disillusion creep into their souls and change their naturally kind and caring personalities. Although they strove to always see the good in people, they were not adverse to drawing their guns and using them when necessary. Both were thankful that so far in their careers they had not had to shoot to kill but knowing the possibility existed, their marksmanship skills were exemplary.

Cat and Marci were different from most of the people in their social circle in that their self-esteem was not raised by frequenting the latest hot spots which sucked a wallet dry with hype and hand stamps. They preferred beer and burgers over the fancy meals served at popular City Place haunts and at restaurants on Snob Island—their name for Palm Beach.

Eight years earlier, they had joined the Palm Beach County Sheriff's Office and, after four years on the streets, had been promoted to detectives in the Homicide Division. In the early years, Marci and Cat often worked separately, but their Sergeant soon realized that, while alone they were formidable, together they were an unstoppable force.

The majority of their peers respected them for their ethics and for working their butts off to put criminals behind bars. There were a few, however, who felt diminished by successful women in the male-dominated profession of law enforcement. Those men assuaged their egos by referring to Marci and Cat as "Thick" and "Thin," a reference to the women's appearance that said more about the men than the women they were describing. Cat and Marci referred to them collectively as "the assholes."

On this Labor Day morning, the sky was glazed with golden hues when Marci and Cat pulled into the lot at Coral Cove Park on Jupiter Island. The sand blowing in from the beach covered the macadam, obscuring the white lines that marked off the parking spaces. Not that finding an actual parking space would have been possible. Between the six Jupiter PD vehicles, two ambulances and what appeared to be at least 40 privately-owned automobiles, the place resembled Sound Advice Amphitheater in the aftermath of a heavy metal concert.

Marci brought the late model Ford Crown Victoria to a stop on the grass that cushioned the children's playground. She and Cat sat quietly, mentally preparing themselves for another day of murder and mayhem. In the glow of the newly awakened dawn, four swings moved rhythmically to and fro, as though ghostly sprites were watching them, witnesses to what had been and what was yet to be.

Marci stared out the windshield as she ruminated aloud. "Two things I really hate—September and this."

"This what?"

With a nod of her head, Marci indicated the swings while nibbling a hangnail on her index finger. "This… the playground so close to a death. Just doesn't seem right."

"That's the new mommy in you talking. Before Sonora was born, you never noticed the grisly stuff."

Marci's response was muffled as she continued to chew on her hangnail.

"I can't understand you if you talk with your fingers in your mouth. Who's the baby—you or Sonora?"

"I was just thinking." Marci removed a wet index finger from her mouth and pointed it at Cat. "Do you remember last Labor Day? We spent it at Blowing Rocks investigating one of the Kalendar Killer murders."

"Peter Colangelo. His memory did cross my mind. Let's hope whatever we find here isn't as gruesome."

"I think of those five people a lot. Probably, too often."

"Me, too. That was a tough seven months. Tough for us. Tougher for the families of the victims."

Marci answered by crossing her middle finger over the still wet index finger and holding them up for Cat to see. "Are you sure you're ready to go back to work?"

"Don't let the black eyes and bandages fool you. I was ready seven weeks ago when you kicked me out of the office and told me I had to rest."

"Did you?"

"Rest?"

"I know. Stupid question." Marci resumed nibbling while staring at the swings a few minutes longer.

Seven weeks earlier:

When Marci arrived at police headquarters, she found her partner sitting at her desk staring at a computer screen. Just two days after a brutal attack, Cat's appearance was shocking. Her long hair was pulled back into a pony tail revealing a badly bruised and disfigured face. Her lips and nose were swollen; her eyes were black. There was a large bandage around her neck; blood oozing slowly through the gauze. Cat's left shoulder was immobilized in a sling.

"What the hell are you doing here?"

"I'm fine… other than looking like the Elephant Man."

"You are not fine, Cat. You need rest. It's only been two days."

"I said I'm fine."

"You're supposed to talk to the department shrink before you can be cleared for duty."

"I cleared myself. What evidence do you have so far? Did you talk to the women in the management office?"

"I really do wish you would go home." Marci pleaded with Cat only to be ignored. "Okay. Have it your way. Nothing. We've learned nothing. The office manager claimed they don't have a maintenance man who resembles your attacker. She has no idea who he was."

"How could that be? How would he know my a/c wasn't working if not through the management office?"

"She's lying. She's trying to protect their corporate ass."

Cat sat quietly, deep in thought. Officers and clerical staff walked by, shooting veiled glances in her direction. Some proffered sympathetic smiles. She scowled back at them. A cadet brought a cup of coffee, put it on the desk without saying a word and hurried away. Cat mumbled her thanks and sipped carefully from the cup; the pain from the deep cuts inside her mouth sending shivers across her shoulders as the hot coffee flowed over them.

"Please go home and get some rest."

"We have other cases. Death doesn't take a vacation because a police officer gets attacked. You work the active ones. I'll work mine."

"You're too close to this."

"I'll do desk duty. You do the field work. I need this, Marci. I need to stay busy."

"Okay. I'm sure you've gone through the mug shots. Anything?"

"No. There's no one in our data base who resembles that bastard."

"You're sure."

"His face is seared into my brain, Marci. I'm sure."

"Once the DNA sample is processed, we can run it through CODIS."

"Unless I'm his first…"

"Then, let's make you his last. Now, go home."

#

Marci shook off the remainder of her reverie and returned to the present. She exhaled a deep sigh and reached for the door handle. As the lock clicked open, she turned to Cat. "You can't pretend the attack didn't happen. You almost died. That's not something you can ignore."

"I'm not ignoring it, Marci. I'm just not letting it rule my life. I'm fine."

Marci nodded her understanding, a finger stuck between her teeth. She gave the door a push with her foot. It swung open and back, crushing her leg and forcing her to bite down hard on her finger. "Shit!"

"When are you going to learn not to do that?"

"Kick the door?"

"Yes, and chew at your hangnails. Get a manicure."

"I'm never getting another manicure." Marci threw a look at Cat that needed no explanation.

"You're ridiculous."

"But irresistible." Marci continued to suck on her finger as though it was a lollipop. "That hurt."

"I'm surprised you have any feeling left in your fingers. Actually, I'm surprised you have any fingers at all the way you bite them."

"I still have the ability to raise one in a single digit salute."

Marci made a fist in front of Cat's face and slowly began to lift her middle finger. Cat playfully smacked Marci's hand out of the way.

"If it wasn't for me always nagging you," Cat defended her behavior, "you'd have ten bloody stumps by now; and you'd be wearing your wedding ring through your nose."

"I know you're talking. I can see your lips moving, but I don't hear a sound. Let's go to work. Neither the law nor the dead like to be kept waiting."

"In my experience, waiting is all the dead will be doing for the rest of eternity so a few more minutes won't matter," Cat informed her while reaching across the seat and pulling Marci's hand out of her mouth. "Don't be so stubborn. If you keep doing that, you're going to get an infection."

"Been doing it since high school—ever since I found out that chubby girls don't make the cheerleading squad."

"You tried out just to annoy Tammy Burns. You never wanted to be a cheerleader."

"I hated Tammy Burns and…" Marci bit skin from her finger, "…my feelings were hurt."

"They were not! You enjoyed every moment she suffered watching you mangle the cheers. Please! Stop biting your finger."

Marci picked the piece of skin from her tongue and flicked it into the air. Cat gagged, "That's disgusting!"

"I hate it when you're preachy."

"You hate it when I'm right."

"That, too."

Through the rearview mirror, Marci saw the coroner's car and van vying for a spot. The last to arrive, the medical examiner and his assistants were forced to park at the curb, half in and half out of the park entrance. "G's here."

"Thanks for the warning."

Marci tossed the car keys to Cat with her usual request, "Hold on to these for me, will ya? I don't have any pockets. And… be nice to G."

Cat grabbed her satchel from the floor and dropped the keys into it as Marci gave the door another shove; this time putting out her hand to stop it from wreaking further damage to her leg. One foot emerged from the driver's side wearing sensible rubber soled shoes with laces neatly tied in a bow.

Dressed in her usual dark pants, man-tailored shirt and blazer, Marci stood beside the car and removed a crumbled tissue from the sleeve of her jacket. On the front of her shirt, the beginnings of a wet spot could be seen where her bra met her rib cage. She pushed her already damp bangs out of her eyes and held them in place with a bobbie pin she retrieved from the car's no longer used ash tray. Wiping the tissue over her face, she lamented to Cat, "I hate September!"

"You already said that."

From the passenger side of the car, another foot emerged. Polished toes peeked out from low-heeled sling back pumps. Cat was dressed in light weight casual clothing and appeared perspiration free. Carefully applied makeup artfully concealed the remains of two black eyes, leaving what appeared to be dark circles from lack of sleep—a plausible explanation accepted by anyone familiar with Cat's dedication to her job. A surgical dressing wrapped around her throat was partially hidden by the collar of her shirt. Despite the bandage's wide width, the raw edges of a deep cut could be seen along the left side of Cat's neck.

Marci walked around the car and looked at Cat's feet with feigned annoyance. "You can't wear those shoes on the beach. Did you remember to bring something appropriate?"

"Appropriate? Like what? Combat boots?"

Cat indicated Marci's shoes with a nod of her head. She reached into her satchel and pulled out a pair of leather thongs. With a practiced step, she tossed her shoes into the car and slipped quickly into the sandals. "Don't worry. I've got my Dolce Vitas right here."

Marci rolled her eyes at Cat as she licked away the sweat dripping from her upper lip. "The model with the magnum—you kill me."

"Don't even say that in jest."

Her face showing instant regret, Marci apologized. "I'm sorry, Cat. You're so damned determined not to let the attack change you that sometimes I forget just how close you came to not being here."

"He got three and a half hours, Marci. He's not getting another minute. Can we go to work now?"

With the wind moaning softly over the dunes and through the palmettos, the two detectives walked side by side toward the bright ball of fire that ruled over the distant waves and the nearby shores. The sun was up, and its power was not to be denied.

"Damn, it's a frickin' scorcher!" Marci again wiped her face with the tissue hidden in the sleeve of her jacket.

"And going to get hotter but we've had this conversation many times over the years. If you weren't so thick headed..."

"I'm not thick headed. I'm professional."

"You're also a sweaty mess and, eventually, you'll be 'tinky." Cat waved her hand in front of her nose, mimicking Marci's 18-month-old daughter. Her voice accurately captured one of the few phrases the little girl could say.

Marci's laugh echoed across the parking lot as she dipped her head to her armpit, sniffed, and then spun around so that she was walking backwards. She lifted her arm and offered Cat a whiff. "Spring time fresh. Smell for yourself."

"No, thanks. Besides, I said 'eventually.' Springtime fresh will become summer stench in a few hours. Trust me."

Cat pulled her sunglasses from her pocket and slipped them

over her squinting eyes. "Did you remember to bring your Foster Grants, Ms. Professional?"

Before Marci could answer, Doctor Mark Geschwer, the much respected medical examiner who was called "G" by everyone, hailed them from the parking lot in his best Jerry Lewis impersonation. "Detective Ladies! Yoo hoo! Detective Ladies."

"Pretend you don't hear him." Cat, visibly cringing, urged Marci to keep walking.

"He's harmless."

A huge fan of the well-known comedian, G's imitations left much to be desired, but his attempts to mimic the king of clowns usually elicited laughs from department personnel. He was fond of saying that it was better to do a lousy impersonation of a comic than a great impersonation of a corpse.

"He drives me crazy." Cat hastened her steps. "I just don't get his fascination with Jerry Lewis. Jerry Lewis! Why can't he admire Richard Pryor?"

"Pryor's dead."

"Yeah, I know, and if G continues speaking in that annoying voice, I might set him on fire."

"Remind me not to piss you off."

G's voice called out to Marci and Cat again, still imitating Jerry Lewis.

"Walk faster," Cat urged, giving Marci a shove.

CHAPTER TWO

Leaving the paved parking lot, Marci and Cat stepped onto already searing sand that burned through the rubber soles of their shoes. Perspiration dripped from Marci's hairline; Cat was unaffected. Marci cursed as she struggled to walk and keep her balance. "Damn! It's hot."

"You're beginning to sound like a parrot. Every day is hot! It's summer! In Florida!" Cat's annoyance at the oft repeated references to the weather was obvious in her tone of voice.

"So, you just confirmed what I said earlier. I hate September."

"You hate June, July and August as well." Cat's face showed no concern for her partner's dilemma. "Hating summer isn't going to change anything. Changing your clothes might be effective."

"I hate all words that start with S... summer, September, sushi, sarcasm."

"Seriously? Sarcasm?"

"Okay. I love sarcasm but I hate salami and salmonella and..."

"You know what I hate... I hate it when I have to suffer because you insist on burning up inside that thermal suit you're wearing."

"It's professional attire, but I don't expect you to understand, Miss Never Breaks a Sweat."

"Hey, don't blame me if you always want to look all bad cop," Cat parried as Marci stumbled and fell into her.

What might appear to the casual observer to be discontent between the partners was in actuality their normal patter. Their conversations were often a give and take of soft barbs which only reinforced their friendship and ability to work together. They knew each other well... so well that they often read each other's thoughts.

"There's sand in my shoes! There's sand in my socks and on my pants!" Marci whined, holding onto Cat's arm to keep from falling spread eagle onto the beach. "You don't happen to have a dust buster in that suitcase you call a pocketbook, do you?"

As Marci bent down to knock sand out of her pant cuffs, Cat's hand disappeared inside her satchel. "I know how much you hate sand in your shoes and, by the way, sand and shoes are S words." Cat withdrew a pair of beach thongs and tossed them in Marci's direction. "Here. I knew you would need these. Just don't expect me to carry those boats you're wearing now."

"You're the best friend and partner ever," Marci gushed with exaggerated appreciation. Hopping from one foot to the other, she pulled off her shoes, stuffed her socks inside of them and quickly covered her scorched soles. "How do I look?"

"Like you're wearing my shoes."

Cat twisted her long hair into a bun at the back of her head and held it in place with a pen stuck through the middle. A flash from her left hand caught Marci's eye.

"What the hell is that?" Marci grabbed Cat's arm and stared at the ring on her finger.

"Kevin asked me to marry him."

"Holy shit! We've been together for over an hour and you didn't tell me?"

"I'm sorry. I just... I don't know."

"What don't you know?"

"Kevin is wonderful. I should be ecstatic, but I'm scared."

"After all you've been through, I'd be worried if you weren't a little scared."

"So, you don't think I'm crazy?"

"Sure. Sometimes. Just not now." Marci admired the large diamond on her partner's finger. "This thing is like the Rock of Gibraltar."

"Too big?"

"Really? Have you ever heard a woman complain that a diamond is too big?" Marci chewed on her hangnail as she interrogated Cat. "You do love him, right?"

Frustrated, Cat grabbed Marci's hand and held it tightly in her grip. "Please, stop doing that and, yes, I do."

Pulling free, Marci picked a piece of skin from her tongue and flicked it into the air. Cat, once again pretending to gag, pulled Marci close and heaved into the breast pocket of her jacket. Marci pushed her away. "Point taken, smart ass."

"Obviously, it isn't because you've got your finger in your mouth again! You don't even realize you're doing it."

"Enough about my fingers. If you love Kevin, trust your instincts. They haven't failed you yet. They won't now."

"It's just…"

"Listen, you're not going to feel safe until we catch that son of a bitch. And we will catch him."

"He's a ghost, Marci. I'm starting to lose hope of ever finding him."

#

Seven weeks earlier:

"Marci, help me. I've been raped."

There wasn't a day—not an hour—since Cat had spoken those words to her best friend and partner that she hadn't relived the details of her attack in gory Technicolor. Time hadn't numbed the emotional pain nor lessened her determination to put her assailant behind bars for life. The bruises to her body were healing; those to her soul were as raw as the day they had been inflicted.

Saturday, June 30, 2007 was the perfect day for sisterly bonding. Cat and Marci had always had a relationship that was more blood than water. Despite the obvious differences in their appearance, they believed that a DNA test would prove them to be twins beneath the skin.

Long planned and eagerly anticipated, that beautiful Florida morning was meant to be the beginning to a day of pampering and shopping. Cat's apartment and Marci's house were within a stone's throw of each other and the Gardens Mall where they planned to spend a few non-work related hours.

First on the day's agenda, however, was a stop for coffee at Starbucks. Sipping scalding hot cups of caramel macchiato on the outside patio, an umbrella sheltering them from the already hot sun, they dreamed aloud about the future. Then, manicure and pedicure appointments where, side-by-side in comfortable leather chairs, they continued their talk of romance, children, vacations, friends and families.

Getting Marci into a nail salon had been a feat worthy of a gold medal, and Cat was not about to let the victory go unnoticed. She continually ribbed her friend about the condition of her feet and hands, comparing them to paws and claws. Marci responded by growling. Laughter followed. There was rarely a moment of silence—usually only while the women clenched their teeth as calloused skin was sandpapered away.

Once they were sure that the dreaded polish smudges could be avoided, Marci and Cat slipped into comfortable shoes and went about completing the rest of their plans. With nothing special in mind, they searched the shops for the perfect outfit for work or play. From store to store, the women looked for that ever elusive blouse or skirt that would turn them from cinder girl to Cinderella.

In the dressing room at Victoria's Secret, they tried on their selections and laughed over the mostly unflattering effects. Unable to suppress their giggles, the sales staff was forced to continually knock and inquire about their insanity. Marci could not resist taking a picture of Cat in a bathing suit with less than adequate coverage to show Ian and Kevin when they got home. The photo was proof positive that Cat's whispered nickname in high school—Tators—had been well deserved.

By noon their stomachs were rumbling and, since this was not a day to be weight conscience, they chose a restaurant known for its over-sized, greasy burgers and extra crispy fries. When each of them ordered diet soda, it was the catalyst for another burst of hilarity. After a quick walk through the remaining department stores, Cat suggested they call it a day.

Kevin and Ian also had plans for that Saturday. While the women were shopping, their men worked on repairing the lawn mower that had sat like a large, green garden gnome in the Welles' front yard for two weeks. As expected, Cat and Marci found them standing in the driveway covered in grease.

Air kisses were exchanged and dinner plans were made. As the guys showered and changed, Marci and Cat put on an impromptu fashion show, modeling their purchases for Sonora Leslie who could not have cared less; the plastic cap of her sippy cup proving to be much more interesting. With exaggerated movements, Cat sashayed across the living room in a Michael Kors skirt and blouse while Marci stomped the carpeting in a blazer and pleated slacks.

Over cold beers, the couples shared tales of the day and then decided to eat at a new hibachi restaurant which had recently opened on PGA Boulevard. The outing was a huge success and all four were delighted with the courteous staff and delicious food. They took in a late movie at the local cinema, and by the end of the evening Marci and Cat agreed it had been one of the nicest days they had shared in a long time.

"I definitely have to find a regular babysitter," Marci confided as she waved her goodbyes.

As the partners would be on call in just a few hours, Kevin

dropped Cat at the front door to her apartment and headed home to Loxahatchee. It was 11:30 pm and many not well-stifled yawns were evident on both of their faces. Cat fell asleep almost as soon as her head hit the pillow, Kneesaa nestled in her arms. Marci did the same after changing Sonora Leslie and climbing into bed next to Ian. At 5:30 a.m., Marci's cell phone rang, bolting her to her feet.

When talking about the events of that morning, Marci told her immediate supervisor, Sergeant Jamison, "… the phone rings in the middle of the night and trouble is always your first thought but nothing could have prepared me for the sound of Cat's voice crying, 'Marci, help me. I've been raped.' I felt like I'd been struck by lightning; every nerve ending was tingling. My ears were buzzing.

Ian was still sleeping and over his snores I heard myself asking, 'Where are you? Are you badly hurt? Have you called the police?' What stupid questions! Of course, she was hurt. She had been raped. And as for calling the police, she called me.

I'm not sure I actually heard anything Cat said after raped. I was moving on instinct, trying to keep her calm; trying to keep myself calm. I told her to not to hang up; to stay on the line with me. Cat was sobbing so hard it was difficult to understand her words but I clearly heard her say, 'Be careful, Marci. He might still be outside. He has a machete!' I remember thinking, 'She been attacked and she's worried about me.'

As much as I anticipated the worst, nothing could have prepared me for the sight of Cat's bruised and beaten face. Thoughts of the Elephant Man kept running through my head. I let myself into Cat's apartment no more than 15 minutes after she called me. She and Kneesaa were lying on the floor of the bedroom. Cat was shaking uncontrollably. In the semi-darkness, it was difficult to see her. Once I assured myself she wasn't in mortal danger, I called you and explained what had happened."

Unlike Marci's report, Cat's had been devoid of emotion. At approximately 2:30 a.m., she was awakened by the sound of someone outside her front door. Kneesaa barked as keys were inserted into the lock.

Since only her parents and Marci had access, Cat assumed one of them was bearing bad news. She sat up in bed. Within seconds, a man was standing in her doorway, machete in hand. Cat jumped from the bed and reached for the gun she kept in the drawer of her nightstand. She was quick but he was quicker. Her attacker, who Cat estimated to be 6'3" and 250 pounds, forcibly threw her face down onto the bed and ziptied her hands behind her back. Although she pretended not to know who he was, she immediately recognized him as the maintenance man who had repaired her air conditioner the previous October.

Kneesaa, forever protective of her mistress, lunged and tried to bite through the attacker's heavy gloves. He swatted her away like a fly, grabbed a pillow case and threw it over her, securing her inside with a knot. Then, he tossed Kneesaa into a corner, where she hit the wall with a loud thud. There had been a soft whimper and Kneesaa went quiet.

"I thought she was dead." Cat said matter of factly. "I thought I was dead."

Keeping tight control on her emotions, more details followed. "When he entered, I was wearing a tee shirt and boxers. After tying my hands behind my back, he took a pair of shorts from my dresser and slipped them over my legs. Then, he shoved a pillowcase in my mouth and said we were going to the bank. He needed money. He dragged me, barefoot, from my apartment. On the way down the stairs, I noticed that one of the zip ties had come lose. The minute he let go of my arm to unlock his car, I spit out the pillowcase and took off across the parking lot. I was screaming but nobody—nobody—paid any attention."

According to Cat's account, she was tackled and dragged behind one of the maintenance sheds. "I fought hard but he was so fucking strong. He taunted me… said, 'You must have taken self-defense. It won't do you any good.' Then, he gave me a hard punch to the jaw which must have knocked me out for a split second—just enough time for him to re-zip tie my wrists. I guess he was worried someone might have seen us because he dragged me back to the apartment.

Once inside, he threw me on the bed and I tried to kick him.

He punched me again in the face. Then, he raped me over and over again. Every time he would force me to open my eyes by pressing the machete harder against my throat. Eventually, my neck felt wet, and I knew he had cut me. Blood was running down my back. He kept singing, 'Miss Blue, Miss Blue, I've got you Miss Blue.'

Hours passed. When the sun came up, he left. He didn't say anything; he was just gone. I crawled off the bed and into the living room. Somehow, I found the strength to stand and, with my teeth, I pulled my pocketbook onto the floor. My cell phone fell out and I used my nose to call Marci. Then, I crawled back to the bedroom and knelt beside Kneesaa. I put my cheek against the pillow case and felt her move. With my teeth and my knees, I got the knot open. She crawled out and together we lay on the floor until Marci arrived."

Under questioning by Sgt. Jamison, Cat admitted that at the time her air conditioner was being installed, she had felt wary of the repairman, who was later identified as Robert Bridgeman, III, a Navy veteran discharged under questionable circumstances. She could not explain her feelings; Bridgeman had done nothing threatening. They hadn't even spoken beyond "The a/c is in the kitchen" and "I'm leaving. Call the office if you need anything." But, something in his demeanor set off an alarm—one Cat had foolishly ignored. And now, he was gone. Like a puff of smoke, he had disappeared into thin air.

"If only I had installed an extra lock on the door when I moved in the way I wanted to."

"You followed the management company's rules, Cat. Don't blame yourself." Tough as he was, Jamison could not disguise the emotion in his voice.

"Well, sometimes," Cat's anger with the choice she had made flared, "rules are wrong and should be broken.

CHAPTER THREE

Still struggling to keep her balance, Marci stood atop a sand dune and did a 360 of the area. At the entrance to the beach, a news crew struggled to carry equipment on the soft surface. Cat saw them at the exact same moment. "Well, now, if it isn't our local gruesome twosome. How nice of them to join us. Get ready for your close-up."

"Not me. I hate cameras. They make me look fat." Marci struggled to keep a straight-face. "Catch the shoes on..."

Before Marci finished speaking, the female reporter tumbled off her five inch heels and landed on her knees in the sand. "I think that's the position she used to get her job."

"You're evil."

Cat, who shared Marci's dislike for this particular on air personality, shook her head in wry amusement. "Be nice. People might have said things like that about us."

"About you, maybe. About me, never. Getting down on my knees is a position I take only in church and even then, my butt is half on the pew."

Just then, G caught up to the Ladies, his multicolored shirt causing Marci to blink rapidly. "Nice shirt, G. Did your son drop his crayons in the washing machine?"

"It is during our darkest moments that we must focus to see the light."

Along with his penchant for Jerry Lewis imitations, Dr. Mark Geschwer was partial to wearing outlandish outfits which caused the uninformed to do triple takes when he passed by. He was also a very well read man who could find a quote to suit every occasion.

"Your words," Marci asked as she covered her eyes to keep from being blinded, "or did you pilfer them from someone famous?"

"Aristotle Onassis."

"I'm going to need a pop culture dictionary. Who is Aristotle Onassis?"

"Jackie Kennedy's second husband. She married him after JFK was killed. He was a multi-millionaire."

"Right. Now I remember. The millionaire Greek guy. I guess there was more to him than money but it certainly wasn't looks. Do you think he was one of those Greeks bearing unwanted gifts?"

"Not unless you are adverse to people jumping at your beck and call."

"Oh, I have that now only in the reverse. Sonora beckons and calls and I run my ass off to get her whatever she wants."

"Ah, children… they do have a way of making slaves of us."

As Marci and G talked, Cat took advantage of the distraction to put distance between herself and the medical examiner. Being aware of Cat's disdain for his comedic abilities, G always did his best to keep his exchanges with her short and sweet. "Nice to see you back at work, Detective." G's normal voice carried softly on the breeze. "How are y…"

"I'm fine." Cat cut G off quickly as she sauntered away.

Feeling a bit foolish for his attempt at pleasantries, the medical examiner looked at Marci and shrugged his shoulders. "How is Sonora doing with the teething?"

Marci answered while holding up a bandaged index finger. "A full set of choppers—and just like me, her bite is worse than her bark."

"So it would seem." G laughed and walked off toward the crowd gathered at the foot of the guard tower. Marci stared after him lost in thought.

A year ago today, Cat and Marci had been called to a crime scene not much different than the present one. In fact, the murder victim was found just a few miles up the beach at Blowing Rocks Preserve—a sanctuary under the care and administration of the Nature Conservatory, one of the world's leading conservation organizations. If facing north, Marci would be able to see the spray caused by waves hitting the Anastasia limestone outcroppings that line the shore.

Unlike Nate Kincaid, who currently lay at the bottom of the 10 foot ladder leading to the lifeguard's perch, last year's victim – Peter Colangelo – was found hanging like a piñata from the branch of a Gumbo Limbo tree just a few feet from the boardwalk running alongside the Indian River Lagoon. It was Labor Day and a red, white and blue banner celebrating the holiday was draped like a sash from one shoulder giving him the look of a beauty pageant contestant.

From Marci's vantage point, Kincaid's body appeared to be the victim of a tragic accident. This would not be the first time a lifeguard had tumbled down wooden stairs rotted by the wind and the rain. Water and salt on the steps combined with their steep incline made for a slippery surface that required constant vigilance when climbing up or down.

Marci mentally ran through what she and Cat knew so far. Local law enforcement had been brought to the scene by a 911 call from a jogger running along the shoreline in the early dawn. Upon arriving and ascertaining that the deceased was on county property and, in fact, a county employee, jurisdiction was transferred to the Palm Beach County Sheriff's Office. The PBSO dispatcher then awakened the on-call detectives and the medical examiner, who was at this moment kneeling beside the corpse.

With the wind offering free dermabrasion, Marci turned away from the scene. She juggled her heavy shoes from one hand to the other as she hurried after Cat, who was talking to one of the officers first on the scene.

"What have we got so far?" Cat inquired of the fresh-faced cop with a tinge of green around his mouth.

From the way he averted his eyes, Cat knew this was his first up close and personal look at a corpse. "His name's Nate Kincaid. He is… was… a lifeguard. Jogger found him just after dawn and called 911."

"Any ideas what he was doing here so early in the morning?"

"Not a one." The young officer was, obviously, pleased to be so near to Cat, whom he had lusted over since he was introduced to her at a Police Benevolent Association fundraiser some months ago. He tried hard not to stare at her eyes, which were ice blue at that moment and felt like they were penetrating his skull. Familiar with the rumors that she could read Marci's mind, he feared she might also be able to read his thoughts. The words sexual harassment flitted about in his brain.

"This beach was closed months ago. Budget cuts. Word is Kincaid had been stationed here but was reassigned to Carlin Park."

"So, why come back here?" Marci chimed in as she joined Cat and her admirer. She dropped her shoes in the sand and reached for the notebook in her jacket pocket.

Without looking at Marci, Cat removed the pen holding up her hair and held it out to her partner. Marci stopped patting herself down and took the pen without offering a thank you.

The officer watched the exchange and blushed. "Ah… damned if I know," he stuttered in answer to Marci's question. "Wish I could be of more help but I'm needed for crowd control." Removing his hat and wiping his forehead on the sleeve of his uniform shirt, he gave Marci and Cat a quick nod of the head and moved off.

G's voice rang out above the wind that had suddenly begun whistling across the dunes. "Hey! Hey! Detective Ladies."

Cat visibly shivered in the oppressive heat. She and Marci began walking toward the guard tower. "Don't forget your shoes."

"Damn," Marci cursed and rushed back to collect her footwear.

Cat, smiling, watched Marci slap her shoes together in an attempt to knock off the sand that had collected in the deep rubber treads. The effort proved futile and Marci tucked one shoe under each arm, leaving specks of amber and white granules spread across her jacket. She returned to where Cat was waiting, a defiant look on her face. "I don't want to hear it, Cat."

"I wasn't going to say anything."

As the two detectives approached G, Cat gnashed her teeth, a sign that she felt trapped in an unpleasant situation. Marci again tried to slap sand off her shoes. In frustration, she pitched them into the sand and kicked them away; her beach thong flying off in the process.

"Son of a…" Marci stomped off after her shoe. When she returned, her sweaty foot was covered in sand. "Yeah. Yeah. Yeah. Sand is an S word. I know."

Cat wisely kept quiet.

"What have ya got for us, G?" Marci spoke through tightly compressed lips in an attempt to keep grit out of her mouth. She moved closer to the body while Cat stayed a few feet behind her.

Studying the victim's sleeping countenance, Cat's first impression was "if looks could kill, Kincaid's face would be a weapon." The best that could be said of him was that he was homely. An excessively large nose and a heavily lined face gave him the appearance of a Shar Pei—the popular Chinese breed of dog known for having winkles and an unpleasant odor.

Since Kincaid's body had been roasting in the hot sun for a few hours, it, too, was starting to smell. Despite the grim scene before her, Cat couldn't help but smile as an image of Sonora Leslie waving her tiny fingers in front of her nose and saying "Tink" formed in her mind. Almost immediately, some of the tension in the air dissipated.

#

Cat loved that kid and was filled with praise for the great job Marci was doing raising her. She was especially impressed to learn that Marci was teaching Sonora sign language.

"Sign language? You're teaching the baby sign language? That's amazing, Marci."

The first time Sonora Leslie signed "I love you" to her Aunt Cat was the moment Cat officially lost her heart. It was also the moment she realized how badly she wanted a baby of her own. The sound of her biological clock ticking was deafening.

"I'm so impressed," Cat told her partner while looking adoringly at the strawberry blonde pixie holding one fist in the air; her thumb, index finger and pinkie pointing skyward.

#

Someone needed only to watch Marci interact with G to know she adored him. Cat was the first to admit that the medical examiner was a decent man who felt deeply for every person who slept the eternal sleep upon his examining table. It mattered not whether they were virtuous or corrupt; G treated everyone with respect knowing that for many he would be only person to mourn their passing. Regardless of his good intentions, since her rape, Cat found G's constant antics annoying. She didn't doubt his integrity and professional ethics; it was his need for comic relief at what she considered inappropriate times that caused waves of nausea to sweep through her body whenever she heard his nasally whine.

In his best Jerry Lewis voice, G fueled the fire. "Come on over here and take a gander," he called to Cat, whose hesitation was obvious in the stiff way she held herself and in the expression on her face.

"Do you do any other impersonations?" she asked, causing G to puff with pride.

"Why, yes. Rodney Dangerfield. Henny Youngman. Jack Ben…"

"Do you think you could do an impression of a professional medical examiner and just give us the facts?"

"Of course, Detective."

There was no confusing the embarrassment on Marci's face

with a sunburn. Cat's rudeness toward G had become more pronounced since the attack. Marci offered G a silent apology, which he accepted with a knowing look in his eyes.

Rolling Kincaid's body onto its side, the medical examiner pointed to some questionable marks in the crease of his knees just above the calf. "Victim appears to be between 50 – 55 years of age."

Cat pressed for clarification. "A little old for a lifeguard, wouldn't you say?"

"He's in good shape and works out regularly though not at a gym. From the muscles in his legs, I'd guess he's both a swimmer and a runner. These bruises are fresh. Death occurred before they had time to fully form."

G laid the body flat in the sand and continued his initial report. "The bruises on his shins and shoulders are also fresh. I'm fairly certain the striations spanning his neck front to back are finger marks."

Marci bent over to get a closer look at the marks; then stood and walked to Cat. "Do you think someone grabbed him and shook him?"

Carefully avoiding the bandage around Cat's throat, Marci put one hand on each of her partner's shoulders. With tempered roughness, she reenacted her vision of the crime, shaking Cat like a rag doll. "Like this?"

Cat stepped away from Marci, a feigned look of annoyance on her face. "Funny. Not."

"That's a possibility," G smiled. "I'll give you a more definitive answer after I get him back to the morgue. Bruising continues for about 24 hours. I should be able to determine their cause by late today or tomorrow morning."

Having listened to the medical examiner express concern over the position of the body and superfluous bruising, Cat and Marci decided to give the case top priority.

"So Kincaid could be the victim of a shake and bake."

"It looks that way, Marci, but why here and why so early in the morning?"

"That's the first question we're going to ask. Until evidence proves otherwise, Nate Kincaid is a murder victim."

Marci turned back to G and with her pearly whites sparkling in the ever rising sun offered a sincere "Thanks." Licking the salt from her lips and batting her eyes, she attempted to tease a faster delivery from the good doctor. "Would it be possible to get a more detailed report later this morning or early this afternoon?"

G laughed at the harmless flirtation and ridiculousness of the request. His office was short staffed and over budget but for the ladies, especially Marci, he always tried to make an exception. "The last I checked miracles were not part of my job description. You'll hear from me when I have something concrete. By the way, this isn't sand stuck in his head wound. I think it's coquina and, maybe, wood. More on that later as well."

As Cat and Marci moved away from the scene to allow the medical examiner to complete his examination, G called out, "Detective Leigh, I'm glad..."

"Yeah. Yeah. I know."

Pinching Cat hard on the arm, Marci admonished her partner. "You could be friendlier to him. He's a good medical examiner and a decent man."

"Ouch! Yeah, I know, but all that comedy stuff at a crime scene is disrespectful."

"You're personalizing. It's normal after an attack."

"Don't shrink me, Marci," Cat responded, anger rising in her voice. "Trust me, near death experiences aren't comical. Real death is nothing to laugh about."

Cat ran her fingers over the bandage hiding the still raw two inch scar on the side of her neck. She turned and walked away from Marci, who followed close behind. A short distance away, the medical examiner motioned for his assistants to load Kincaid's body into a bag.

"Marci! Get your shoes!" was the last thing G heard before following his team out to the parking lot.

CHAPTER FOUR

Cat and Marci had always found the public's fascination with death and dying, well, fascinating. Rarely did they arrive at the scene of a crime and not have to wade through a sea of onlookers. The morning Nate Kincaid's body was found was no different except that the majority of thrill seekers were women—lots of women—all lined up along the walkway, watching the police and coroner at work. What made this group stand out was not just their large number but also the air of familiarity that emanated from them.

Standing beside Cat, Marci did a rough count. "There have to be at least thirty yakking women up there on the ridge, Cat. How did they get here so fast?"

"Don't know, but did you notice their clothes? No one is wearing gym shorts or sweats. The day has barely begun, yet they all look party perfect; not a hair out of place or smudge of mascara on their cheeks. You'd think they were going someplace special."

"A possible murder scene is pretty damned special in my book." Marci always paid extra attention to onlookers, knowing that perpetrators often returned to watch from among the gathered crowd. A woman was not beyond consideration as a murderer. Letting her eyes roam over the friendly group, Marci saw that most of the ladies carried cups of coffee imprinted with the image of birds in flight—the logo of a nearby breakfast spot, The Seagull Diner. She made a note in her pad to stop by the restaurant on the way back to the office.

"Seagull Diner must make one hell of a cup of coffee. We'll have to try some before going to the station."

"I hope they have takeout. I'm hungry." Cat's stomach rumbled and she rubbed it as though in excruciating pain. "I don't know if I can make it to lunch."

"You're always hungry. You eat twice as much as me and you never gain a pound. It's just not fair."

Cat grabbed Marci by the lapels of her jacket. "You should be melting in this ridiculous, excuse me, *professional* getup. I expect you to pool into a puddle of perspiration. If you faint from heat exhaustion, I'm not picking you up."

"Dr. Robertson would be so proud of you."

"What are you talking about?"

"Alliteration. You just formed an entire thought using alliteration. You used to hate it when he made us do that in English class."

"Great. Will that keep your knees from buckling?"

"Fainting is for sissies. Anyway, my wardrobe comes with built in exercise equipment." Marci lifted her thick soled shoes into the air like weights. "These make pretty good dumb bells." The realization that she had left herself open for another zinger, forced her quick response. "Don't!"

Cat merely shrugged her shoulders as happy voices uttering the deceased's name reached their ears. Snippets of conversation carried on the wind and from them the detectives deduced that all the ladies had known Nate Kincaid and, yet, despite the occasional sniffle, no one really seemed sad.

"A bit too lighthearted for a crime scene, wouldn't you say?" Marci scanned the crowd trying to put a face with a voice.

"Definitely. Go use your magical powers of interrogation. See what you can find out."

Marci once again dropped her shoes and maneuvered her way up and over the sand dunes. In her mind, she formulated the questions she would ask the members of the girls' club waiting on the hill.

Tossing her jacket over a nearby bush, she retrieved her notepad from her pants pocket. Then, holding the pad in one hand, she searched for a pen with the other, suddenly fearful that the inevitable had happened. Marci's pockets were to pens what washing machines were to socks.

Cautiously, she approached the spectators, hoping not to scare away any potential witnesses. To her surprise, the women milled towards her. They were eager to talk and the more they talked, the more Marci realized that she and Cat were going to be kept busy following a trail of former lovers, all of whom had reason to hate Nate Kincaid.

Thankfully, the pen materialized. It had fallen through a small hole in her pocket and gotten caught on her underwear. Although a goodly amount of reaching was required to get it, Marci was not known for giving up easily. Once she had the pen in hand, the interrogation moved quickly.

While Marci gathered names and contact information, Cat walked the beach searching the crime area for evidence. Eventually, she made her way back to the tower where Kincaid's body had lain just a short time before. She climbed the stairs, noting the slickness of the wood.

On the deck, she quickly tagged a thermos, paper coffee cups and a bakery sack with a bit of uneaten croissant and a few loose grapes in the bottom. The sack was greasy and Cat, hoping the buttery substance would yield a fingerprint or two, dropped it carefully into an evidence bag.

As she worked, she sang softly to herself, *"Love is in the air. In the whisper of the trees. Love is in the air. In the thunder of the sea."*

The song, written in 1977 before Cat was born, had recently been used in an episode of the popular television show Desperate Housewives. On nights when corpses and crime stats kept her awake, Cat was inclined to numb her senses watching what she classified as stupor sensitive programs. Unfortunately, one of the side effects of those shows was the inability to get soundtracks out of her head. Cat was usually careful not to let Marci hear her singing because then she would have to admit where she had heard the tune. Marci did not like the women of Wisteria Lane.

"Watching that crap kills brain cells," Marci warned every Monday morning, knowing Cat had tuned in the night before. "Be careful or the self-absorption of those characters will rub off on you."

Since Cat was probably the least affected-by-materialism person Marci had ever met, her fears were totally unfounded and she knew it. She just couldn't resist teasing her best friend.

Cat's favorite comeback, "Yeah, like MWF increases your I.Q." was a jab at Marci's love of midget wrestling.

Squinting in the glare of the sun, Cat studied the railing surrounding the guard tower. She immediately knew that there was little possibility of getting prints from the oft-used barricade which was scarred from years of exposure to the elements.

Finding a few skin cells would be nice but, again, such evidence was rarely useful when found in public places. From the corner of her eye, Cat saw a bit of tissue wadded up and lying near the old bench under the watchtower's only window. Picking it up in her gloved hands, she noticed that the crumbled mass seemed to be stuck together, as if with glue. She detected a faintly familiar scent on the paper and realized that Kincaid's reason for being at the beach probably had nothing to do with swimming. Cat dropped the tissue into a new evidence bag, confident that the experts in the lab would confirm her suspicions.

Standing at the top of the stairs, Marci silently watched Cat work. She was happy to hear her best friend singing even if the reason for the song irritated her. Cat's mental health was a priority for Marci. Love being in the air was a sure sign that Cat was healing inside and out.

"If I was a betting woman, I'd say that choice of song was prophetic. Let me guess where you heard it. Desperate Delusional Divas. Right?"

"Funny. It's a good song."

"It was a good song 30 years ago."

Rather than answer, Cat held up the evidence bags for Marci's inspection. They offered just the distraction that she was hoping for. "What do you think was going on here?"

"Looks like breakfast a deux. One of our heartbroken lovelies, perhaps?"

Marci took the bag with the tissue. "What's in here?"

"Proof of sex on the beach I suspect—the activity not the drink. What did you find out and why do you smell like you fell into a vat of eau de cologne at a perfume factory?"

"Oh. Thank you!"

"Come again?"

"Earlier this morning, you were certain I would offend in my professional attire. Now, I'm rose water sweet."

"Not exactly. You still stink just in a different way."

"Overpowering, right? I've never understood why some women bathe in this stuff."

"Just stand downwind and tell me that you found our murderer."

"Strange bunch," Marci nodded toward the women on the hill while draping her jacket over the railing. The sweat stains under her armpits had reached her waist and spread across her chest.

She dropped her shoes to the deck; one of them bounced and fell over the edge to the beach below. "Shit."

"Marci, your shirt is soaked. You look like someone sprayed you with a hose." Cat reached into her satchel and pulled out an oversized PBSO tee shirt. "Sometimes, I feel like your mother. Here."

"You know I wear these clothes just to annoy you, right?"

"Well, you're doing a good job of it. We're two for two today—first sandals, now shirt. Don't even think about underwear."

"What? You won't share your peek-a-boo panties with me?"

"No, and if you keep dressing like Dr. Watson, I'm going to request a new partner."

"You're Watson. I'm Sherlock. Actually, we're both Sherlock and since you love him as much as I do, you would never get rid of me." Marci put her hand over her heart in exaggerated shock.

"Don't be so sure." Cat laughed at the image of Marci—sweat stained shirt, sandals too big for her feet, perspiration dripping from her forehead. "You are a sight to behold. Why do you insist on wearing cement blocks on your feet?"

"We can't all have picture perfect tootsies like you, now, can we?" Marci prepared to throw the remaining shoe at Cat; then placed it carefully on the deck. "Don't let me forget my orthopedics when we leave."

"Deal. Tell me what you learned."

"All of them claim to have known Kincaid for years and swear he was a really nice guy."

"I gather you didn't buy what they were selling."

"There was something in the way they chose their words, and they all used the same words almost to the point of being rehearsed. They're all icky sweet and sooo very sad. Something tells me there's more to this story. Of course, none of them were here this morning."

"How'd they find out he was dead?"

"Said they were having breakfast at the diner and heard a cop talking about a dead lifeguard."

"All of them? Having breakfast at the same diner? And they immediately assumed it was Kincaid? That's interesting."

"Yeah. I thought so, too."

"And you think Desperate Housewives is fiction."

"There's something weird about them. Either they are lying or they mainlined the better part of the Domino Sugar inventory."

"You're cynical, Marci. Maybe Kincaid really was a nice guy."

"I'm not saying he wasn't, but there's something more going on."

"Let's not jump to conclusions. Remember Sequin? The stripper from T's Lounge? We were damned positive she had killed her John."

"Yeah. She was sorta happy/sorta sad he was dead."

"But she didn't kill the slime bag."

"Okay. I get your point. But when that many women know the same guy and use the same superlatives to describe him... Think about it. How many women have you met while sunbathing at the beach?"

"None."

"Exactly. How did these broads meet? If it was through Kincaid, then the reason was not friendship. Single women do not like competition."

"Are they all single?"

"I didn't specifically ask that question but the word "dated" came up often enough to give me reason to speculate."

"What if they all did date him? Wouldn't that be cliché!"

"Kincaid—the Casanova of Coral Cove—a lifeguard who seduced all the single women at..."

"We don't know for sure they're all single."

"You're right but a lifeguard who seduced all the women at his beach would make a good plot for a movie."

"Only if it's a murder mystery. I've never been friendly with women who dated my exes even if I hated them once the relationship was over. We females just are not that open minded."

"You're right again and..."

"Could you repeat that?"

"I said 'You're right agai...' Don't be a smart ass, Marci."

"Can't help it. That's where my brains are situated. Anyway, hate does bind people who otherwise would have no interest in each other."

"Like me and my rapist. I hate him and I'm stuck with his memory for the rest of my life."

Marci reached out to touch Cat. "Time does heal, Cat. You have to have faith."

"Faith?" Cat choked out the word. "Faith is just another word for gullible, and I stopped being gullible the minute I felt that machete slice into my neck."

#

Seven weeks earlier:

The parking lot outside Cat's apartment was dark. The light from her bedroom window shone through the curtains like a beacon at a Hollywood premier. A man sat in his car—lights off, engine idling. His head was tilted back; his eyes mere slits. He waited and watched. When the window went dark, he exited the car and slowly, soundlessly, crossed the macadam.

At Cat's front door, he took a large key ring from his pocket, inserted one of the keys into the dead bolt lock and slowly turned it. The door opened, making a noise only Kneesaa heard. She growled. Then, she growled again—a deeper, more guttural sound.

"Quiet, NeeNee." Kneesaa ignored Cat's command, and the next time she growled the sound coming from her throat signaled danger approaching. Cat sat up and rubbed her eyes. In the doorway, the outline of a large man holding a machete was clearly visible.

#

"Let's arrange a time to interview our potential Miss Havishams at the station. This might be better than that soap opera you like. What's it called? The Wrinkled and Raunchy?"

"And everyone thinks I'm the funny one."

Marci chuckled as she changed the subject. "From my observations, I'd say the median age of the sob siblings is about 50? Not exactly young but not old either. And for the most part, they're all still pretty good looking."

"What about raunchy? You think they all participated in some form of beach calisthenics?"

"Anything is possible. Let's do one last walk around. Make sure the CSIs know what to do with the evidence you tagged and then head over to that diner everyone seems to favor."

"Good idea. I really am hungry."

"When aren't you?"

"Don't forget your jacket and shoes," Cat reminded as she headed down the staircase.

Marci kicked off a sandal to wipe the sand from her feet and in so doing, she stepped on something sharp. Her yowl of pain brought Cat back up the staircase.

"What happened?"

"I stepped on something… something sharp." Marci moaned as she hopped about the deck.

"It was probably a splinter."

"That was no splinter."

Marci got down on her knees and rubbed her hands over the worn wood. "Well, I'll be." She pulled the bobbie pin from her hair and pried at the planking trying to dislodge her find.

"Lookie here." Marci held up a small, round shiny object for Cat to see.

"Is that an earring?" Cat moved in for a closer look. "Those look like engraved initials on the front."

"Yes, they do."

"Going to be fun finding the owner."

"Things are really getting interesting." Marci dropped the earring in an evidence bag, grabbed her jacket and one shoe and hurried after Cat.

"Don't forget your other shoe." Cat's reminder carried across the sand.

"Shit." Marci turned around and headed back to the guard tower.

As the partners made their way back to the parking lot, Marci shared some of her own fears about aging. "You know, Cat, fifty will be here before either of us realizes it. If we're half as well preserved as the women I met this morning, we will be sitting pretty."

"Maybe the coffee they were drinking was laced with collagen. Imagine the money Starbucks could make—one collagen latte, unsweetened, fat free milk, no whipped cream."

"Order me two; I just got a hot flash," Marci quipped just as Cat stepped on something half buried in the sand coating the macadam and twisted her ankle. "Hell, Cat, are you okay?" Marci's quick reflexes kept Cat from falling over face forward.

"Yeah, I think so."

"You do know this is absurd, don't you?"

"What are you talking about?"

"Because I stepped on something, you have to step on something. Why do you have to be so competitive?"

"You're kidding, right?"

"You're always copying me. Tell me something you don't copy."

"Your wardrobe. And thanks for your concern. What did I step on? I felt like I was roller skating."

Marci dug in the sand and held up a ballpoint pen. "With the compliments of Premier Publishing House. Never heard of it."

"Books. They publish books. You know, those things with pages. The pages have words on them."

Marci snorted and Cat, anticipating Marci's reaction, easily caught the pen which was heading like a missile toward her.

"We can always use another pen considering how many we, meaning you, lose."

"My gun is loaded. Don't tempt me."

"I'm trembling," Cat shot back while making a big display of dropping the pen into her bag.

"Lot of good it's going to do us at the bottom of that... that shopping bag you call a pocketbook."

"Oh, ye of little faith."

"Oh, me of past experiences. Where are the car keys?"

"Ah..." Cat searched her satchel for the keys but came up empty. Wincing, she hobbled into the grass and dumped the contents of the bag. The keys and numerous pens fell to the ground along with assorted other stuff. "Viola!" Cat held up the keys.

"Yeah, viola my a…"

Wagging her finger in Marci's face, Cat admonished, "Uh uh, Mommies don't curse."

She gathered up her belongings and dropped everything back into the satchel—all except one pen. This she clipped to the side of the bag, giving Marci a meaningful look. "Just in case you need it. Let's go."

With a chuckle, Marci and Cat headed back to their car, which though unmarked, shouted cop so loudly it practically brought speeders to a standstill on the Interstate. Cat got behind the wheel and steered them out of the parking lot and back to the main road.

"You sure you want to drive?"

"Yeah. It's my left ankle. Won't affect my lead foot one iota."

"Can't blame me for hoping." Marci hit a button on the door and the passenger window rolled down. "Damn! I stink and it's not perspiration! Why don't women understand that less is more?"

"Probably for the same reason they think bigger is better. Of course, when it comes to dividends, diamonds and dicks, they're right."

"The three Ds. What all women seek and all men lie about," Marci winked at Cat. "Now, if only we could figure out which asset made Nate Kincaid so unforgettable."

"We'll know soon enough," Cat laughed as she held her nose and waved a silent "phew" in Marci's direction.

CHAPTER FIVE

With Cat at the wheel, the detectives traveled south on U.S. Highway One. Since the northern Palm Beaches were not known as a hot spot for murder, Marci, a West Virginia girl by birth and a workaholic by choice rarely had an opportunity to visit the many attractions in her own community. She was enjoying this little sightseeing tour and nearly jumped out of her seat at the sight of the Jupiter Lighthouse jutting into the inlet.

"There's the lighthouse. I forgot we had a bit of history right in our own backyard. Did you know that it was built in the late 1800's on the site of an Indian midden?"

"Midden?" Cat glanced quickly in her partner's direction before gluing her eyes back on the road ahead.

"Yeah. Midden. Sometimes, it's called a shell heap. What it amounts to is a dump for domestic waste. Impressed?"

"So, it's a crap trap. Yup. I'm stupefied by the extent of your knowledge," Cat answered, her eyes rolling back in her head.

"Don't be. I had to look it up on Wikipedia after I heard the word on Jeopardy. I'm just a fount of useless information."

"Don't underestimate the power of a useless tidbit. You could be the next office trivia champion all because you know midden means big, heaping pile of shit."

"Says the person who has won the last two years."

"Just blond luck."

"Well, if you win again, you have to share the pot with your devoted partner."

"I do?"

"Yeah. You midden know nutin' if not for me."

"I think I'm going to be sick, and it's mostly because I also know the reason why your eyes are brown which, now that I think of it, fits right in with this conversation."

Marci and Cat dissolved into fits of laughter. The sun flashed off Cat's engagement ring, bringing the conversation back to where it had begun earlier in the day.

"I honestly don't know what to say, Marci. I love Kevin. I know he loves me. But when I think about how quickly things can change…"

"Change for the good. Kevin is part of the good changes in your life."

"I know."

"Then, let's focus on the good. Tell me how he proposed. Did he go down on one knee?"

"We went to Moe's Southwest for dinner."

"You returned to the scene of the crime. Very apropos."

"I suppose."

"What do you mean, 'I suppose?'"

December 2006

Cat and Marci were enjoying a lunch at Moe's Southwest— their favorite place to eat on the run place while on duty. Across the dining room, Cat spied a lone male wearing nicely creased pants, a dress shirt and tie. Their eyes met and both quickly looked away.

"Marci, there's the cutest guy sitting a few tables away. He's just my type."

"What type is that?"

"Considering the way he's dressed, I'd say employed. He's also about the right age, tall and built like someone who could hold his own in a fight."

Talking over a mouthful of rice and beans, Marci asked, "Can we arrest him for anything?"

"Why would you want to arrest him?"

"Duh! So you can meet him."

"There's got to be a better way than handcuffing him to the table. He keeps looking at me. What should I do?"

"Seriously? You learned all of this stuff in Flirtation 101. Smile. Bat your eyes. Get up, walk over and introduce yourself."

"I can't do that. What if I'm imagining his interest?"

"What if you're not. Take a chance. In the meantime, I'll think of a reason to arrest him."

"You're no help." Cat's appetite was lost. She pushed the food around on her plate for a few minutes and when she next looked up, the man was gone. Disappointment washed over her. "Damn. He left."

"I told you we should arrest him."

Cat stared out the window hoping to get a last look at the stranger. Suddenly, she felt Marci kick her under the table.

"Why are you..."

Marci kicked her again and just at that moment, Cat noticed a pair of long legs standing a foot away. She looked up to find a napkin and a business card waving in her face.

"Hi. My name is Kevin. I think you're the most beautiful woman I've ever seen. I... I... Here's my business card and cell phone number. If you're interested, I'd like to get to know you."

And with that, he dropped the card and the napkin on the table and was gone.

"Well, partner, what are you going to do?"

Picking up the napkin and the business card, Cat placed them on seat beside her. She picked up her fork and tapped it against the side of her plate. "What any good detective would do. Investigate him."

"Ah, romance."

#

Cat made a sharp right turn onto Donald Ross Road and slowed as she approached the entrance to Seagull Plaza. Marci kept pushing for details. "So, how did Kevin propose."

"Well, we got our food and sat down. Just as I'm about to take a bite of my taco salad, Kevin says, 'I grabbed some extra napkins. Here. You might want this one.' And that's exactly what he gave me—one napkin."

"One? Obviously, he's never watched you eat."

"Yeah. Well, this one was kinda special. Kevin had drawn a heart on the napkin." Cat smiled at the memory. "He wrote, 'The last nine months have been the happiest of my life. Make the rest of my life just as happy. Marry me.'"

"Oh, my god, how sweet! What did you do?"

"I started to cry."

"Ohhhhhhhhhh…"

"You're missing the point, Marci. I cried because I didn't know what to do. I felt trapped. Kevin got down on his knee and put the ring on my finger."

"Right there in the restaurant? In front of everyone? You were sort of trapped."

"Ya think? Everybody started cheering and clapping. The manager took our picture."

"So, now you're famous at Moe's. Guess we won't be doing any undercover work there."

"Thanks for finding humor where there isn't any."

"Cat, this is a good thing. Really. I'm so happy for you. Now, I'm gonna cry."

"Here." Cat reached into her satchel and handed Marci a stack of Moe's Southwest napkins. "Help yourself."

"Thanks." Marci blew her nose in one of the napkins, crumbled it up and put it back in Cat's pocketbook.

"Hey! That's gross."

"Now, we're even for the midget wrestling remark."

"Fair enough."

"Cat, I know we've lost some forward motion on your case, but we'll find the bastard. We won't stop looking until he's behind bars."

"I won't be able to sleep until he is.

#

Seven weeks earlier:

Outside Cat's apartment, the sun was barely up. Still zip tied, badly beaten and shivering in pain and fear, Cat crawled to the hallway and, using her teeth, pulled her pocketbook from the top of the credenza to the floor. She used her face and teeth to find her cell phone and with her nose, called Marci.

"Marci, help me. I've been raped."

That was all Cat was able to say before she began to sob

uncontrollably. Through her tears, she warned Marci, "Be careful. He has a machete."

Cat could hear Marci yelling her name as she crawled back to the bedroom. Kneesaa, though still wrapped in the pillowcase, was showing more signs of life. As Cat used her teeth to untie the knot that held Kneesaa captive, the pup whimpered. When the pillowcase was open, Kneesaa crawled out and nestled against Cat's chest. Like two wounded warriors, mistress and devoted ally laid on the floor together waiting for Marci to arrive.

#

Cat pulled the unmarked car into a handicapped parking space and flipped the visor to display their PBCSO—ON DUTY identification card. She retrieved her heels from the back seat, opened the door and swung her still sandal clad feet out. Quickly tossing the sandals over her shoulder, she wiped sand from between her toes, slipped into her shoes and stood up.

"Don't forget your orthopedics, Marci."

Marci, who was already heading for the restaurant's entrance, was still wearing Cat's beach thongs. She turned and stomped her way back to the car. "Keep it up and I'll lock the windows on the way back. The combination of B.O. and perfume is deadly," she threatened as she opened the rear car door and grabbed her regular footwear.

The Seagull, a popular strip mall restaurant a few miles south of Coral Cove Park, had a waiting line snaking around the outside seating area that marked the entrance. Even at this late morning hour, the parking lot was full and all the tables were taken. Cat and Marci stood in the open doorway and surveyed their surroundings. At the entrance to the main dining room, a sign reading *SEAT YOURSELF* was positioned haphazardly on a tripod.

The interior space was taken up with booths and small tables. There were a few serving stations from which the wait staff could grab coffee pots and utensils. The servers were in constant motion taking and delivering orders but, despite the hurried pace, appeared to be friendly and helpful. Most took a few extra minutes to chat with their customers and many seemed to be on a first name basis.

On the other side of the restaurant, near the checkout counter and kitchen, four booths and four large tables filled the open space. There was plenty of room to walk around even with customers vying for the last piece of chocolate cake or bran muffin in the bakery display case near the cash register.

To Cat and Marci this room seemed the perfect spot for a large group to meet and make plans. Marci signaled the nearest waitress with her badge. "Proprietor around?"

"Hi, officers. I'm Dolly, the morning manager."

Dolly talked and walked at the same time. She was balancing four plates of eggs and bacon with assorted sides, which she placed in front of customers at a nearby table. She then turned back to the detectives, who were waiting patiently. "I'll be right with you. Just give me a sec to refill these coffee cups."

When Dolly finally stopped her forward motion, Marci and Cat held out their IDs as Marci made the introductions. "I'm Detective Welles. This is Detective Leigh. We have some questions about a group of women who ate here this morning."

"Oh, you must mean the Belles of the Beach. That's what we call them because all they talk about is some lifeguard they dated."

"How often do they meet here?" Cat continued to scan the restaurant as they talked.

"Breakfast once a week for the past year. They're always pleasant. Seem to know each other well. Good tippers. Did something happen to one of them?"

"No, they're all fine," Marci assured her. "Did you ever hear them mention the lifeguard by name?"

"Yeah. His name was Tate. No. Nate. Nate King or something like that. I'm pretty sure about the Nate part. I only heard them talking while I was serving."

Cat could see that the waitress was anxious to get back to her customers, but she was determined to get the information she and

Marci needed. "Did any of the other waitresses serve them?"

"No. Just me. This is my section and I'm here six days a week."

"Six?" Marci's face registered doubt.

"We're closed Mondays. I'm a waitress, the morning manager and a co-owner."

"Lots of hats," Marci smiled encouragingly, hoping to elicit gossip.

"Lots of work. Really, detectives, I've got to get back to my customers."

Cat wasn't letting her get away that quickly. "Is there anything else you can tell us? Something that stood out in your mind?"

"Well, one lady seemed to be the leader. She acted like the president of a club. She always paid the bill and she always paid in cash. Don't know her name."

"Describe her." There was an echo as both partners spoke.

"Taller than me. Maybe five foot seven. Average weight. Long dark hair and dark eyes. Nice teeth. Really nice teeth. Her smile grabbed your attention."

"Anything distinctive about her?"

"Well, yeah, now that you ask. Her hair. She wore it parted in the middle, and she had a wide grey skunk stripe down either side of her head. Natural, too, I think. Is that distinctive enough?"

"You didn't think to mention that right away," Cat inquired over her grumbling stomach.

"A year ago, it was memorable. Now. Not so much."

"Well, if you think of anything else, you know, like she had only one leg or three eyes, gives us a call." Cat handed Dolly her business card and walked away.

Marci apologized. "My partner gets grumpy when she's hungry. Thanks for your help."

"Should I assume their days dining here are over?"

"You should never assume anything," Marci said as she turned and walked away. At that moment, her stomach rumbled, reminding her that the stale bag of pretzels she had munched on the way to work that morning did not constitute a healthy breakfast.

"Cat, I'm starving. And, by the way, your people skills are rusty."

"Ask me if I care. Those muffins look delicious. Want one?"

"How do you know they're delicious? Maybe they taste like crap."

"Why is it that suddenly our conversations revolve around fecal matter? Have you ever had a muffin made from crap. Do you even know what crap tastes like?"

When Marci didn't answer, Cat continued to badger. "Well, do you want one or not?"

"Sure. And, yes, I do know what crap tastes like. So do you. What else would you call that heart attack waiting to happen that comes out of the vending machine at the office?"

"Point taken. Order me a blueberry muffin. Get whatever you want. My treat. I've got to go to the bathroom."

"Want something to drink?"

Cat yelled over her shoulder as she hurried away, "Now that you mention it, order me a lemonade."

#

Seven weeks earlier:

Cat laid on the floor, blood seeping from her mouth. She could feel her face swelling and imagined her appearance to be grotesque. She was thirsty but too weak to make her way to the bathroom.

Noticing blood on Kneesaa's coat, she momentarily stopped breathing until she realized the blood was coming from a deep cut on her own wrist. She tried to wipe it away, but she was losing feeling in her arm and only succeeded in making it worse.

Kneesaa licked her face and her wet, scratchy tongue helped to alleviate both the physical and emotional pain Cat felt. She began to doze; the sound of police sirens and the whooping of an ambulance brought her back to the present. She struggled to sit up; her back pressed against the wall. Through eyelids that were swollen nearly completely shut, she could see the flash of strobe lights illuminating her bedroom.

A police radio squawked an unfamiliar voice announcing arrival at her address. Footsteps on the stairs and the sounds of EMTs entering the apartment helped to steady her heart rate. Cat felt a hand on her arm. She tried to focus her eyes. Marci was kneeling beside her. "I'm here, Cat. You're going to be all right."

Two emergency medical personnel lifted Cat in their arms and carried her to the sofa in the living room. Marci picked up Kneesaa and cradled her. In the light of a table lamp, the EMTs examined Cat's face and bandaged her wrist and neck. "You'll need stitches. The wrist cut is deep but he missed the artery. Your neck will need stitches as well. Not as deep as the wrist, thank God."

Cat smiled her understanding and smiled her thanks to the paramedic as he wrapped her neck and arm mummy style for transport to the hospital. It was only then that Cat realized how much blood had been absorbed by her shirt. Pink when she had gone to bed, it was maroon from the collar to the hem. She moved her head cautiously from side to side. Still attached. She would live. She reached for Marci's hand.

"Water, please."

#

Sipping lemonades and carrying a white paper bakery sack similar to the one found at the crime scene, Cat and Marci left the restaurant.

"There was no one at the scene this morning that fit that description. Her I would remember."

"But she was here at the diner, Marci, which makes me wonder why she did not go along for the ride to the beach."

"That's the first question we'll ask when we find her."

"One more thing..." Cat grabbed Marci by the arm.

"What?"

"STOP biting your finger. Eat the muffin. I promise you, blueberries taste better than cuticles. Cuticles taste like shit."

CHAPTER SIX

On the way back to the station, Cat and Marci paid a visit to Ocean Rescue headquarters in Juno Beach, hoping to get their victim's home address and some background information. They spoke with Kincaid's immediate supervisor, Lieutenant Kenneth Charles, who had only glowing reports of his employee's service to the people of Palm Beach County. His distress at Kincaid's passing seemed sincere but only just—much like the women at the beach.

"Nate's been... was a lifeguard with OR for 18 years. He was 33 when he was hired. Old for a newbie, but he had lots of experience. Lived and worked at the Jersey shore as a kid."

"Eighteen plus 33...," Cat did the math quickly in her head. "... that would make him 51."

"Yeah, he was 51 last May. We had a party for him. I'll get the exact date for you."

"Was he married? Children?"

"*Was* being the definitive word."

The Sergeant's voice was muffled as he bent over a file cabinet drawer. "Divorced a long time ago. Bad scene. One son. As far as I know, he doesn't have any contact with the kid."

Marci had her pad at the ready. The job of taking notes always went to her. "You have the best handwriting in the department," Cat declared whenever Marci tried to convince her to take over the job.

While she may have had perfect penmanship, Marci was also notorious for losing ballpoints the way oak trees lose their leaves in the fall so, as expected, she patted her pockets and came up empty. Scanning the room for a possible alternative, she saw Cat twirling the pen found in the parking lot like the experienced majorette she had been in high school, a knowing look on her face.

As Lieutenant Charles continued rummaging through a file drawer, Cat and Marci viewed the photographs covering the walls—glamour shots of the Sergeant in his younger body building days.

"That you?" Cat nodded toward the picture of an athletic looking twenty year old.

"Yeah. I thought I was quite the Mr. Atlas in my youth. Now, the heaviest weight I lift is a glass of wine with dinner. Here it is. Nate's birthday is…. was March 20th." Charles held out a file to Marci.

"Eighteen years is a long time. Any problems that you remember?"

"Not a one. Nate was a good worker. Rarely missed a day. No complaints although his politics sometimes ticked off the higher ups."

"What do you mean?" Cat's antennae were vibrating.

"He spent some time as a union rep and wasn't afraid to fight for what he felt he… we deserved."

"After all these years, you must have formed an opinion of him beyond his glowing qualities as an employee. What was your personal impression of him?"

"Nate was a great guy. Really. Everybody loved him—the ladies especially. I've lost count of how many women he seduced, but he once told me he estimated about 800. The guy was a legend."

"I'm not sure that statistic is one worthy of admiration. He seems like the love 'em and leave 'em type to me." Cat's feminist spirit challenged Lieutenant Charles. "Is that what happened with his wife and son?"

"Don't really know. Nate hated to talk about either one of them. Actually, he just plain hated his ex-wife. The kid… I could never get a good read on how he felt."
"And you don't know why they got divorced?"

"Nope. He really was a friendly guy, Detectives. Ask anybody." Despite the admiring tone of his voice, Lieutenant Charles' praise reverberated with hidden jealousy for his colleague's proficiency with women.

Further conversation revealed that Nate Kincaid had been a charmer who had raised the pickup line to heights only otherwise reached in poetry by Lord Byron. He was college educated, well read, loved the arts and had a natural ability to bull shit his way through any discussion. Friends of both sexes had been abundant.

"So you have nothing bad to say about him? Eighteen years and the two of you have never had a disagreement?" Marci raised quizzical eyes from the pad in her lap.

"Yeah, sure. We didn't always get along, but we weren't enemies. Just the usual ego stuff. Nobody likes the boss, and Nate could be pretty set in his ways. He hated it if I changed his shift or made him work on a holiday."

Cat moved closer and stood toe to toe with the Lieutenant, forcing him to take a step backwards and stumble into a chair. "You can be honest with us, LT. You can't hurt Nate Kincaid's feelings. Just tell us what you really thought of him."

"Well, I don't know if it's important or not, but Nate seemed to work in the present and live in the past. His tower radio was always tuned to the oldies station and he favored old black and white films. If you got him talking about his misspent youth in Asbury Park, he couldn't shut up. That's when he seemed happiest, and I always felt he became a lifeguard so he didn't have to grow up."

"A bit of a Peter Pan, huh?" Marci, realizing that with a little prompting the Lieutenant could fill in a lot of the blank spaces in their investigation, led the conversation in the direction they needed it to go. "You said he was college educated?"

"Nate had been lots of things. He said he had worked as a photographer, a teacher, a writer, a director of community theater. I think he even acted in porn movies as a teenager but it was being a lifeguard that provided an easy living with limited responsibility. Plus, lifeguards—even old lifeguards—are babe magnets as his success rate will substantiate."

"Suddenly, I'm all ears. Tell us more."

As Charles talked, Marci wrote hastily in her pad using a form of shorthand only she and Cat could understand.

Cat picked up a photograph from Lieutenant Charles' desk and turned it toward Marci, coughing to get her attention. Marci squinted at the image of a thirty something, thin, blonde woman in a barely there bikini. "This your wife?"

"That's my beauty." Charles' chest puffed with pride. "We've been married a little over three years."

"Second marriage?"

"Yes. We met on the beach at Coral Cove."

"Does she know you're a babe magnet?"

"Why else would she be attracted to an old codger like me?" Charles laughed at his perceived cleverness.

"Let me rephrase that. Does she know you're still a babe magnet?"

"Hey, I look but I don't touch. Don't tell my wife I said that."

Marci closed her pad and put the pen in her pocket. "We appreciate your time, Lieutenant. If we have any more questions, you'll be hearing from us."

By the time Cat and Marci left their meeting, they had a much clearer picture of the deceased. They stood in the parking lot enjoying the breeze from the ocean and discussed what they had just learned. Marci skimmed the pages of her notebook, checking off items that needed further investigation.

"Babe magnet? Seriously, if Lieutenant Charles is a babe magnet, I'm Gisele Bundchen."

"Know what really bothers me?" Cat ruminated. "Charles should be more upset that Kincaid is dead. They worked together for a long time."

"He did seem to envy Kincaid's success with the women. Maybe he feels his death will open the playing field. How did you like that bit about Kincaid doing porn movies?"

"Is there a correlation between the size of a man's nose and his penis? If so..."

"I thought it was feet. Seriously, I was hoping the dear Lieutenant was our killer."

Cat again slid into the driver's seat. "Yeah. Me, too, but that would have been too easy and, anyway, the former Mr. Atlas is really Mr. Wimp. At best, he might have slapped Kincaid to death."

"Now, who has a cruel streak?"

"Well, as per our earlier discussion, when it comes to diamonds, dividends and dicks, I think we might have a clear winner."

Back at their desks, the partners set about filing reports and transcribing notes. Rather than waste time picking up a late lunch from the deli, they finished what was left of their muffins and completed their meal with less than fresh sandwiches from the vending machine in the lobby of One Police Plaza; washing it all down with stale lukewarm coffee. The burnt taste sent shivers along Cat's spine as she choked on the grinds that lined the sides of the styrofoam cup.

"Remember when we talked about eating crap earlier? Well, this is pure diarrhea." Cat pitched the cup into the trash can next to her desk. A dark brown oily liquid seeped slowly onto the floor. Cursing, she put the cup back on her desk and dropped a wad of Kleenex over the puddle. "Shit."

"I think we've already established that," Marci laughed.

"Detective Leigh?" A courier with a mop of electrified orange hair stood in the doorway of the bullpen.

Cat's head snapped around and waved. "Over here."

The courier crossed the open area in five long strides, dropped a manila-colored envelope into Cat's outstretched hand and turned away. He left the office even quicker than he had entered. No signature needed.

Cat stared at her name printed in big, bold black marker on the front of the envelope but she made no move to open it. Instead, she ran her finger slowly over the word emblazoned on the flap -- CONFIDENTIAL.

"What's that?" Marci craned her neck to see who had sent the envelope.

"The DNA results from my attack. Why does it take so long to get rape kits processed?"

"Backlog and crimes against women don't get the priority treatment they deserve. What are you waiting for? Open it."

Cat hesitated and Marci threw herself across her desk, reaching for the envelope. Cat slapped her hand away, broke the seal with her fingernail and removed a sheaf of papers. "Nothing. They found fucking nothing."

"Take a deep breath. You know that DNA is mostly a movie prop. We don't need it. We know who attacked you."

"I just wanted something—a hair, a fiber, a cell, something— to prove those hours were real."

"Prove it to whom? Not me. Not anyone in this office. Not the D.A."

"In court…"

"You know better than that. Rape cases like yours rarely hinge on physical evidence. You're the best eye witness we could have."

Frustrated, Cat threw the papers in the air. They were picked up by the current from the overhead fan and fluttered across the open space. Marci chased after them. "I'll put them in your file."

The next hour was spent completing reports. Marci took a magnifying glass from her drawer and used it to study the inscription on the earring found at the lifeguard's tower.

"Even magnified, it's hard to make out these letters."

"Engravings and monograms are not my taste," Cat countered, taking the magnifying glass and earring from Marci's hand. "Let me see."

"Well, what do you think?"

"I can't make it out. Send it to the lab. Let them worry about it."

Marci returned the earring to the evidence bag. Without thinking, she reached for the coffee cup on her desk and brought it to her lips. "Agh! Gross! This stuff is toxic."

"Yeah. We need a pot of our own. A Mr. Coffee would be great."

"Maybe, we can make it a line item in the 2020 budget," Marci suggested.

Cat picked up her own cup and once again tossed it in the trash, this time not caring that the contents spilled onto the floor. "By then, I'll need a new stomach. Can you believe we started this day on the beach before sunrise?"

"It's well past dinner. The rest of the paperwork can wait. I'm starving."

"Me, too."

"How did I know you were going to say that? It's just so unfair how much you can eat and not gain weight."

"Tall genes. What do you say to burgers and brews at O'Shea's? Kevin's working late so I don't have to rush home."

"Wish I could say the same." Marci slammed her desk drawer closed and turned the key. "Ian is keeping the baby up so that we can share a little family time."

"Understood. I'll grab a fast bite and head on home."

Marci and Cat made their way through the now empty squad room. They switched off the lights and headed for the elevator. The clock over the assignment board glowed 7:30 pm.

#

Seven weeks earlier:

As the paramedic wound a bandage around her throat, Cat glanced at the television and saw that the time was now 6:30 am. Four hours had passed since her attacker let himself into the apartment.

"It was that damned maintenance man, Marci; the one who almost knocked you down the stairs after fixing my a/c."

"Tell me what happened… as much as you can remember."

"I remember it all. Clearly. I was sleeping. Kneesaa barked. She never barks; you know that." Cat flinched in pain as the EMT secured the bandage around her neck.

"I can wait to take your statement. We don't have to do this now."

"Yes! We do! I don't want to forget a single detail. He was standing in the bedroom doorway holding a machete. I jumped out of bed and reached for my gun in the end table. He was faster. Threw me back on the bed, face down, and zip tied my wrists. They started to cut into my skin. Kneesaa tried to bite him. He grabbed her and shoved her into a pillow case. Then, he threw her across the room. She hit the wall and cried out. I thought she was dead."

Cat reached for Kneesaa, who was curled up next to her on the sofa. She wet a finger and tried to rub the blood out of her fur. Marci put a hand out to stop her. "We'll get her a bath. She's fine. Can you go on?"

"He wanted money. I had 64 bucks in my wallet. He took it; then he held that fucking machete to my throat and raped me." Cat's chest began to heave; she started to hyperventilate. The paramedic put a brown paper bag over her mouth.

"Breathe. Deep. Slower. Okay. You're okay."

"Let's do this at the hospital." Marci took Cat's hand and held it tightly.

"No. We have to do this now before I forget... before he hurts someone else."

"I swear, Cat, we'll put the bastard behind bars. He won't get away with this."

#

In the parking lot of One Police Plaza, the two friends hugged good-bye; a habit they had gotten into since Cat's close encounter with death. Awareness that this could be the last time they saw each other had been given them a new perspective thanks to Cat's rapist.

Marci watched Cat pull out of the parking lot with trepidation. Despite Cat's bravado, Marci knew her partner was still shaken by events of that night. Cat's survival was a miracle made possible by wits, wiles and perfectly honed observation and mediation skills. Cat had literally talked her way out of death.

Together, the partners now spent many of their off hours, as few as they were, working with the Office of Victim Services. They were determined to make victim a word that every criminal feared. To that end, they spoke at women's clubs and civic groups across the state about the need for people to take responsibility for their own safety.

To her credit, Cat never shied away from the details of her attack. Since many women find talking about the physical aspect of an assault embarrassing, Cat always emphasized that rape had nothing to do with sex. "It's about control, ladies. Control and humiliation—not sex."

She always ended her presentations by stressing, "When it comes to rape, a penis is a weapon, much as a gun, a knife, a baseball bat or a fist is a weapon. Once you understand that, you will no longer be afraid to talk about being assaulted, and you must talk about it if you are to heal."

As Cat's car faded from sight, Marci worried that their newest case, filled with talk of Nate Kincaid's prowess with women, might cause Cat's nightmares to return. As the moon ascended to its rightful place in the sky, Marci's sensors were on overdrive.

CHAPTER SEVEN

The car had barely stopped when Marci jumped out and rushed to the front door. Through the picture window she could see Ian lying on the floor with Sonora and both appeared to be sleeping. She smiled; the two greatest loves of her life always filled her with unspeakable joy. Tiptoeing across the living room, Marci threw her jacket on the couch, kicked off her shoes, and knelt down next to Ian, gently touching his shoulder.

To her surprise, he wrapped her in a bear hug and pulled her to the floor. "I thought you were a burglar."

"Oh, really? Is this how you capture a burglar?" Marci interrogated as Ian rolled on top of her and planted a big kiss on her lips.

"Maybe. Depends on the burglar."

The sound of their laughter awakened Sonora, whose cries were immediately silenced by the sight of her mother. Marci rose and picked up her beautiful baby girl. "Hello, my angel. Mommy's home."

#

O'Shea's, a popular eatery on trendy Clematis Street, was a hangout for law enforcement personnel of every rank. There was rarely a night when the bar was not overflowing with people. Business men, construction workers, surfers, bikers, sexy young girls and proper middle-aged ladies—all were welcomed. Known for being a popular meeting place for the singles' crowd and, considering how many relationships had started on its dance floor, the bar's reputation for being "lucky" was well deserved. On this night, not even the outside tables provided a seat for weary workers needing a place to relax.

Cat made her way through the crowd blocking the front door,

nodding to fellow officers as she slid between close-pressed bodies in deep conversation. She found a space at the bar and leaned in to place her order. Suddenly, she grabbed the guy next to her by the throat with one hand and, with the other, she pulled a plastic toothpick from a glass on the bar and shoved it up his nose. "You filthy pervert. You grabbed my boob when I came through the front door and I let it go. Now, you cop a feel of my ass. Ain't gonna happen again, man."

"You're hurting me. I didn't do nothing. You're crazy."

Cat's assailant—a puny, long haired, tattooed wannabe biker known to everyone as Tail Light—kept shouting denials as other police officers drew close. Cat's hand was pried from Tail Light's neck by a young cop in uniform. She moved backward and threw the toothpick on the floor. "You're lucky there wasn't an ice pick handy." Cat's anger got the better of her and she moved in, hoping to wipe the grin off Tail Light's face.

"Detective, let me handle this." A blue sleeved arm blocked her path.

Visibly shaken, Cat turned and headed in the direction of the ladies room. Once inside, she entered a stall, sat on the edge of the toilet seat and cried.

#

Side by side on the couch, Ian and Marci played with Sonora, but despite Marci's obvious delight with the baby, Ian sensed something was wrong. "Bad day?"

"Another maybe murder."

"There's something else."

"It's Cat. She's isn't herself. I'm worried."

"She's an intelligent woman, Marci. And she's strong."

"I know but she's changed. She's less tolerant. Less like… Cat."

"Give her time."

Bending her head to Senora's belly, Marci cooed, "Mommy loves you so much. I'm never going to let anything bad happen to you."

#

Having spent her anger in a sea of tears, Cat flushed the toilet and cautiously peeked out of the stall. Coast clear. Standing under the harsh fluorescent light above the vanity, she studied her face in the mirror. "Old," she said aloud.

Summoning up her dignity, she exited the bathroom and made her way back to the bar. All eyes were on her. Tail Light was handcuffed and being held in place by a nightstick pressed into his stomach. He was being read his rights by the young officer who had come to Cat's rescue. Cat waited patiently for him to finish.

"I'll follow you to the station."

"No need. You have about a hundred eye witnesses here who will swear that he molested you and you defended yourself. Case closed. Go home."

"I'm sorry for overreacting."

"You did what needed to be done. I'm glad I was here."

"Me, too. Thanks."

Walking along Clematis Street to the nearby parking lot, Cat cast a wary eye on darkened doorways and alleyways. Whenever she was alone, she followed a strict routine—walk quickly to the car and unlock the door, check the back seat before getting in, lock the doors. She did this faithfully every day—morning and night. Never again would she be caught unprepared. On nights like this night, she added a Bluetooth to her routine.

#

"Kevin asked Cat to marry him," Marci brought Ian up to date on the biggest news of the day.

"That's terrific! That's great news. It is great news, isn't it?"

"Of course."

"So why don't you seem overjoyed?"

"She said 'Yes' but she's not sure."

"Cat and Kevin live together. Yes, I know she moved in after the assault, but she must feel he's the right one or she wouldn't have done that. They're practically married already. What's not to be sure about?"

"I don't think she trusts herself to make big decisions anymore. She's lost some of her confidence."

"That's a temporary condition. Other than you, I don't know anyone as grounded as Cat. Plus, she's safe with Kevin. He loves her. She loves him. It's all good."

"I said the same thing." Marci stood on tiptoe and kissed Ian. "I love you."

"Of course, you do. I'm great and so is this little girl of ours, who just happens to need to be changed." Ian held Sonora at arm's length, offering her to Marci who wasn't the slightest bit offended by the smell coming off her daughter's diaper.

"Is this how you welcome mommy home? Well, I guess it's only fair. Aunt Cat had to deal with my stinkiness earlier today. I'll bet she put you up to this."

#

As soon as she had the wireless connected to her cell phone, Cat called Kevin. "I'm just heading out, sweetie. It's been a long day. I've missed you."

Kevin's deep reassuring baritone soothed Cat's nerves. His voice on the other end of the call made the drive seem shorter. They chatted the whole way home.

"I'm turning onto Clydesdale now. Be home in two seconds."

As Cat pulled into the driveway, her headlights picked up Kevin waiting patiently in the open doorway. She drove into the garage and stepped out into his waiting arms. The closing garage door served as a barricade against the evils in the world.

"I am so glad you came into my life." Cat held tightly to Kevin. Taking his hand, she put it to her lips and kissed it. "You are my knight in shining armor."

As they walked arms around each other's waists into the house, Cat let her mind wander back to the day they met.

#

December 2006

The napkin and the business card Kevin had given Cat at Moe's Southwest were tucked safely in her pocketbook. She looked at them from time to time over the next three days. Should she? Shouldn't she?

Unlike the matter of fact way Cat made decisions on the job, in her personal life she was more contemplative. Never one to act on impulse, her decision making process was based on level headedness and clear thinking. Unsure of what to do, she did what she knew best— a records search. When nothing untoward turned up, she bit the bullet and called him. It was a good decision.

In the living room, Kevin had a faux fire blazing on the hearth. Even though no real heat was generated by the sterno-fueled flames, Cat stood with her hands out, trying to draw the chill from her body.

"Babe. Notice anything?"

Kevin's head was practically arrow shaped, so hard was he trying to get Cat to look at the mantle. Holding center stage, a silver frame had been placed between pictures of Cat and Kevin at the Miami

Zoo. Inside, two sets of napkins proudly proclaimed the love he felt for her.

CHAPTER EIGHT

The last to leave were the first to arrive, and the phone was ringing at 6:45 when Cat stepped off the elevator. Marci was already at her desk. "Are you all right?"

"Yeah. Why wouldn't I be?"

"Last night's adventure is all over the station. Why didn't you call me, Cat?"

"You have a life. You can't live mine."

"I'm not just your partner. I'm your friend—your best friend. What did Kevin say?"

"Didn't tell him and neither will you."

Cat's thoughts returned to the night before, guilt at not telling Kevin about Tail Light weighing heavily on her conscience. She could still feel the pressure of Kevin's body on her own as they made love. She smiled remembering how Shadow, Kevin's husky, and NeeNee had jumped on the bed and tried to nestle between them. Both she and Kevin had yelled at the dogs, "Get down," without losing their rhythm. Afterward, they remained entwined until Kevin's breathing signaled he was asleep. Cat extricated herself from his arms and went to the bathroom.

Two furry bundles of black and white were sprawled on her side of the bed when she returned, and Kevin was snoring contentedly. Cat grabbed his tee shirt from the floor and slipped it over her head. In the living room, she sat on the sofa with only the light from the full moon to guide her movements. After a few minutes, she reached under one of the cushions and removed a large envelope. From it, she took photos of herself, badly beaten, and a stack of crime scene reports. She began to read them for the hundredth time.

"Cat! Are you hearing me? Captain Jameson wants to see you." Marci's voice brought Cat back to the present.

"About what?"

"He's the Captain. What do you think he wants? There are no secrets around here." Marci stood and walked away, her back to Cat hiding the fact that she was worried by the encounter with Tail Light and even more worried by Cat's current pretend nonchalance.

Cat crossed the bull pen and knocked with feigned self-confidence on Captain Jameson's door. "You wanted to see me, sir?"

"Heard there was an incident at O'Shea's last night. Are you…"

"I'm fine, Captain. Nothing to worry about."

"I'm not worried, at least, not about the incident. That little shit isn't going to file charges. I am worried about you."

"Like I said… I'm fine."

Captain Jameson pointed to a chair. Cat shook her head, indicating her desire to remain standing.

"That wasn't a request, Detective. Sit."

"Yes, sir."

"You need to take control of your emotions, Cat. Things like this will happen from time to time. Some will be accidents. Others—like last night—won't. I don't want to be worried that you'll overreact."

"Yes, sir."

"If you need help, get it. Don't make me the bad guy."

When Cat returned to the bull pen, the phone on Marci's desk was ringing. The insistence of the flashing light on the call button signaled someone or something important on the other end.

As Cat grabbed for the receiver, she saw Marci heading for the squad room kitchenette. When Marci returned with two cups of instant coffee, Cat, still holding the receiver, was perched expectantly on her desk. "That was G. He says he has the answer to why Kincaid was so popular with the ladies."

"Let me think. Faux coffee or a decomposing body. Decisions. Decisions." Marci pretended to struggle with making up her mind. "Decomposition it is!"

During the phone call, the medical examiner, who had seen just about everything in his thirty plus years in the morgue, hinted to Cat that he had uncovered something "huge." Eyes twinkling with curiosity, Cat and Marci decided to visit with G before heading over to Kincaid's condo; a search warrant having been approved. The coffee mugs were left teetering on a pile of file folders on Marci's desk as the partners made their way to the elevator.

"Want to talk?"

"Not about last night. We need to catch my rapist. I won't be able to rest until he's behind bars and on the receiving end of a broomstick every night."

Entering a morgue was disconcerting for most people, but Doc G's sterile little world was even more so for the uninitiated. His fondness for the comedians of yesteryear was evident in the waiting room and in his private office. Rather than anatomical charts, the walls were covered with posters of "the Greats," as he called them—Jerry Lewis, George Burns, Jack Benny to name a few.

On the wall over his desk hung a plague inscribed with a quote by Red Skelton, *"No matter what your heartache may be, laughing helps you forget it for a few seconds."*

Considering all the heartache a medical examiner had to deal with on a daily basis, those, he often said, "… are good words to live by."

Cat and Marci had long since stopped being surprised by the contradictions they found in G's office. On the bright yellow walls of the exterior halls and the stark white of the examining room, life and death, laughter and tears had found a place to co-exist in peace.

"What took you so long?" G greeted them warmly as they entered his lair. With a sweep of his arm, he guided them into the main autopsy room. "The sticky stuff on the tissue you found was semen. Our surfside Don Juan had sexual intercourse shortly before his death and, since no condom was found at the scene, the tissue served as a repository for his seed. Female ejaculate was also on the paper so I would say our mystery woman also used the tissue to clean herself."

"I guessed as much," Cat nodded in agreement.

"Forgive me." Marci noticeably shivered. "No matter how often I hear these reports, I can't help but feel like a Peeping Tom."

"There's always an element of voyeurism with cases involving sex," G assured her. "There's no reason to be embarrassed."

"I keep seeing triple Xs in my head. Please, just go on with your report."

"There is something very telling about Mr. Kincaid's post mortem condition and, even being aware of your dislike of overt sexual situations, Marci, I still think you both need to see it. Follow me."

What Nate Kincaid lacked in classic good looks, he made up for in a less obvious but more coveted way. Perhaps, the endowment fairy sneezed while waving her wand over his groin, but the bulge under the sheet covering his body had nothing to do with a missing gym sock.

"If I appear a little waxen to you…," the medical examiner advised his favorite ladies, "… it is not due to the nature of my job. This hue is a classic example of green with envy."

On that remark, G uncovered Kincaid with a flourish and allowed Marci and Cat full view of the corpse. "Eleven inches plus a little extra for good measure. This guy should have been in porn movies. He would have made a fortune."

"He was and although his measurements are impressive, I

doubt they had anything to do with his death." Marci blushed her response.

"Perhaps not in the literal sense, Detective, but Mr. Kincaid's substantial girth and length might well have been the catalyst for murder by an amant jaloux—a jealous lover. There were quite a few women at the beach, were there not, and I think more than his name was on their lips."

"That's disgus…"

"Hate, my dear Marci, I was referring to hate."

Cat stared at Kincaid's body, but it wasn't his penis that had her attention. "G, what about those marks on his shoulders? They look like thumb prints?"

"Good eye, Detective. They are thumbprints. Take a look at this."

G lifted Kincaid's upper torso so the partners could see his back. The imprint of eight fingers were visible—four on each shoulder—proof that someone had gripped Kincaid hard and, possibly, pushed him off the tower. "They've darkened considerably since yesterday."

Marci nibbled her fingernail as she often did while formulating an idea. "The fingers look small. Are you thinking a woman?"

"That would be my assumption. The recipient of Mr. Kincaid's affections most likely had her legs wrapped around his waist for an extended period of time. Holding her up while thrusting forward and back against the wooden railing caused the bruising on the backside of his legs. The finger marks on his shoulders are the result of the lady holding on for dear life. The lesion on his forehead was definitely caused by wood from the tower. There were tiny splinters in the wound."

"So much of the wood used to build the tower and ladder has deteriorated that it would be impossible to determine exactly where the fragments came from. We found nothing in a search of the immediate area," Cat interjected. "Nowhere did it appear that a piece of wood had broken off."

"There are other towers on the beach, Cat. How many did we see? There were three just in the area we surveyed and the beach goes for miles. Since all the towers are in bad shape, it's possible the wood came from another location."

"There was blood on two ladder rungs, most likely left by the cuts on the front of his legs." G continued with his findings. "Both legs have similar markings. I'm positive the wounds are the result of losing his balance and hitting his shin against the edge of the steps. The head wound is harder to define but he could have hit the frontal bone on a step when he fell forward trying to catch himself. Unfortunately, no evidence of impact was found on the staircase at the level required for his height. The actual cause of death was the fall from the tower ladder and impact with coral buried in the sand. Was he pushed? Only the denizens of the deep can tell you that for sure."

"So, we're looking for a woman. Do you think that in the throes of passion…"

"No. The sex act had already concluded by the time Kincaid fell to the beach." G suddenly stopped speaking and reached for Marci's hand. "Please stop that. If you keep biting your cuticles, you're going to get an infection."

"What is this—an intervention? First Cat. Now you."

"Consider it my professional medical opinion. What you are doing is unhealthy and, to be truthful, retch worthy. Do you know how many germs are on your hands at any given time?"

"Okay. I get it. What else did you find?"

"I'm pretty sure he was unconscious or, at least, dazed before he hit the sand. The actual cause of death was focal brain injury—both coup and contrecoup. In the fall from the tower ladder, his head smashed against a large piece of coral buried in the sand, causing the skull to bend inward and impact with the brain. I extracted pieces of the coral from the wound."

Cat looked closely at the rest of Kincaid's body, trying hard not to focus on his genitals.

"Viagra," G stated, a smirk in his voice.

"What? What about Viagra?"

"That's why he's still standing at attention. I found Viagra in his system."

"Interesting, but I didn't ask, and I wasn't looking."

"Sorry. I misinterpreted the direction of your gaze."

"I was looking at his knee. His one knee is badly bruised."

"Both of them actually, front and back, into the crease above the calf. There are also scrapes extending downward from one knee in front. My best guess, the scrapes and some of the frontal bruising are from the fall, but the rest could be the result of rough sex, especially the bruising on the back side of the legs."

Marci removed a piece of skin from her tongue and, after checking that neither Cat nor G were watching, wiped it on the leg of her pants. She sucked on the finger to stop the bleeding while she spoke. "For some people, tempting fate is the ultimate turn on. Having sex in public… Maybe they hoped to get caught in the act or… Jeez, I just don't know. Danger has never been an aphrodisiac for me."

Marci and Cat moved away from the autopsy table as G pulled the cover back over Kincaid's body. The ladies expressed their appreciation for his quick analysis and got his confirmation that a written report would be on their desk by mid-afternoon.

As they were about to close the door behind them, G stopped Marci with a tap on the shoulder. In his fingers, he held a band aid and a tube of antiseptic. "Detective, a moment, please."

Cat and Marci left G's office in silence. Already late for the planned search of Nate Kincaid's apartment, they headed for the parking lot. Even after they were settled in their car; even after the engine had roared to life and Cat had shifted into drive; even after they had driven the five miles to the highway entrance, they did not speak.

They were on the northbound ramp to the I-95 when Marci, no longer able to control herself, snorted and an avalanche of giggles filled the car. "Wow. I had a hard time keeping my mouth from gaping open." Marci spread her hands to simulate the length of Kincaid's bounty.

"I know." Cat laughed as she pushed Marci's hands further and further apart. "You never were any good at geometry. As much as I tried to look everywhere—anywhere—else, I kept going back to his groin. No wonder those women loved and hated him."

Wiping tears from her eyes, Cat pulled the car into traffic. She and Marci now knew the answer to the question they had bandied about in the beach parking lot. Of dividends, diamonds and dicks, Kincaid had been amply blessed with the last.

#

With search warrant in hand, Cat and Marci led their team of four investigators into the condo that Kincaid had called home. With them were Detective Maurice "Moe" Di Lorenzo, Detective Damian Mack, Sergeant Paulie Padrone and Officer Keith Kennedy.

Inside the front door, sneakers and sandals were scattered haphazardly, as though kicked off and forgotten. Two full trash bags were leaning against one wall. Since the garbage pail was overflowing, the dumpster didn't appear to have been a popular destination.

On first inspection, the two bedroom/two bath unit, constructed in the 1940s, looked the same as when it was first built. Square footage-wise, it was small by present day standards and sparsely furnished. Except for the kitchen, no attempt at modernization had been made. Most of the carpeting had been removed. Pockmarked bamboo flooring covered the main living area and the master bedroom. The wood flooring was marred and scarred by what appeared to be the imprint of high-heeled shoes.

"See those little circles in the flooring? Those are caused by the metal caps on high-heels. Must have been a lot of ladies dancing their way into Kincaid's heart or he into theirs."

"How do you know that?"

"Kevin and I used to have bamboo in the living room and dining room. He was always telling me to take my shoes off. The few times I forgot, I left holes just like those which is why we now have tile." Cat stood above one of the damaged areas on the floor and placed the heel of her shoe into one of the indentations. "Perfect fit."

"I gotta give you that one, Cat. The floor feels gritty, too. I'll bet Kincaid wore those sandals at the beach and just kicked them off when he got home. That's something I know about because I'm always yelling at Ian for tracking in sand from the golf course."

A gust of wind from the open patio doors lifted a week's worth of newspapers from the floor. Marci sniffed the air. "Nice being this close to the ocean. I can smell the salt."

In the dining area, a small round table and two old and beaten wicker chairs took up a corner. A tablecloth covered the top and draped down the sides but was mostly hidden under piles of mail—opened and unopened letters, bills, and flyers advertising pizza and Chinese food.

A sofa covered in a neutral nubby fabric and one matching over-sized chair provided the only seating in the living room. Six empty water glasses were lined up on the floor in front of the sofa. A barely visible outline of what Cat imagined to be Kincaid's backside could be seen on the dusty wood, evidence that he preferred leaning up against the furniture to sitting on it.

There were no coffee tables or end tables—nowhere to put the little mementos that made a house a home. Looking around, Marci & Cat realized that tables were unnecessary. There was nothing to display. Aside from some well-chosen paintings on the walls, the condo was devoid of warmth and individuality. If ever a space shouted detached, this was the place.

"Marci, doesn't it strike you as odd that a man known for seducing hundreds, maybe thousands, of women has not one knick knack or picture—nothing personal—to remind him of his successes?"

"With a track record like his, I doubt that he was much

interested in saving ticket stubs or locks of hair."

Off a short hallway, the doors to two bathrooms stood open. The smaller of the two was decorated with posters from old horror movies. On the vanity, a child's toothbrush, an egg timer and a cup with a hippopotamus handle gathered dust. A shower curtain imprinted with images of Dracula, Frankenstein and the Mummy provided a childish yet chilling touch. The room appeared caught in a time warp.

Sgt. Padrone, a man so fanatical about his appearance he starched the crease in his trouser legs, pushed the curtain aside and groaned. "I knew I should have worn my old uniform today. This case is going to cost me a fortune in dry cleaning bills."

The tub was filled with diving gear, fishing rods, a small surf board, beach toys and assorted other outdoor equipment—and everything was coated with a thick layer of sand. Padrone's voice carried throughout the apartment as he called to Cat and Marci. "Detectives, your report should include a notation that Kincaid preferred showers to bubble baths."

The master bedroom closet, badly in need of painting, was small and crammed with jeans, tee shirts, boxes, scuba tanks, basketballs and holiday decorations, among other things. Baby clothes and toys were stacked on the floor. After taking into consideration what she had seen in the bathroom, Marci pinpointed another aspect of Kincaid's life that needed looking into. "Cat, come see this. As if the bathroom wasn't creepy enough, Kincaid still has onesies and rattles stored in this closet. His kid should be a teenager by now, wouldn't you say?"

"I'd say I'm not surprised, Marci. Look around this place. Nothing has been thrown away in years not even the garbage." As Cat bent closer to look at a pile of clothes, they toppled from their precarious perch. Hidden under a baby blanket was a floor safe.

Calling for one of the youngest members of the team, Marci instructed Keith Kennedy to "Get it open or get it down to the station. I want to know what he was hiding in there."

The second bedroom, the only carpeted room in the apartment, seemed to serve a dual purpose. A bed was pushed up against one wall while most of the remaining space was lined with floor to ceiling bookcases. The carpeting was littered with papers and books making it difficult to fully open the door. The paperbacks and hard covers that should have filled the bookcase shelves were scattered about the room.

Cat's first reaction was that the makeshift office had been ransacked. Squeezing in sideways, she kicked some of the debris out of the way, clearing a path for Detectives Damian Mack and Moe Di Lorenzo to follow. Although it was noon and the Florida sun was shining brightly, the office/bedroom was dark. The double window facing the front walkway was covered with tightly closed venetian blinds. One small lamp with flickering 60 watt bulb barely dispelled the shadows.

"Pull up those blinds, Moe. Only bats could see in here." Cat squinted into the blackness. Having entered lots of cramped and damp places in the last ten years, she was accustomed to working in less than optimum conditions, but the eerie feeling she was experiencing at this moment had nothing to do with a lack of light and space.

In every corner and crevice of the room, balled up and discarded papers were thrown haphazardly. A quick glance was all that was needed to discover Kincaid fancied himself a novelist and screenwriter, albeit a frustrated one. A cabinet partially buried under piles of clean and dirty laundry held evidence that Kincaid had found a modicum of success in years past.

Two tightly crammed drawers and the floor served as his filing system. Despite what appeared to be nothing more than the beginnings of many conceived but never completed stories, Cat's fine-tuned senses told her there were secrets hiding among the discarded pages of dialogue and character studies.

"Jesus. What a pig sty! My allergies are going to kick into overdrive. Just hook me up to oxygen now." Erudite Moe Di Lorenzo coughed loudly as he pulled the cord on the venetian blinds, sending millions of dust particles into the air.

"Are you positive that you're a big, tough homicide investigator?" Damian Mack teased. "Check your pants. See if you left anything home this morning."

A game of verbal badminton ensued as Moe Di Lorenzo defended his manliness with a quick chop shot. "Yeah, and who was the one screaming like a little woman about the roaches on the Kilmo case?"

"Roaches are disgusting. Dust is just dust. It's everywhere. Grow a pair."

"Enough already." Cat's voice made it clear they were there to work. "Use those obviously intelligent minds to uncover some useful information."

A desk weighed down by a pile of papers resembling the Leaning Tower of Pisa drew Cat's attention. A three wheeled chair—one wheel missing—tilted precariously sideways in front of the desk, like a drunken sentry protecting a hidden treasure. Another pile— this one books—was balanced haphazardly on the seat. Not wanting to send the books crashing to the floor, Cat carefully lifted the many paged volumes, one by one, and placed them on the floor. This activity allowed her to see under the desk where she found an almost equally as high stack of manila folders.

"Moe, I know what an avid reader you are so take this pile of folders and see if you find anything useful."

Begrudgingly, Moe took the 50 folder high stack and cleared a spot on the floor to sit down. He gave the first few folders a quick once over. "I'm an avid racing form reader not novels. These are manuscripts."

"Maybe you'll luck out and the stories will be filled with lots of sex and violence."

"Doesn't interest me. I saw that every day in vice. Not recommended bedtime reading."

"Well, give it your best."

Cat balanced herself carefully on the wobbly chair and reached over to turn on the computer which was partially hidden by a holey beach towel once three times its present size. For a brief moment, the monitor glowed a dull green and then brightened as the AOL home page filled the screen. Kincaid's user name and password were saved for easy access to his inbox. Cat did a double take when she saw the amount of mail he had received.

Speaking to twice divorced Damian Mack, a forever marine who was crouched nearby sorting through hundreds of balled and crinkled pages torn from as just many notebooks, she posed a question. "Mack, you're doubly doomed, right? Do you do any of this online dating stuff?"

"A two-time loser, that's me. Sure. Sometimes. Haven't had any luck at it. Why?"

"Kincaid has hundreds of emails from women. I didn't know there were so many dating sites. PlentyofFish. Match.com. Flixster. Myspace. Facebook. eHarmony. OKcupid. Talkmatch. This list is endless."

"There are as many sites as there are people desperate to use them."

"You might want to take some pointers from our vic. He has 1536 read and unread emails. I estimate that about 900 of them are from single women. Some of these emails are months old."

"Makes sense. Since real trash never got thrown away, why would the internet variety?"

"I suppose. Have you ever heard of Big, Black and Beautiful or Triple Naked Naughtiness?"

"They sound a little progressive for Mack's tastes." Moe Di Lorenzo's disembodied voice echoed from inside the closet he was now searching. "He's more a missionary, in the dark, hole in the sheet kind of guy."

"Funny! Real funny, Moe. Since we're talking about color, there's something I've always wanted to ask you. What's with the mafia ensembles? I'll bet even your underwear is black."

"What's wrong with wearing black?"

"You look more like a criminal than a cop."

"Good. Maybe the real criminals will be afraid of me."

"Takes more than clothes to make the man."

"Go fu…"

"Pete must find working with you a barrel of laughs. Are you sure he's out on paternity leave and not applying for a transfer to another precinct?"

Moe Di Lorenzo knew that Damian Mack was kidding. The men were good friends who hung out together when neither had a date, which was often.

Moe's partner of five years, Pete Shonto, had just become the proud father of twin boys. Anxious not to miss the first days of their life, he began a three-week vacation the minute the infants' heads popped out of the womb. Pete telephoned Moe every morning and afternoon to report on his sons' latest developments. Moe referred to those calls as "snooze alerts" because, at less than a week old, sleeping was what the Shonto boys did best.

The philosophy in Homicide Division was that "it takes two," which usually referred to the how and why of a murder investigation. The saying also paid heed to the fact that solving a case was work intensive and not something that could be accomplished by a glory hog.

Since a team of one was no team at all, Moe was always available for any investigation in need of an extra pair of eyes and hands. When he heard that Cat and Marci were short staffed, he offered to go along for the search of Kincaid's apartment.

Before Moe could snap at Mack with another zinger, an obviously embarrassed Keith Kennedy interrupted from the doorway where he had been listening to their conversation. "No wonder the mattress cover in the master bedroom is so stained."

Turning away from the computer, Cat shot an inquiring glance at the red-faced young officer. "What are you talking about?"

"All those emails from woman. The mattress on his bed is… Go see for yourself—that is if you can stand the sound of Marci gagging."

"If Marci is on the verge of vomiting, that must be one hell of a mattress."

"She pretending but she's intent on making her feelings known to everyone within earshot." Kennedy stuck his finger in his mouth in imitation of Marci's not so subtle commentary.

"That bad, huh?"

"The bed's unmade except for a blanket thrown over the mattress. When we pulled it back, we found one of those quilted covers stained with, um, semen… lots of semen. This Kincaid guy had not been sleeping alone."

"How are you doing with the safe?'

"Still working on it."

"Any chance of getting DNA from that cover?" Mack asked the beet red Kennedy.

Not one to miss an opportunity to get in a jab, Moe Di Lorenzo spoke from the confines of the closet. "I know it's been a while since I've done any mattress dancing, but other than Kincaid, whose DNA would you expect to find? Even if we found female ejaculate, what would we compare it to? There's no database of women who fell for assholes and then killed them."

"Okay, guys, this conversation is getting more ridiculous by the moment." Struggling to hide her amusement, Cat instructed Kennedy to "Wrap up the cover and take it to the station with the rest of Kincaid's personal effects. If you can't get the safe open, take it with you when we leave."

Returning her attention to the computer, Cat focused on the outgoing emails. There were nearly a hundred and each one contained the exact same message from Kincaid, who was obviously an expert at cutting and pasting. Not a word varied in what amounted to a cyber pickup letter.

"Okay, gentlemen, listen up and take notes. Kincaid was quite the smoothie."

'Dear Desirable Stranger. Like you, I love the arts. I have season tickets to a number of well-known theaters, including the Maltz, Lyric and Florida Stage. I often attend concerts at the Florida Fairgrounds. What type of music do you like? I see we share a passion for travel. Paris is the most beautiful city in the world. You can't help but fall in love when you are there. Perhaps we can discover the magic and the passion together.'

Pausing in her recitation, Cat confessed her distaste for the cavalier manner in which Kincaid seduced the unsuspecting women. "Suddenly, Marci isn't the only one wanting to retch."

"Keep reading, Cat. Could be I will learn something." Moe Di Lorenzo seemed genuinely interested even as he cast a wary eye at his partner. "And Mack, shut your trap. That's wasn't an opening for you to join the conversation."

Cat picked up where she had left off.

'In the meantime, the view of the fake lake from my apartment is charming. Would you allow me to make you dinner one evening? My skills are limited, but I can make us a delicious salad, and we can share a glass or two of wine while listening to music and the waterfall below my balcony. I'm an expert at massage and would gladly rub the weariness out of your feet if you will let me.'

Again, Cat stopped reading. She pinched her nose as she skimmed through the rest of the emails and personal history. "I detect the scent of virtual bullshit. Mack, you need to read our vic's profile. He knew how to flatter women; really played up to their fears of getting old and becoming less desirable."

"Fear isn't my chosen method of seduction." Mack rose from his knees to a standing position and stretched his legs.

"Well, it worked for Kincaid. He even admitted to being

frugal—that's code for cheap—and they still wanted to date him. No fancy restaurants or hotels for this guy. He was a coupon clipper and made sure the ladies knew it. From his letters, his frugalness appears to be a point of pride with him."

"I don't consider myself cheap, Cat, but the Breakers isn't exactly on my speed dial either."

"Bear with me. He didn't spend money on quality dining or travel accommodations, but when it came to the arts, he dangled concert and theatre tickets the way a pedophile does candy. The women practically begged to be invited to these shows. Seems he got himself caught in the web of deceit a couple times, too. He invited two women who were friends to the same play."

"Guess he was hedging his bets. How'd that work out for him?"

"Seems the women shared their online dating experiences and from the sound of their emails, they were pissed."

"Enough to kill him?" Mack asked.

"Life in prison for missing a Leonard Cohen concert? I don't think so."

"Who?" There was an echo in the room as both Mack and Moe voiced the same question.

Cat ignored them and continued scrolling through the dating websites. The more she read, the more she realized that underneath Kincaid's flattering words were some deep seated resentments toward women. She wondered if he had had mother issues but before she could pursue the matter further, Officer Kennedy shouted his success at opening the safe.

"Detectives, there's more than $25,000 in here. All small denominations— singles and fives, a few tens—nothing bigger. What do you want me to do with it?"

"Bag it. Tag it. And dream of what you could do with it if it was yours," Marci ordered from somewhere in the condo.

Cat, who was finding the lifeguard lothario more intriguing by the minute, went back to searching his computer. Kincaid's emails were rife with simmering sexual innuendo and something more. There was a subtle undertone of distrust, as though he expected the women to hurt him and, therefore, was determined to hurt them first. His was a self-fulfilling prophecy.

From his very first letter of introduction, Nate Kincaid extended his version of flowers and candy—an invitation to dinner at his condo, wine, music and a massage. Any woman who lived more than a thirty-minute drive away was passed over for someone within "pop over" distance, making convenience a priority even in his love life.

"Padrone," Cat yelled to the sergeant coordinating the search, "get me the list of women who were at the crime scene this morning. I have a feeling they all knew our lover boy more intimately than they admitted. And I don't think he was the nice guy they all claimed he was."

Shutting down the computer and disconnecting it from the wall, Cat lifted the laptop and prepared to leave the room. Mack's voice, filled with tension, stopped her before she took one step.

"Cat, I may have found our first clue. This was wedged between the wall and the bookcase." Mack held up a large expandable file with one hand. In the other, he held a stack of letters showing signs of age. "Love letters of a sort sent from father to son."

Mack passed the letters to Cat one by one. Each was addressed to Jason Kincaid; each had been opened, read and reinserted into the original mailing envelope. In addition to the envelopes being stamped RETURN TO SENDER, the letters bore messages in red magic marker emboldened across the pages. DROP DEAD. GO TO HELL. FUCK YOU. FUCKING BASTARD. There were others as well.

"I'd say the kid had no love lost for his father."

"I'd have to agree. Find him. You and Moe check out the address on the envelopes. Find the wife, too. I want to know what happened to this family."

Cat carried the computer out to the living room. Glancing at the dining table piled with letters and bills and the floor covered with old newspapers, she realized that Kincaid was a hoarder in all aspects of his life. The undeleted emails and the trash by the door were indications that he threw nothing away—except for people.

CHAPTER NINE

Stepping into homicide division's bullpen two mornings later, Marci was accosted by the sound of female voices rising and falling in a fevered pitch. If she hadn't known better, she would have thought she had time traveled back to her college dorm during pledge week.

"Morning, Moe" she greeted the still partner-less detective. "How many former loves do we have here this morning?"

"Twenty two and counting. The conference room looks like party central. They brought breakfast—pastries and coffee."

"Nice of them but the party's over. Let's split them up. You, me, Cat, Mack and Kennedy. Get as much information as you can without feeding them any lines. See what jives and what sounds rehearsed."

"I'm on it, Marci. By the way, Mack and I drove to Port St. Lucie last night to check out the address on those envelopes. If the kid lived there, he's long gone. Nobody we spoke to had ever heard of a Jason Kincaid."

"Okay. Don't give up. There has to be something in the personal effects we took from the apartment to point us in the right direction. Go over his financials. Look for alimony and child support payments."

"Will do. Paulie wants to talk to you. He's got some info on the money we found at the condo."

Marci walked quickly toward her office, anxious to drown out the abnormal sound of gaiety that echoed off the old plaster walls. Her annoyance barometer was reaching a dangerous level. "This is Homicide Division, dammit. Happiness is not allowed here," she muttered half to herself.

Stopping at Sgt. Paulie Padrone's desk, Marci raised her eyebrows, soliciting some input on the windfall in Kincaid's safe.

"Tips." Padrone smiled an answer to her wrinkled brow.

"Tips? People have been calling with tips about the money?"

"No. The money is tips. Kincaid worked as a valet at one of those ritzy enclaves on the island. Club manager says he pulled in about two hundred a night, five nights a week—all in tips. That's $4000 a month over the seven months of season. Cash. No taxes. No IRS breathing down his neck."

"Four thousand dollars a month for parking cars? We're in the wrong business."

"Tell me about it. I'm thinking of calling the club manager back and asking for Kincaid's job."

"You and me both. Okay. Turn the cash into Evidence. Let's see where this case goes. If no family comes forward, we're set with donuts and coffee for the next five years."

Marci walked off in the direction of the shared-space office she and Cat were now using, stopping midway to continue her conversation with Padrone. "The keys to his apartment were in his pocket. It could have been the simplest heist in history.

"Yeah?"

"There was no alarm on the apartment. Kennedy opened the safe easily and he has trouble opening a cell door with a key."

"I can smell wood burning."

"The safe wasn't that heavy. Even an average-sized man could have carried it."

"And I repeat… Yeah?"

"But not a woman."

"Where are you going with this hypothesis?"

"I'm not sure. Kincaid's life was full of passion. Secrets and lies had to be a part of his M.O. How else could he juggle a date book the size of the Manhattan Yellow Pages. His death, obviously, had nothing to do with an easy windfall. One of these ladies holds the answer and I want it. Time to talk to the bimbos."

With a purposeful stride, Marci covered the remaining distance to the office. She dropped the file folders she was carrying on her desk, took a deep breath and turned back toward the conference room to claim her first interview of the day.

Women–blond, brunette, redhead, tall, short, curvy and chesty, skinny and flat chested, pudgy and just plain fat, white, black, Asian, Hispanic—came and went for three days and little if anything of use was learned. On the last day of interviews, as the afternoon sun bounced off the green and whites separating One Police Plaza from the public parking facility reserved for civilian employees and visitors, four very tired investigators met in the now quiet conference room. Moe was the only one missing, having left early in the day to follow up on a lead.

"Who wants to start?" Cat's yawn took in everyone at the table.

"If my suspicions are correct," Damian Mack ventured, "I think we all just participated in a well-orchestrated presentation of The Many Loves of Nate Kincaid."

"No shit." Marci fairly spit her response. "I could have saved us a lot of time by playing back the taped statement of Lady Love No. 1. All their answers were the same."

"It was like talking to the Stepford Wives." Arms behind his head and legs up on the table, Keith Kennedy was leaning so far back in his chair that his comments were directed at the acoustical ceiling tiles.

Around the table they went, sharing insights from their days trying to crack the polished countenances resulting from Botox injections and laser resurfacing. Damian Mack was eager to offer his observations.

"My nephew has a knack for reciting movie dialogue. These women sounded just like him; like they were parroting lines from a script. 'Kincaid was a nice guy. He showered me with affection. Told me I was beautiful. He was a great lover.' As if we needed convincing he was well endowed. We've all read the autopsy report."

"Yeah. If I have to hear blessed by the gods one more time," Kennedy rocked his chair into an upright position, "I'm going to puke. So what if he had a big dick. Every one of these women thought he was devoted to them. They believed they were the love of his life until they weren't."

"I'm not sure there is an actual correlation between being devoted to someone and being well endowed. That's more the male perspective if by devoted you mean good in bed."

"You could have fooled me from all the talk on those gossip shows."

"For women, actually being in love is a bigger turn on than size. Right, Cat."

Cat, who had a habit of rolling the pad of her left index finger over her thumbnail while concentrating, joined the conversation. She rested her forehead on her cupped hand as she gathered her thoughts. "It's abnormal not to be resentful when you learn that the tender words you took as truth turn out to be nothing more than trash talk. Kincaid recycled his lines more often than the Solid Waste Authority does garbage. Nothing he said was ever genuine."

"So, what are you saying?" Kennedy, the youngest of the group and still somewhat of a novice with women, had a look of befuddled innocence on his face. "They forgave him because he had a big snake in his trousers?"

Three seasoned officers of the law answered in unison. "Idiot!" The empty styrofoam coffee cups thrown in his direction added emphasis to their words.

"Women don't like to be used," Marci lectured. "When someone like Kincaid comes into our lives, we plot revenge. Our first thought is to cut off that dick you can't seem to ignore. We usually settle for putting a cigar in the gas tank of your car or slashing a tire. This time, maybe, those women were pushed too far. The mob mentality might have put them over the edge."

In the silence that followed Marci's statement, Mack and Kennedy contemplated their own crotches. A barely discernible shiver crept up their spines and exited through their scalps.

"Don't you find it interesting that not one of these women remembers meeting a brunette with striped hair, yet she paid for a year's worth of breakfasts?" Cat's voice vibrated with question marks.

The loud huffing and puffing of an out-of-breath Moe Di Lorenzo distracted everyone from answering. He stood in the doorway, a satisfied smile forming his normally down turned mouth into a happy clown face. "I found him. The kid. He's in his second year at Palm Beach Community College. Gardens' campus. Wants to make movies. Wants to be a writer just like his daddy."

Marci stopped biting her finger and looked toward Cat, who was already looking back at her. Their eyes meet and, without saying a word, they stood and gathered their belongings.

"Did you get a home address, Moe?"

"Yup. Registrar was very helpful. Want me to come with you?"

"All three of you. A little fear could work in our favor." Marci was already heading out the door. "Nothing like the sight of five police officers to scare the shi… to encourage the young man to talk."

The elevator doors were just about closed, sealing the five detectives inside, when Paulie Padrone's hand sneaked through the narrow gap. "G called. He's finished the autopsy and wants to speak with the Detective Ladies asap."

"Please call him back. Tell him we're on the hunt." Cat jabbed the close button with a vengeance. "We'll meet with him later in the day."

"There's something else. Call came in. The Jupiter police found a body. Female. Raped. I think it's your guy, Cat. Chasewood Apartment on Center Street. She didn't make it."

"Tell them we're on our way."

"Already did. They're expecting you."

The ride to the first floor was silent and uncomfortable. Cat was visibly shaken. She rummaged through her satchel trying to hide the emotions that were playing out on her face. As the elevator doors opened, she tossed the car keys to Marci with shaking hands. "You drive."

June first to November 30th was rainy season in Florida and when it rained, it usually poured. The same could be true for murder. One body could easily signal a coming deluge of death and Cat and Marci were about to discover that death—even the death of a stranger—could be very, very personal.

When Marci and Cat arrived at Chasewood Apartments, the entry way was blocked by a Jupiter police cruiser and two uniformed officers. Marci stuck her head out the window and was instantly recognized with a "come on through" wave of the hand.

Entering the victim's apartment, Cat was struck by the similarities to her own attack. Crime scene investigators and medical personnel filled the living room and hallway. A trail of blood led to the bedroom where the body of a young woman, mid thirties, laid on the bed, covered to the neck with a sheet. Her long blond hair had been combed into two ponytails atop her head and tied with wide green ribbons. She looked posed and peaceful. G, his back to the door, was giving his preliminary findings to the detective in charge. Cat's gasp caused him to turn around.

"You shouldn't be here, Detective."

"She shouldn't be dead. We should have expected another attack." Cat ran a shaking hand along the scar on her neck. "We've got to put this bastard away."

"I'm confident this scene will yield much more evidence. We will catch him, Cat."

"We need to do it fast. I have a bad feeling in the pit of my stomach."

CHAPTER TEN

As darkness fell, two unmarked squad cars pulled up in front of the house on Monet Court. Just a few blocks from the college campus, Jason Kincaid's home defined student housing—a paint job ten years overdue and an unmown lawn decorated with beer bottles sprouting weeds in the remains of lager and ale. Detective Moe Di Lorenzo rang the bell and added urgency by pounding hard on the door.

A few hours earlier, Keith Kennedy had tracked down Nate Kincaid's paramour on the morning of his death by searching through the emails on his computer. Patty Murphy had assured the detective, in a lilting brogue that conjured up images of leprechauns and rainbows, that Kincaid had been alive when she left the lifeguard tower.

Ms. Murphy also mentioned seeing a young man rushing through the parking lot when she arrived in the early hour. She had not gotten a good look at him but, in the semi-darkness, his appearance was so similar to Kincaid's that she actually called out to him. The teen did not respond or slow his pace. In fact, he walked faster. Ms. Murphy was distracted when her name was called from the direction of the beach.

"Patty. I've been waiting for you. Come be with your lover."

Patty Murphy smiled as she recited how Kincaid had beckoned to her. In that moment she confessed, she forgot about the boy completely.

When the front door opened and the five law enforcement officers gazed upon Jason Kincaid's face, they understood the reason for Ms. Murphy's initial confusion. Standing before them was a clone of the vic—years younger and with a much fuller head of hair, but the large nose and deep set eyes, as well as a mouth full of pearly whites, sent shivers from tail bone to scalp. They knew corpses could not walk and talk, but Jason Kincaid gave new meaning to life after death.

Marci held out her badge and ID while introducing herself and her colleagues. "I'm Homicide Detective Marci Welles with the Palm Beach County Sheriff's Office. These other individuals are Detectives Leigh, Di Lorenzo, and Mack. This is Officer Kennedy. We'd like to talk to you about your father."

"Uh. Okay. Sure. Come on in," Kincaid's son stuttered as he tried to control the surprise on his face. "What's with my father? Something happen?"

As the officers purposefully closed the short distance between inside and outside, Jason Kincaid stepped back to allow them entry into the house. The décor was typical college dorm design; in other words, a total shambles. Clothes were strewn on the furniture, beer cans littered every available surface, books, CDs and DVDs were scattered on the floor. The Xbox which sat atop an old 50" television with a badly scratched screen was paused on Level Two of the popular video game Call of Duty: Modern Warfare. Asleep in a popasan chair was one of Kincaid's housemates, his body twisted at such an awkward angle it hurt for the no longer as flexible officers to look at him.

"Can you wake the contortionist and ask him to leave the room?" Moe nodded his head in the direction of the snoring boy.

"What's this all about." Jason Kincaid's voice quivered with the beginning of nervous energy. "Why can't he stay?"

"Protocol."

Moe nudged the chair with his foot, which startled the sleeper into a sitting position. Although his eyes sprang open, he was far from awake."Beat it, Quasimodo." Moe pulled him from the chair. "Make yourself scarce for awhile."

With darting eyes, the teen looked from one officer to another and then at Jason. He was confused but not so much that he didn't recognize trouble when he saw it. Hastily, he bolted from the room and up the stairs to the second floor.

"When it comes to subtlety, Moe, you don't have any." Cat picked up the conversation with the younger Kincaid. "Where were you Tuesday morning between 5:00 and 7:00 am?"

"Here. Asleep. My first class is at 8. Why?"

"You didn't go to Coral Cove Park to see your father?"

"I haven't seen my father in years. Not since my tenth birthday party."

"What happened at the party?" Mack, who had been quietly picking through the debris on the coffee table, bounced a small cellophane bag of pot in his palm which was effective in getting the younger Kincaid's attention.

"Not mine. We had friends over last night. Someone must have left it here."

Mack held the bag of weed aloft in his left hand. In the right, he dangled a package of rolling papers. "We don't care about the pot, although we will take it with us. You know. Since it's not yours. The owner can claim it at the station at anytime."

Keeping the conversation moving, Marci asked, "How old are you? Nineteen? Twenty? That's a long time not to have contact with your father."

"My parents got divorced when I was really young. My father was resentful of every penny he had to pay in child support, and he treated my mother like shit. When I visited him, he always tried to turn me against her. I stopped going."

"Courts don't usually allow a kid to just bail on visitation because he doesn't like his old man."

"Courts don't like kids to commit suicide either. The judge took my threat pretty seriously."

"I imagine he would, but what if he hadn't? Would you have killed yourself? Ten years old is awfully young to go all Charlie Rocket on yourself."

"Who? What?"

Sensing an emotional outburst, Cat changed the subject. "Let's get back to Tuesday morning. You said you were here, asleep, because classes don't begin until 8 am. Can anyone corroborate that for us?"

"I don't know. We all have different schedules. It's not like we check up on each other. Everybody just comes and goes."

"What if I told you an eyewitness saw you at Coral Cove Park that morning?"

"I'd say that person was wrong."

"Sure. A clear case of mistaken identity." Moe dangled a set of handcuffs. "Want to change your answer?"

"I wasn't at the beach on Tuesday."

"Guess both you and that bag of pot that isn't yours will be going to the station until your memory improves. Must be true what they say about a brain on drugs."

"I don't do drugs."

"You don't lie well either. Turn around. Put your hands behind your back."

"What are you arresting me for?"

"We're not arresting you... yet. But when we do, it will be for murder." Marci instructed Moe, Mack and Keith to transport Jason Kincaid to the station as she and Cat headed out to their long overdue meeting at the morgue with G.

"Get in touch with his mother. Ask her to come to the station. Pick her up if you have to but don't tell her we have the kid. I'm curious how she will react when she realizes her son is a murder suspect. And, for God sake, find the skunk lady."

CHAPTER ELEVEN

Despite his best efforts, Doc G was unable to definitively determine whether Nate Kincaid's death was an accident or a homicide. He concluded that the lifeguard's injuries could very well have been caused by a slip and fall from the tower ladder. His written report, which he personally handed to Cat and Marci, was disheartening for everyone involved in the case.

County of Palm Beach
State of Florida

Case No. 68534
Victim: Nate Kincaid

Upon questioning by Detectives Welles and Leigh, Ms. Patricia Murphy, a guest of Nate Kincaid on the morning of his death, stated that, at the time of her leaving, the victim was alive and headed toward the ocean to cleanse himself.

Her statement would be in keeping with the residue of sodium, chlorine, magnesium, sulfur, calcium, and potassium found on the victim's body, hair and clothing. A sufficient amount of sea salts were found in his nose and throat to confirm that he had submerged himself in the ocean for an extended period of time.

As there is no conclusive evidence to the contrary, the possibility exists that, upon his return to the tower and his subsequent climbing of the ladder, the victim's feet, wet with salt water and covered in sand, caused him to lose his balance. The scrapes on the front of his left leg could have been caused when his left foot slipped off the step and traveled through the opening at the back of the ladder.

Such action would have pitched the victim forward, causing his forehead to come into contact with a step at a higher level. From the size of the contusion in the center of the frontal lobe, it is probable that dazed or unconscious, he fell backwards off the ladder, landing on a substantial piece of coral partially buried in the sand at the foot of the tower.

Nate Kincaid's death was the result of both coup and contra coup brain injuries resulting from violent forward acceleration and the sudden stop of the brain as it hit the sides of the skull.

~Signed: Mark Geschwer, Chief Medical Examiner.

"Detectives, I wish the results of my examination had turned up something concrete. I will continue to go over the evidence found at the scene just in case my staff has missed something. Which reminds me, I stopped at the lab this morning to check on that earring you found. The engraving remains a mystery."

"Any epithelial cells?" Cat asked, holding her breath in anticipation of good news.

"Too small a surface."

Daylight had gotten away from them and, with the moon rising on the horizon, Cat and Marci were feeling somewhat dejected. They entered the squad room expectantly, hoping that Moe Di Lorenzo, Damian Mack and Keith Kennedy had good news.

The limited access interrogations rooms were in a separate section of the Homicide Department, out of view of prying eyes and ears. Cat punched in her pass code and pushed back the door for Marci to enter first. Through the two-way glass, they could see Di Lorenzo and Mack hammering away at Jason Kincaid. Jason had his lips pressed together so tight they appeared glued. All three looked frustrated.

"We found the letters your father wrote to you. He kept them in the original envelopes. You know, the ones you wrote tender endearments on—Fuck you, Go to hell, Die you bastard. Remember them?" Moe DiLorenzo raised an inquiring eyebrow.

"I didn't kill him."

Damian Mack bent over the table and leaned in close to Jason Kincaid's face. "Your father's girlfriend puts you at the scene of his murder. Granted he was still alive at the time, but I think you returned later in the morning and killed him."

"You think he had the guts to murder his father?" Di Lorenzo feigned surprise. "He looks kind of wussy to me."

"Hey, even a wuss can be pushed too far. Right, Wuss?" Damian Mack continued to taunt Jason in an attempt to get a reaction.

"I didn't kill him."

"That's all he keeps saying," Keith Kennedy informed Cat and Marci. Since he had been lingering outside the interrogation room listening to the interview, Officer Kennedy was able to fill Cat and Marci in on what had happened so far.

"We're not getting anywhere. He just keeps saying he wasn't at the beach and he didn't kill his father."

"What about the mother?" Marci knew that the maternal instinct to protect one's child could be used to their advantage.

"Mack got her number from the kid's cell phone. He wouldn't give it up at first but Mack can be very persuasive. I called and left a message. She hasn't called back. Oh, by the way, her name isn't Kincaid. It's Fitzpatrick. Doranda Fitzpatrick."

Suddenly Jason Kincaid's voice rose to a shout. "All right. All right. I was at the beach but I did not kill my father. Not that he wouldn't have deserved it. That prick was always giving my mother a hard time. You probably don't know this but she wrote a book about him, and he threatened to destroy her."

"What's in the book?" Moe Di Lorenzo was suddenly smiling.

"It's fiction but it's also true; a story about a lifeguard who preys on lonely women. He pretends to love them but when they are no longer useful to him, he... he... you have to read the book. It's based on interviews my mother has had with a lot of the women my father screwed, literally and figuratively."

"Sex and jealousy. Perfect motives for murder. Maybe it's your mother we should be interrogating. How did your father find out about the book?"

Neither Moe Di Lorenzo or Damian Mack let on that they had already met some of the women in Doranda Fitzpatrick's book. They certainly weren't going to tell Jason Kincaid that the ladies had told a completely different story than the one they were hearing from him.

"My mother told him. Stupid! Stupid! Stupid! I begged her to fuck him for a change. Figuratively, of course. I wanted the world to read that book and know him for the asshole he really is."

"Your mother didn't agree?" Mack pulled a chair up to the table and looked at the obviously angry young man with renewed interest.

"The book was her revenge. For years she has seethed with hate for the way he treated us. Yet, on some level, she feared his reaction. She wanted him to know she hadn't used any real names."

"And her consideration meant nothing to him. He still threatened her." Moe DiLorenzo sensed something big coming and didn't want to lose the momentum.

"He was a bastard."

"And you killed him to protect her."

"I did not kill him. We fought. I threw a punch and missed. He flicked me away like I was a piece of lint on his jacket. He laughed at me. I left because, you're right Detective Di Lorenzo. I am a wuss."

"Let's go back to Tuesday morning. Where was your mother?"

"I don't know. I'm not her chaperone. She's lives by herself."

"We've been trying to reach her. She doesn't answer her phone and there's no one at the house."

"She's probably in New York."

"In New York?"

"Meeting with her publisher."

"What's his name?"

"It's name. Premier Publishing."

In the outer office, Cat dropped to her knees and began searching through her pocketbook. Frustration overrode her normally calm demeanor. She dumped the contents of the bag on the floor and rummaged her way through an assortment of tissues, makeup, notebooks and keys until she found what she was looking for. "We have a winner." Cat raised the pen found in the parking lot at Coral Cove much as a priest would raise a chalice at Sunday mass.

"What time do you think publishing companies close?"

"I keep telling you. I didn't kill my father." Jason Kincaid's voice was heavy with choked back tears.

"If not you or your mother, who would have wanted your father dead?" Moe Di Lorenzo's patience was being strained.

"It would be easier to find out who didn't want him dead. Now, please, leave me alone!"

Jason Kincaid, stood, knocking over his chair, and directed a stream of curses at the detectives interrogating him. His fists, pounding on the table, sounded like taiko drums to those watching from outside.

Marci rapped quickly three times on the glass, a signal for Mack and Moe to end the interrogation. By the time they exited the room, a decision had been made. "Put him in a cell. I don't want some attorney to claim we browbeat him to force a confession. We've got until late tomorrow to arraign him or set him free. A night in jail should be an eye opener, and if need be, we'll book him on drug possession."

"Go home. Get some rest. Be back here at 7 a.m. Breakfast is on Marci and me but don't expect the fancy stuff Kincaid's sweethearts supplied. Bagels and coffee—that's it." Cat's tone registered urgency and weariness.

"And," Marci added, "by morning, Mom should be plenty worried about her darling boy. Let's see if we can't play them against each other."

Once Jason Kincaid had been secured in a cell, the five investigators headed home. Cat and Marci considered stopping at O'Shea's for a beer, but realizing that even one drink might put them to sleep at the wheel; they hugged and said their goodbyes.

Marci was relieved. She had feared a reenactment of the bar scene from a few nights earlier. Cat's emotions were still riding a roller coaster of highs and lows. Morning seemed to come more quickly with every passing day, and both women needed to sleep or their powers of deduction would be seriously handicapped. "I feel absolutely weary. What about you?"

"Yeah. I don't know which is worse physical or emotional exhaustion."

"You haven't mentioned the Chasewood Apartments' victim."

"What about her?"

"The hair ribbons. The machete."

"I'm afraid to let myself hope, Marci. Let's just focus on Kincaid for now.

Heavy rain fell as the two friends, who both drove a white Jeep Liberty, pulled alongside each other at the parking lot exit. Thunder shattered the silence and cloud to ground lightening filled the skies. They waved; then Marci turned left and Cat turned right, disappearing into the enveloping darkness.

CHAPTER TWELVE

The evening thunder storm which followed Cat and Marci home turned into four days of unrelenting rain. Law enforcement personnel referred to extended periods of wet weather as Nature's Crime Stopper since criminals were less inclined to get wet than they were to dirty their hands with ill gotten gains.

With no new cases requiring their attention, the detectives used the time to follow up on leads and file reports. Cats' initial call to Doranda Fitzpatrick's literary agent became a game of phone tag with Cat doing most of the chasing. When they finally spoke, the agent proved to be cooperative to the point that he answered questions before Cat asked them.

"The title of the book is *800 Women*—a reference to the number of females Doranda's ex had taken to his bed. The book is fiction but based on actual statements made by the women she interviewed. Doranda is nothing if not persistent. She used the internet to blog about the book; she put adds in papers in every city she knew he had lived. Eventually, the women flocked to her. We anticipate great sales and have what I consider to be a clever marketing campaign in the works. We're giving away gold earrings engraved with the Chinese numerals for 800."

Cat's quick intake of breath preceded her next question. "What do the earrings look like?"

"I can fax you a photo. They're very delicate. Quiet lovely, in fact."

"How many pairs of earrings are you giving away?"

"We ordered a thousand pairs. Doranda got enough to give one set to each of the women interviewed. I don't know the exact number. The rest will be used at book signings and special events. You know, Detective, good marketing is as much a matter of luck as creativity.

The title of Doranda's book just happens to coincide with a renewed interest by the literati in China's history.

The Capital Museum in Beijing put artifacts on exhibit which indicate that China's literary history is 800 years older than carapace bone script. Lots of Chinese history buffs are buying earrings, tie clasps, money clips, necklaces and rings engraved with the number 800."

#

With the sun barely up, Cat sat, coffee mug in hand, on the arm of a still somewhat soggy deck chair overlooking the acre of property she and Kevin called their backyard. The four day deluge had left the lawn and trees looking greener; the flowers bigger and brighter. At the birdfeeder, cardinals and blue jays quarreled over who got the biggest serving of sunflower seeds while two very energetic squirrels ran back and forth across the top of the fence that enclosed the property, performing a gold medal worthy balance beam routine.

This porch—this yard—they were to Cat what church was to other people. Here was where she came to pray, to solve problems, to bury her troubles and to find peace. Watching Shadow and Kneesaa as they frolicked in the grass brought a smile to her lips. She felt excitement course through her body. Cat had always believed that to all things there was a season and the season for solving the Kincaid case and finding her attacker was now.

No sooner did Cat pull out of the driveway then her cell phone rang. She didn't need to look at the caller I.D. to know it was Marci. The ring tone—country star Blake Shelton's "Ol' Red"—gave her away. Shelton was Marci's not-so-secret crush.

"Have pity on me. I'm not on duty yet."

"There's been another murder."

The scene was all too familiar when Cat and Marci pulled up to the abandoned house in Riviera Beach. Police cars and crime scene vans lined the street. A police officer so young he didn't appear to shave barred the front door. Cat and Marci flashed their badges.

The interior of the house had been damaged beyond repair. Every piece of wiring and plumbing that could be sold had been ripped out of the walls. The kitchen and bathrooms were empty except for huge holes where cabinets once hung and toilets had stood. The carpeting was filthy and showing signs that it had been used as a port-a-potty by animals and squatters living in the area. In the middle of what once was the dining area, a body covered with a tarp held G's attention.

The victim, a twenty something female, had been sliced with what could have been a machete. The only part of her body not damaged was her face. Her long blond hair had been combed into pony tails and tied neatly with wide pink ribbons atop her head.

"Raped?" Cat's voice was filled with anger.

"Yes. Slicing was done postmortem, thank God. None of the cuts which, if my count is correct, number 52, are deep or life threatening. Death was by strangulation most likely during the rape. From the way the blood has pooled, I surmise that after ejaculating he lifted her into a sitting position and held her upright while he parted and combed her hair. Then he laid her back down and cut her."

"Sick bastard," Marci's voice was barely above a whisper.

"Aren't they all? Let me show you something. Come around and stand over the victim's head. Good. Now look down at the wounds. What do you see?"

"Christ. It looks like a palm frond. The cuts—the leaves actually appear to be moving." Both Cat and Marci were dumbfounded by the revelation.

"Our sick bastard considers himself an artiste."

#

In the hope of both finding a flaw in G's report of Nate Kincaid's death and unearthing new information, Marci and Cat decided to re-question Patricia Murphy about her morning romp at the beach. Murphy lived 20 minutes from the new crime scene which gave Cat and Marci time to talk on the way.

"This is my guy, Marci. I just know it. We've got to stop him before he kills again."

"It's not our case, Cat. The best we can do is follow the investigation from the sidelines and ask G to keep us abreast of any new developments."

"He's going to make a mistake and I want to be there when they take him down." Cat peeled away from the red light; the screeching tires adding intensity to her words.

Patty Murphy, well spoken, well-dressed, perfectly coiffed and made up, vividly described her sexual escapade with the deceased Nate Kincaid without a smidgen of embarrassment. She readily detailed how she had gripped his waist with her legs and dug her fingers into his shoulders to keep from falling. She confirmed that Kincaid's physicality had him banging not only her but also his calves against the railing he was using for support.

Nate Kincaid, Ms. Murphy assured Cat and Marci, was alive and well when she left Coral Cove. He was planning to go for a swim and then leave for his regular assignment at Carlin Park. To the best of her recollection, no one was in the parking lot when she left.

"How would you describe your relationship with Mr. Kincaid?" Cat asked.

"I guess… Well, we were dating. I think exclusively."

"How did you meet?"

"On the beach at Carlin Park. I was snorkeling and he joined me. We just hit it off."

"Are you single?"

"Yes. No. Separated from my husband."

"Any chance of reconciliation?"

"Why are you asking?"

"Just trying to put all the pieces of the puzzle together."

"We were talking about getting back together until I met Nate."

"Have you ever met Doranda Fitzpatrick?"

"Who is she?"

As no better explanation for the bumps and bruises Kincaid's body had sustained could be found, the Ladies knew that G's report would stand as written.

"Ignorance is bliss, Patricia Murphy has no idea she was just another notch on the bed post." Marci mentally checked Kincaid's latest conquest off the suspect list.

"Number 801. The man should go into the Guinness Book of Records."

"On a different note," Marci attempted to lighten the mood, "have you written your speech yet for the Victims' Rights luncheon. It's quite an honor for you to be chosen as the keynote speaker."

"Public speaking is not high on my bucket list. I've got it written but I'm not sure if I'm saying what I want to say."

"Let me hear it. Knowing you, you have it completely memorized by now."

"I do. You have to be honest if you don't like it."

"Let her rip."

"'Scars reveal where we have been. They don't have to dictate where we are going.'

Quite a profound statement, wouldn't you agree? One might think that a great orator had given voice to that sentiment. Not so. Believe it or not, those two sentences were part of the closing dialogue on an episode of Criminal Minds.

Never did I think I would find inspiration on a weekly crime drama. The boob tube so often lives up to its nickname that I sometimes imagine brain cells collecting at my feet if I watch for too long. I learned a valuable lesson. If we listen when people speak; if we remain open to suggestions and advice, we grow. We grow wiser and safer and more confident in ourselves and in our abilities to navigate through this life.

On a slide rule of least important to most important, the words uttered by Joe Montegna, one of the stars of Criminal Minds, are proof that Hollywood is still home to a few good writers. Where they gain value is in their truth. Scars, both the visible and the invisible kind, are a compendium of life's less smile-inducing moments. Rather than being etched in our minds and on our bodies with ink, they are indelibly written in raw, red, raised flesh and painful memories.

Painful – no one can deny that being raped is painful. The fear alone is impossible to describe. The physical abuse is torturous made more so because, no matter how fit a woman may be; no matter how much self defense training she may have, nature did not give us the same body mass as a man. Defending ourselves is almost impossible. That being said, it isn't physical strength that wins a war. It is fortitude. It is determination. It is the power of the mind and the spirit.

If a genie were to pop out of a bottle and offer me the opportunity to switch genders, I would refuse. Not be a woman? I've never been prouder of my gender than I am today. As I look around this room, I see great power and deep, deep wells of caring. The pages of our history books are filled with people of great achievement; people deserving of acknowledgement and celebrity. But I would rather celebrate you. Celebrate us.

We are strong. We women have within us the ability to get through the most difficult situations and remain whole. We are the caregivers. We are the nurturers. We are The Little Engine That Could... and we can. We can turn being victimized into being victorious. Alone we are formidable. Together we are unstoppable.

How you choose to view your scars will determine how successful you are in healing and moving forward. I like to think of mine as pennies tossed into a wishing well. As memories ripple to the surface, I ask that hate be short lived. I ask not for revenge but for justice and peace. I ask for continued strength to face whatever lies ahead. So far, my requests have been granted.

Today, I add one more wish to my list—that each of you finds within yourself that same strength. To a certain extent, my wish is wasted. I'm wishing for something that already exists. Strength is within you. All you have to do is reach down and take hold of it.

I'd like to leave you with this image. As a result of being sexually assaulted, I have a very deep scar on my left wrist put there by the zip ties used to bind my hands. Over that scar I now have a teal blue ribbon tattoo. The color teal makes me recognizable as a survivor of sexual assault.

Many people have asked why I wanted to mark myself so publicly. The answer is simple. Since I have to remember what happened for the rest of my life, I want to remember that I survived."

Cat took a deep breath. "What do you think?"

"You have a tattoo?"

"Not yet but I will tonight."

"It's wonderful. I think I'm going to cry."

CHAPTER FOURTEEN

"Lady here to see you." Sgt. Paulie Padrone popped his head in the door of the conference room where Cat, bandage covering her wrist, and Marci sat surrounded by the evidence collected so far in the Kincaid case.

Damian Mack and Moe Di Lorenzo sat nearby writing reports on the events of the previous day. The only member of the investigative team missing—Keith Kennedy—was bringing Jason Kincaid from lockup for another go round of interrogation.

On the floor were boxes filled to overflowing with Kincaid's personal effects. The middle of the conference table was cluttered with dirty paper plates, half eaten bagels, open containers of butter and cream cheese and soggy paper cups holding the remains of cold coffee.

As Padrone continued to speak, the four detectives looked at him with heightened curiosity. "Says she's the boy's mother."

"Well, don't that make the day more interesting?" Moe Di Lorenzo voiced aloud what everyone else was thinking.

"More interesting than you realize. Wait until you meet her." Padrone disappeared before he could be asked to explain.

"Do you think she'll let us keep the $25,000 if her son is convicted?" Damian Mack clutched his stomach which was gurgling loudly. "I don't know how much more bad coffee I can drink. That money could keep us in Starbucks for a long time." He rushed off to the bathroom without waiting for a response.

Pushing back their chairs, Cat and Marci fixed their faces with the stern look of professional homicide detectives. Side by side they walked across the bullpen.

"Good morning, Mrs. Kincaid. I'm Detection Leigh and this is my partner, Detective Welles. We're handling your ex-husband's case." Cat intentionally used the wrong surname hoping to solicit a reaction, but her own surprise at seeing Doranda Fitzpatrick was difficult to hide.

Standing before them was the mysterious skunk lady, and she was just as Dolly, the waitress at the Seagull Diner, had described her—long dark hair, dark eyes, nice teeth and a killer smile. The killer part, Cat realized, was merely speculative at this point in the investigation. Neither was she the bimbo Cat and Marci had expected.

Truth be told, none of the women interviewed deserved that classification. They were all educated, attractive and, for the most part, self-assured and successful. The former Mrs. Kincaid, however, beat them all in two very obvious ways. She was very beautiful, classy and definitely not the kind of woman who would be attracted to an aging lifeguard and part-time valet.

"The name is Fitzpatrick, Detectives. Doranda Fitzpatrick. I haven't used Nate's last name since I gleefully left the courthouse after our divorce many years ago. Please, call me Doranda."

"All right, Doranda," Marci made nice-nice with their guest. "Sgt. Padrone informed us that you have a story to tell.

"Yes, but first... is my son all right? Are Jason and I suspects in Nate's death?"

"Should you be?"

"No, but I am the ex-wife and as the saying goes, "Hell hath no fury..."

"So, then it was you who pushed your husband from the tower."

"I'm curious. Does that tactic ever work?"

"The way this works...," Cat said, steel in her voice, "we ask the questions."

"Fine, Detectives. I'm innocent."

"Prove it. Where would you like to start?"

"At the beginning, of course."

Doranda's flippancy did not endear her to Cat and Marci, who had for years dealt with criminals hiding behind false bravado. Marci nodded her head in acknowledgment of the obvious. "Once upon a time it is then. Please. You have our undivided attention."

"My son did not kill his father."

"That seems more like the end of the story than the beginning."

Since Cat was still staring at the skunk stripes in Doranda's hair, she let Marci lead the interrogation.

"Beginning, middle or end... he didn't do it."

"You seem pretty certain of that. Convince us."

"I was at the beach Tuesday morning but you already suspected that. I had just parked my car when I saw Jason run to his and drive away. About the same time, Nate's love interest arrived."

"Is she one of the women you interviewed?"

"No. She's just the latest conquest."

"And after that lady left, you killed him?"

"No, detective. I did not kill Nate. I often wanted to but I didn't."

"Then why were you there, Ms. Fitzpatrick... Doranda? What brought you to Coral Cove Park last Tuesday morning?"

"Two years ago, I began writing a book based my relationship with Nate. It's about to be published. Recently, I sent him an advance copy. It was a foolish thing to do and he was furious. On Monday, while Jason and I were having dinner, he called and spewed vile threats. Jason was afraid for me. That is why he went to the beach—to warn his father to leave me alone."

"And to kill him if he refused?"

"I've already told you that Jason did not kill Nate. How many times do I have to say it?"

"A lot more." Cat joined the conversation by holding up her hand and counting off on her fingers.

Tears of frustration and fear appeared in Doranda's eyes. "Every morning I call Jason's cell phone to wake him up. He's a heavy sleeper and never hears the alarm clock no matter how loud we make it. For reasons only a teenager understands, the ringing of the cell phone penetrates the fog. He always answers but...."

"... not Tuesday morning." Cat finished Doranda's sentence for her.

"Correct. I know my son, and I knew he had gone to the beach. Nate's routines never vary. Tuesday is... was always fuck day. I'm sorry."

"No problem. Go on."

"As I already told you, when I arrived, I saw Jason running to his car. A woman was on the walkway, and I assumed correctly that she was Nate's latest conquest. For a moment, it appeared she was talking to Jason, but then I saw Nate and realized he was calling to her. I waited a little while and then walked to the tower. Nate was leaning against the guardrail."

Doranda Fitzpatrick stared at Cat and Marci. "His lady friend was wrapped around his waist, holding onto his shoulders with all her might. The position was quite familiar to me."

"You watched?"

"No! Of course not! I was afraid Nate might see me, so I went back to my car and waited until the woman left. I started to get out of the car... to go talk to him.... and changed my mind."

"Why?"

"I got tired. Not sleepy tired—the emotional kind. I was tired of fighting and losing the battle of words. Nate was good with words. He could always twist them in his favor. I just didn't want to go through that again. I left the beach and drove to the coffee shop where the ladies and I were meeting for breakfast.

A while later we heard a Juno Beach police officer say that a lifeguard had been found dead at Coral Cove Park. My reaction was pretty intense. The ladies pressured me to tell them what I knew and I did. They left and drove to the beach."

"Did they think death was a spectator sport?" The public's reaction to tragedy never surprised but often disgusted Marci.

"They saw it as justice, not vengeance."

"But you didn't see it that way?"

"No. Nate's death scared me. I wanted to go home so I could prepare Jason before he heard it from someone else."

"And give you both time to perfect your alibis." Cat wasn't asking for confirmation. Hers was a statement of fact.

"I'll tell you again. We did not kill Nate. Not me. Not Jason."

"Then who did?"

"All women and no one woman, Detective. Maybe some former and present husbands as well. Add in fathers, sons, brothers, daughters, sisters. All of us and none of us."

"Cryptic comments don't interest me. I'm going to ask you one more time. Do you know who killed Nate Kincaid?" Marci hovered so close to Doranda that their knees were touching. "You have one second to start talking, or I will arrest you and your son for murder."

"May I tell you my story—from the beginning—as you agreed earlier?"

"We're all ears."

"I became involved with Nate while I was reeling from what I considered to be the ultimate betrayal in my then marriage," Doranda began her narration. "The betrayal had nothing to do with affairs or sex or drugs or anything of that nature. What actually happened is irrelevant to this story, so I will not complicate matters by discussing it.

Nate and I had met, perhaps, a year or two earlier, when we were employed by the same firm. Everyone liked him. He was witty, intelligent and, I don't really know how to explain it, but he had a way of making a woman feel she was the sole focus of his attention."

"So, he was a good guy?"

"Yes, at first. I remember a day... Nate had come to work early and I was still at my desk. He came up behind me and began massaging my shoulders. Suddenly, he jumped back, claiming an electrical charge had passed from me to him He said it was a sign that we were connected somehow. Personally, I thought he was nuts... but sweet.

Truth be told, Nate was a great playmate but a lousy mate. I'm sure by now you are aware that he was blessed with a larger than average penis. The first time he was introduced to me that trait was more important to our host than whether Nate was smart or funny or kind. It was important to Nate as well, but he pretended it wasn't. After our marriage ended, I wondered if being recognized for such a carnal distinction all his life had numbed his ability to feel real emotions."

Doranda Fitzpatrick stopped speaking to collect her thoughts. "May I see my son?"

Marci and Cat exchanged glances in silent agreement.

"We'll take a short break."

CHAPTER FIFTEEN

As if planned, Keith Kennedy knocked on the office door just at that moment. "Kid's in the interrogation room. Ready when you are."

"You have to believe me. He's innocent. Please, let me take him home."

"Doranda, an eyewitness puts your son at the scene of a murder. You're his mother. How much credence do you think we should put in your avowal that he didn't kill his father?" Cat's faced registered sympathy for the pained expression in Doranda Fitzpatrick's eyes.

"I'm going to call a lawyer."

"That's a good idea. Get one for yourself as well." Marci blocked her path as she headed for the door. "We're holding you for further questioning and as a possible accomplice in the death of Nate Kincaid."

Turning to Keith Kennedy, she ordered, "Officer, let Ms. Fitzpatrick make her phone call. Then, put her in the room next to her son."

With Marci following close behind, Cat headed in the direction of the waiting and anxious Jason Kincaid. A request for representation by an attorney only prevented the detectives from further questioning Doranda Fitzpatrick. Jason was an adult in the eyes of the courts. He had not as yet asked for a lawyer.

"All right, Jason, let's talk more about your relationship with your father."

"Did my mother call? Is she here?"

"We have briefly spoken with her."

"Am I getting out of here? Why can't I see her?"

"Let's talk. Then, we'll see what arrangements can be made."

"I've already told you I did not kill my father."

"That's for us to decide. Tell us about your childhood."

"It's a boring story. I always felt that my father pretended to like me. I would visit him on weekends and when I had time off from school. We did a lot of things together—the zoo, parks, the beach. When I behaved as he thought I should behave, he seemed to care. When I didn't... He rarely hit me but he was very good at loading me down with guilt trips. He wanted me around to have fun but he really didn't want to be bothered with responsibility. He was always the injured party although I was the one being hurt."

"You said that you threatened to commit suicide."

"Yeah. I just couldn't stand being around him anymore. I was too young to understand why I was afraid of him but I was definitely afraid. Mom had to go to court. The court made me see a psychiatrist. The psychiatrist sent us to family therapy. In the end dad walked away. I'd like to think it was because he was concerned about my well-being, but the reason was probably that I stopped being a playmate. I had become a problem."

"Your mother also referred to your father as a playmate. Why do you think that is?"

"Because as long as dad was doing what he wanted to do—which meant no drama—he was happy."

"What happened after you no longer had to see your father."

"I got better. I felt normal. Actually, I felt like I had been on a ship in a violent storm and suddenly the waters were calm. My mother insisted I continue to see a psychiatrist for a few years and it helped. Eventually, I understood it wasn't me. It was him."

"But you still hate him."

"No. I don't hate him. What I hate is that I never had a father—a real father—to love. Now that he's dead and I should be feeling sad, I don't feel anything at all. Can I see my mother now?"

"Soon."

Cat and Marci returned to the interrogation room where Doranda Fitzpatrick waited for her attorney.

"My lawyer is on his way, but since I have nothing to hide, I would like to continue my story. I'm not trying to burden you with unnecessary details, but Jason and I will be best served if you understand what we have been through."

Marci and Cat nodded their assent and Doranda Fitzpatrick continued to fill in the details.

"As I said, I met Nate on the job. I worked in the office and he worked the night shift as a valet parking cars so we really didn't see each other. However, occasionally a group of us would meet for dinner and drinks and Nate would join us. We began to spend more time together. He invited me to come to Coral Cove on my day off which I did. Coral Cove had not as yet been closed to the public. At the time, I didn't see Nate for the master manipulator he was."

"Are you saying he set a trap for you?" Marci was beginning to see the method to Nate Kincaid's madness and her interest in his methodology was piqued.

"In a sense, yes. I was married at the time, but that marriage was crumbling. I badly needed someone to listen to my fears. Nate made himself available. Rather than encouraging me to save my 20 year commitment, he convinced me to let him fill the void. Hindsight allows for a much clearer perspective. By the time I realized what a selfish and amoral man Nate was, it was too late."

"You say he was amoral. Please explain." Cat pulled up a chair and straddled it. Over the years, she had found that proximity to a suspect loosened the tongue. It was always easier to get a suspect to talk if the interrogator remained quiet and close.

"Nate never suffered guilt or pangs of conscience. He went after what he wanted with a vengeance and cared nothing about who was hurt in the process. I got pregnant soon after we married. Jason was eight when Nate and I divorced. For two years, we shared joint custody. Then Jason suddenly refused to have any contact with his father. He threatened to kill himself if I made him go for his weekly visits."

"Did he ever tell you why he didn't want to see his father?"

"I didn't need to ask. They were the same reasons I wanted to get away. Jason wasn't abused—not sexually or physically. Emotionally is another story. Nate had a way of working himself into your head and planting terrible seeds of self-doubt."

"Did your son see a doctor?"

"Yes, I insisted. I took him to the same psychiatrist I was seeing."

"And how did that go?"

"Hard to say. He was so young. Healing took time—a long time. He's a well-adjusted young man now. I hate the thought that Nate, even in death, might drag Jason back into depression. Years of therapy have helped me to see Nate as the very clever, charming sociopath he was. He had the ability to discern what was missing from someone's life and, like a shape shifter, fill that void. It was all an act; a mask he wore."

Doranda Fitzpatrick sighed. "Eventually, the mask slipped."

"How long was the mask in place during your marriage?" Marci was fascinated by the workings of the human mind and always interested in the details of people's lives.

"We lived together for two years before marrying. The relationship began to falter almost immediately after the 'I do's.' I started to question my sanity, but I could not face another divorce. I remember feeling that the early pleasure of being with Nate had turned into a walking on eggshells uneasiness. He wanted me to let my hair go completely grey and hated that I wore nail polish and makeup. I thought it was all so weird. Most men want the woman in their life to look her best. Still, I stayed, and the streaks in my hair, the ones you both keep staring at, took root."

"Sorry," both Cat and Marci mumbled just the right amount of forced embarrassment.

"My mother always said my father was the cause of her grey roots." Marci ran a finger through a few strands of her hair. "I keep a bottle of Miss Clairol under the bathroom sink just in case my husband has the same effect on me. Go on with your story."

"Nate began to undermine my self-confidence, using humor and sarcasm to pick at my insecurities. If I complained, I was too thin skinned to take a joke. He always seemed to be waiting for me to do something wrong so he could play the victim.

"Victims are our specialty." The look on Cat's face left no question about the meaning of her remark.

"Okay." Marci attempted to spur the conversation along. "This is all a very fascinating look into your life but what does it have to do with your ex husband's death?"

"I apologize but you need to understand how Nate's mind worked and the effect he had on people. No one was real to him, especially the women he wooed. They were merely the leading ladies in a fantasy he had created in his mind, probably as a teenager. Eventually each actress would begin flubbing her lines and missing her cues. Nate merely dropped the curtain and reopened with a new star. The cycle repeated over and over again."

"I still don't see how this helps our case or your case," Marci pressed.

"I know you interviewed a lot of Nate's old girlfriends. I'm sure you are wondering why all those women told the same story. They did, didn't they?"

"Yes, almost to a word. How did you know?"

"I also interviewed those women as research for my book.

They were all anxious to meet me, and once we began talking, we realized that our stories were exactly alike. The words Nate used to seduce us, the places he took us, the dinners he prepared, the music we listened to, all the trips, concerts and plays. Everything right down to the first time he bedded us was exactly the same. I grew to hate spinach and blueberries, an almost daily part of Nate's diet." Doranda Fitzpatrick made a feeble attempt at a smile.

"There's one big difference between their stories and your story, Doranda. They only said he was wonderful. Can you explain why that is?"

"Embarrassment is one reason. We all felt like fools after we found out how we had been tricked. It's been years since Nate has been a part of my life but when I look back, my skin still crawls."

"Everything you've told us is a reason for you or one of the other women to kill him."

"That's true, but we only killed him in our dreams. None of us is capable of killing him while awake. Now, I would like to see my son."

CHAPTER SIXTEEN

As Cat and Marci were about to lead Doranda Fitzpatrick into the adjoining interrogation room, Captain Jameson motioned for Cat to join him in his office.

"Ah, crap, what now?" Marci's finger found its way between her teeth before Cat was even out the door. She had been trying somewhat successfully for weeks to break the habit that everyone hated and all it took was a nod from the Captain to start her nibbling again.

When Cat entered Captain Jameson's office, she was confronted by two IAD detectives, each with an austere look on his face and an attitude so forbidding they could stop a stampeding herd of buffalo in their tracks.

"Detective Leigh, I'm Sergeant Ryan. I think you recognize Chief Reynolds. We'd like to ask you some questions about a recent incident at O'Shea's Pub."

"What about it?"

"Isn't it true, Detective, that you were recently a victim of a violent crime?"

"It is."

"And what crime was that?"

"You already know what crime. I was raped."

"And isn't it true that you underwent therapy after the attack?"

"That's standard procedure for any officer involved in any type of violent interaction."

"Would you say that the attack has affected your attitude on the job?"

"No. What are you getting at?"

"During the altercation at O'Shea's, you claimed a customer assaulted you."

"He did."

"You shoved tooth pick up his nose and told him he was lucky it wasn't an ice pick. Yes?"

"What's going on? Did that little pervert file charges?"

"Just answer our questions."

"He grabbed my ass and my breast. I stopped him before he grabbed anything else."

"You threatened him."

"I defended myself as I have been trained to do."

"Where in the police manual does it state that shoving a toothpick up an assailant's nose is a recommended defense maneuver?"

"I made what I considered and still consider an intelligent decision. You're acting as if I drew my weapon in a crowded bar and endangered the patrons. I didn't. I chose to subdue Tail Light, quietly I might add, without inflicting any harm to his person unless you consider removing a little snot from a little snot-nosed punk harmful."

"Do you think your behavior at the bar was erratic or out of character for you?"

"Actually, I think I was amazingly controlled which I contribute to being a professional law enforcement officer with enough on the job training to know how to react in a potentially dangerous situation. Is there anything else you need to know?"

"No. We just wanted your side of the story. Everything you said confirms eyewitness accounts. We're done here."

The reunion between mother and son was emotional. Less than an hour after Doranda Fitzpatrick made her one phone call, Richard Greenberg entered the police station, the flaps of his black leather trench coat opening out about him like the wings of Satan. His presence immediately calmed mother and son, who knew that their legal rights would now be handled in a manner that could make even the most arrogant prosecutors question their abilities. In a deep baritone voice that gave added credence to his substantial power, Attorney Greenberg made his exact intentions known.

High priced and high profile, R. L. Greenberg, Esq. was hailed among defense attorneys as a heavy-weight in the courtroom. With what seemed absolute ease, he turned impossible-to-win cases into knockouts. He was also revered for his silver tongue during closing arguments.

"You have no evidence with which to hold my clients," Greenberg stated with assurance when Cat and Marci refused his demand for release. "No fingerprints. No DNA. Not a strand of hair or piece of fiber that links my clients to the victim."

"An eyewitness puts Jason Kincaid at the scene on the day his father died."

"Yes, Detective Welles, an eyewitness who stated my client was leaving the scene and that Nate Kincaid was still alive. Alive enough to engage in some pretty strenuous exercise, I'm told."

"He could have come back after the woman left."

"Could have come back?" the attorney parried with a Cheshire Cat smile. "He could also have gone to school and completed a full day of classes, which he did. I have here a signed statement from the registrar."

With an attitude of intellectual prejudice, Greenberg passed the notarized form to Cat, who was having difficulty hiding her dislike of the attorney.

"By the way, she asked me to apologize for not returning your phone calls. I believe her explanation was, 'Not enough hours in the day,' and we all can understand that, can't we? According to the attendance roster signed by each of his teachers, Jason was on time for all four of his Tuesday classes starting at 8 am and ending a little after two. By then, Nate Kincaid was resting on a stainless steel examining table in the morgue."

"His mother…" Marci began.

"His mother already stated that she was at the beach but left without speaking to her former husband. All of the women you interviewed will confirm that she had breakfast with them at the diner. Unless she has a clone, it is impossible for her to have been in two places at once. Let me save you some time here just in case you are going to bring up the pen that you found in the parking lot. Yes, I know about the pen. I have hundreds of pens from banks, restaurants, insurance companies, even one from Ms. Fitzpatrick's publisher. And no, I was not at Coral Cove on Tuesday morning. I was having root canal. Want to see?" Greenberg made a half-hearted attempt to pull his cheek away from his slightly open mouth.

"Not necessary. We still have questions for Doranda."

"If my client is willing…"

"I am. I have nothing to hide."

"Then, let's begin." Marci sat down at the table. "Do you know who killed your former husband?"

"No, I don't. Every woman he ever dated at some point wished him dead but none of the women you met—the women I interviewed—are murderers. Of course, those women are only a small percentage of Nate's conquests. The only thing I know for sure is that Jason had nothing to do with his father's death. He was only at the beach to protect me. When he left, Nate was alive and horny."

"So you say."

"I'm sure the woman he was with will testify to that fact, if she hasn't already."

"Do you know what the felony murder rule is, Doranda?"

"What are you getting at, Detective?" attorney Greenberg moved to protect his client.

"I'm just trying to explain to Ms. Fitzpatrick how the system works. Doranda, did you know that a person can be charged with murder if they are involved in a felonious act that ends in the death of another human being even if that death was accidental or committed by another party? In other words, if you killed your former husband and Jason was there, he can be charged with murder as well. Same is true in the reverse."

"I did not kill Nate. Jason did not kill Nate. We were not at the beach tower together. The most we are guilty of is wanting Nate dead not making it happen."

"And we are through here. Thank you, Detectives. It's always a pleasure seeing you— both of you." Richard Greenberg turned smartly in his $2500 shoes and glided in the direction of the confinement and release area of the station. Smugness radiated from his every pore. Doranda and Jason followed at his heels like obedient puppies.

Cat kicked hard at the chair she had been gripping; her resentment of the attorney sounding loudly as the chair slid across the floor. "Release them," she ordered Keith Kennedy.

CHAPTER SEVENTEEN

For three weeks, Cat and Marci went over every bit of evidence from every possible angle in an attempt to link Doranda Fitzpatrick, her son, or any of the women attached to the Kincaid case to the crime of murder. Their efforts were fruitless.

The work week ended on a dark note, except for the announcement by Captain Jameson that IAD had closed their investigation into the O'Shea's incident. "Next time you feel compelled to do a nasal reconstruction on a suspect, Detective, be sure to keep me in the loop."

At near nine pm on the Friday before Halloween, a weary and frustrated Marci and Cat headed home, another torrential storm adding to their somber moods. As was their routine, they pulled up next to each other in the parking lot for one last wave before turning in opposite directions.

The roads were almost empty; most people having had enough sense to get where they are going and stay there. Thunder rattled the car windows while lightening bouncing off the roadway caused the few drivers still en route to their destinations to tap their breaks more often than necessary.

As Marci drove, she pulled band aids from four of her fingers with her teeth. On days like today, she was inclined to do a lot of damage to her cuticles despite her best efforts to stop gnawing away at them like a beaver with a pile of wood. The band aids were a pre-emptive strike meant to keep her from biting when the urge hit her. In frustration, she spit the bandages to the floor and pushed the button on her CD player. A children's song—one of Sonora's favorites—filled the silence. Marci reached over to change the tune, then stopped.

Taking a deep breath, she let the song continue, singing along with it. "Ten little monkeys jumping on the bed. One fell off and bumped his head. Momma called the doctor and the doctor said, No more monkeys jumping on the bed. Nine little monkeys jumping on the bed…"

#

By the time Cat pulled into her driveway, the storm had somewhat abated. The garage door did not open when she hit the remote button and the motion detectors did not illuminate the yard when she exited the car. As she walked the darkened sidewalk to the front of the house, she rummaged in her satchel for her keys. The porch light was off and she hesitated before stepping up to the door, still searching for her keys in her purse. A voice suddenly came out of the dark.

"Miss Blue. Miss Blue. I've got you Miss Blue."

Cat stiffened as her rapist stepped out of the shadows. He was barely visible, but she could clearly see the machete hanging at his side.

"I named you Miss Blue because of your eyes. I didn't know you were a cop. Then, I saw you on that report about the dead lifeguard. Miss Blue turned out to be a lady in blue."

"Why didn't you kill me like you did the other women?"

"I always planned to come back for seconds. Once I saw that report, I knew I couldn't wait any longer. You were good. I really hate having to kill you."

"Wish I could say the same."

As her rapist raised the machete over his head, Cat dropped her bag. With a steady hand, she fired her gun.

An hour later police vehicles, the medical examiner's van, an ambulance, and several trucks from local tv stations were spread out over the lawn and driveway. The house lights had been turned back on and spotlights panned back and forth over the grounds. The body of Cat's rapist was lying face up on the porch and G was making a cursory examination. The cause of death was obvious. Cat shot him through the heart. Marci and Kevin stood on either side of Cat, daring anyone to approach.

"Detectives," G called softly to Marci and Cat. "Come here. Look at his back. Here. Just below the left shoulder."

In the dim light cast by the single bulb in the fixture over the front door, names written in an old-school calligraphy could be seen tattooed in matching colors on the rapist's shoulder—Miss Pink, Miss Green, Miss Purple, Miss Orange. A bandage covered the skin below the last name. G pulled the covering away, revealing a new tattoo—Miss Blue.

"What the hell is that?" Marci's voice was filled with rage.

"A list of his victims including me. Looks like we've missed a few."

"Miss Orange and Miss Purple. We'll find them."

"Yes, we will. I owe them that."

The Monday morning news found Cat, Captain Jameson and Mike Brickshaw, the Sheriff of Palm Beach County, in the spotlight. A local news anchor interviewed them about the events of the past week. After a short statement by Captain Jameson, Sheriff Brickshaw expressed his admiration for the expert manner in which Cat conducted herself in the face of almost certain death.

"I am relieved that a predator has been removed as a threat to society and that Detective Leigh is safe. I am awed by the comportment she displayed during last week's attack. She is the perfect example of highly trained law enforcement at work. The control and quick thinking she displayed while face to face with her would-be killer is ingrained in all the members of the Palm Beach County Sheriff's Office."

Sheriff Brickshaw turned and looked at Cat with respect and admiration. "I'm very proud of her as I am of every officer under my command."

The reporter then turned to Cat and asked if she would like to make a statement. Confidence written all over her face, Cat took a deep breath and began to speak.

"For as long as I can remember, July has always been one of my favorite months. The fourth was not just a day to celebrate our country's birthday; it was the day my family gathered to celebrate our love and kinship. Red, white and blue signified patriotism and loyalty—not blood and bruises. Now, July is the month I celebrate being alive.

After my attack, I was terrified to live alone. No matter how many locks were on my door, I feared someone would break in. I knew I was lucky to have survived my night of horror, and I always wondered what would happen if my attacker returned. I worried I wouldn't be as lucky the next time and I almost wasn't. I understand how survivors of violent crime feel, and make no mistake, rape is a violent crime.

Consider that the most brutal aspects of assault are almost always reported in the press and a description of the weapon is included. If a knife is used, we read about the length of the blade. If battering is the cause of injuries, we learn that a baseball bat or an iron pipe was the weapon of choice. A shooting report includes the type of gun and caliber of bullets. When discussing rape, a penis is a weapon—nothing more. Rape is not about sex. It is about power and control.

After being raped, everything that once was normal in the lives of survivors seems surreal. We dread going to sleep because we are plagued by nightmares. Awake, the sound of a dog barking or a tree branch hitting the window causes momentary panic. Relationships are difficult because survivors lose trust. We become intolerant of human failings. If a man doesn't meet our expectations —and only a saint could—he doesn't get a second chance.

Survivors often become incapable of allowing someone new into their lives. Immediately after my attack, only those closest to me—my fiancé who at the time was my boyfriend, my mom and dad, my brother, a few friends—knew that the happy expression on my face each day was part of my makeup. Apply lipstick. Smile.

It's hard work pretending to be someone you're not but, as kind as most people are, they don't want to be burdened with other people's sorrow. As a result, many survivors never really grieve for the loss of their innocence, security, trust and independence. Grieving is weak. Survivors are afraid to be weak.

The death of Robert Bridgeman closes a chapter in my life but it opens a new chapter for the Palm Beach County Sheriff's Office. Bridgeman was a serial rapist. We have connected him to the murders of Kelly Fontaine of Jupiter and Daniela Panzarino, a West Palm Beach resident. We will not stop investigating until we have gotten justice for every woman who was brutalized by him."

CHAPTER EIGHTEEN

The front page of the Palm Beach Post was decorated with jack-o-lantern images smiling a treat or treat greeting. The two-toothed pumpkins belied the stories of madness and murder that were the primary news topics locally and nationally. The article reporting Nate Kincaid's death to be an accident was hidden away in the local section between the latest winning lottery numbers and an article about a man accused of killing his boss in the parking lot of a home improvement store.

The case against Dobson Jenkins was strong but Marci knew a clever defense attorney would twist the facts. They always did. She and Cat had been tasked with solving the crime in 2005 and, although they had been able to quickly amass all the evidence needed to arrest Jenkins, it had taken two more years to bring him to trial. Marci and Cat had been served with subpoenas to appear earlier in the month so for the past few weeks they had been spending their off hours reviewing their notes on the case.

Jenkins, a construction worker in his late 50s with a history of drug use and domestic violence, shot his boss, James Picinich, when the two men stopped to buy supplies for a bathroom remodel they were working on together. Jenkins arrived at the store first and waited in the early morning darkness for Picinich to arrive. The men argued and Jenkins shot Picinich, leaving him to die in his car. Customers at the store called police when they heard the shots; a unit was nearby and the officers pursued Jenkins onto the I-95. During a high speed chase, Jenkins rammed another car, forcing it into the guardrail, and continued north. He was eventually stopped when his car slid into a roadblock placed across the highway. A dozen officers with weapons drawn were enough to convince him to throw his gun out of his truck and surrender peacefully.

Under questioning, Jenkins claimed that Picinich was having an affair with his estranged wife and that Picinich had influenced her to take out a restraining order against him. When Cat and Marci interviewed Mrs. Jenkins, she was sporting two black eyes and a swollen lip the size of a basketball. She claimed that Picinich had provided nothing but moral support and legal advice in the form of a business card from the attorney he had used for his own divorce.

The Jenkins/Picinich case took up half a page while Kincaid's death notice barely took up an eighth of a page. Marci threw the newspaper on top of the evidence collection boxes which were stacked in a corner of the conference room waiting to be taken to storage. The one unresolved issue was what to do with the $25,000 found in Nate Kincaid's safe. Neither Doranda Fitzpatrick or Jason Kincaid had made a claim. Since the police department was under no obligation to remind the family of the money's existence, everyone from the Chief on down was wondering if the windfall would be theirs to keep.

Marci was partner-less for a few days as Cat was giving testimony in the recently reopened Eugene McWalters' case which she had investigated before she and Marci began working together. With no new murders in their queue, Marci decided to give her desk a good cleaning and began the process of shredding years of no-longer-in-business restaurant menus, birthday cards, charity dinner invitations and assorted other junk. Hidden under a pile of departmental memos she found the advance copy of Doranda Fitzpatrick's book that had been taken from Nate Kincaid's apartment. Emblazoned in black and gold on a scarlet-hued cover, the title, *800 Women*, intrigued her.

Not caring who overheard her talking to herself, she queried aloud, "Could one man really have sex with that many woman?"

Making herself comfortable—feet on her desk and coffee cup within easy reach—she flipped open the cover. Three hours later, she was hopping from one foot to another as Cat stepped off the elevator and was immediately pushed back in.

"Whoa. Slow down. Where are we going?"

"To pay a little visit to Doranda Fitzpatrick."

"Now? I've been in court for half a day. I'm tired."

"Believe me, you're going to feel re-energized very quickly. Read the last chapter, Cat. Just read the last chapter." Marci handed

Cat the book and fairly pressed her nose between its pages.

"Okay. Okay. I get it. You want me to read."

"Just the last twenty pages."

As Marci drove, Cat utilized her self-taught speed-reading techniques to get through the final chapter of the book. Closing the cover, she sat and stared out the window.

"Yeah. My reaction exactly." Marci was practically jumping in her seat. "I can't wait to ask the former Mrs. Nate Kincaid a few questions."

Twenty-five minutes later, she parked the unmarked squad car in the driveway of 1342 Meadowlark Lane in Jupiter. As she and Cat made their way to the front door, anticipation showed in their steps.

Doranda Fitzpatrick did a fairly good job of hiding her surprise as she welcomed the detectives into her home. "It's a beautiful late afternoon, isn't it? I was sitting out on the patio. Please, come this way. May I offer you something to drink, Detective Welles? Detective Leigh?"

"No, thank you," Marci answered for herself and Cat. She held the author's book and casually flipped the pages as they walked and talked.

Doranda Fitzpatrick opened the double French doors to a private patio surrounded by bougainvillea bushes and a wall of bamboo. Small solar lights edged the path and a copper fire pit, already blazing, warmed the early evening air.

Cat stood near the pit and inhaled the scent of burning wood. "When I lived in New Jersey, I loved the smell of a fireplace burning on a cold night. My dad bought cords of wood, and we would stack them outside the back door. No driftwood in Bergen County. Did you collect all that?" Cat tipped her head in the direction of the pieces of sun bleached and misshapen wood stacked nearby, waiting to be added to the flames.

"I know it's really too early in the year for a fire, but there's something very relaxing about staring into the flames. As for the wood, I enjoy walking along the beach. Whatever I find comes home with me."

Cat and Marci exchanged glances as they took seats on one side of the portable camp fire. The unspoken consensus was clear. Like Nate Kincaid's soon-to-be cremated body, his murder weapon could be a pile of ashes by now. Doranda Fitzpatrick pretended not to see the exchange as she took a seat opposite Cat and Marci.

"We want to ask you about your book." Marci held the work of fiction up for Doranda Fitzpatrick to see. "The final chapter has an unusual title—*Sand in Their Coffee*. Does it have any significance?"

"Actually, it does," Fitzpatrick acknowledged. "As you know, Nate was fond of bringing his ladies to the beach. He always brought hot coffee in a thermos and fruit or Danish to satisfy the hunger roused by those pre-dawn romps. Early mornings at the beach can be very windy. The tower offered no real protection from the elements. Sand was everywhere, even in the coffee. Nate always joked it was the sugar he sweetened the day with for his honeys."

"His honeys. I heard that term quite a few times during the investigation." Cat crossed her arms in an unconscious hug of herself.

"Nate used many quaint forms of endearment; I've forgotten half of them. His delivery was almost robotic so often did he speak them."

Marci turned the book over and opened it from the back. "You told us you started this book two years ago."

"Yes. That's correct."

"And it's fiction?"

"Well, yes and no. It's published as a work of fiction, but we all know—both of you, me, everyone involved in this case—that the background story is true."

"How true? The wife in your book actually kills her former husband."

"No, she doesn't, Detective Welles. You've, obviously, read the book. You *know* perfectly well it was an *accident*." Doranda pronounced her words with intentional emphasis.

"I called your publisher. He said it takes as long as a year once a book is edited to get it shelf ready. Yet, Nate Kincaid dies in your story in almost the exact same way he did in real life. Can you explain that?"

"As I have already told you, Nate was a creature of habit. You don't live with someone for years and not anticipate their reactions, especially to unwelcome events."

"So, you knew he would be pissed off about the book; but to predict his death by falling from the tower ladder... That's seems almost clairvoyant."

"There are only two possible scenarios if you are going to kill a lifeguard—drowning or falling. Drowning would have been implausible, especially in Nate's case. He was an exceptional swimmer. He rarely talked about it but he actually went to college on a swimming scholarship and, if not for a broken nose while diving into the pool, would have had an excellent chance of going to the Olympics. I chose falling because of the condition of the tower and the beach after the hurricanes of 2005. I can't tell you how many times I slipped on those stairs when I would visit Nate at the beach."

"What do you mean 'condition of the beach.'" Cat's voice held deserved admiration for Doranda Fitzpatrick's composure.

"Beach erosion was severe after that season. In many places, rock formations that had been buried under yards of sand were exposed. Towers that had been ten feet above the beach now had a twenty foot drop with which to contend."

"And..." Cat waited patiently for the remainder of the explanation.

"Sometimes, life imitates art. "

"Or, you could have gotten away with murder." There wasn't a bit of admiration in Marci's voice.

"The similarities between the book and actual events are mere coincidence, Detective. Writing it was akin to throwing a penny into a wishing well."

"You wished your former husband would die?"

"There is a quote by David Joseph Schwartz. He was a motivational speaker who died in the late 1980s. I apologize if you already knew that, Detective Welles. I wasn't being condescending." Marci ignored the apology. She recognized condescension when she heard it.

"What's the significance of this quote?"

"'Believe it can be done. When you believe something can be done, really believe, your mind will find the ways to do it.' I found the way to rid Nate from my life by writing a book. I never physically touched him."

Cat slid to the edge of the chair, stood up, and took a stance in imitation of what she imagined happened at the beach. "You were at Coral Cove the morning your ex husband died. You stood at the top of the ladder, where he could see you, and waited, knowing that his anger would propel him to do something careless. He reacted aggressively, slipped and fell, and you left him there to die."

Doranda Fitzpatrick now stood as well. She turned and walked toward the French doors that 20 minutes earlier she had ushered the two detectives through with insincere welcome. Her movements signaled the visit was over. "You have a wonderful imagination, Detective Leigh. Perhaps, you should be a mystery writer."

Marci took her place beside Cat. The three women stared at one another. Only one knew the truth of what had happened to Nate Kincaid. The other two surmised but had no proof. The one who knew had no intention of aiding the struggling detectives.

"Your work, Detectives, should have taught you that life, in its own way, really is fair and that justice is eventually served just not always in the way one would expect. I've enjoyed our visit. Thank you for stopping by." Doranda Fitzpatrick escorted Cat and Marci to the front door. She watched them as they walked to their car and, hopefully, out of her life.

"By the way, neither Jason or I want the money you found in the safe. What the IRS doesn't take, you can have. The donuts and coffee are on us. Enjoy."

Before Cat and Marci could respond, she closed and locked the door with an audible click. Anger appeared as a mask on Marci's face. She and Cat sat in the car reviewing their conversation with the ex-Mrs. Nate Kincaid.

Cat's face was also set in a mask but the emotion was totally different. "She's right, you know."

"About?"

"Justice being served. Emotional rape is just as damaging as a physical assault."

"What are you saying, Cat? That you're glad they're getting away with murder?"

"If we had evidence, I would arrest her and plant her ass in jail, but we don't."

"And you're okay with that?"

"Not so okay that I don't plan to track down every woman on that list whom we haven't yet interviewed."

"Doranda Fitzpatrick or one of her sidekicks is a murderer, Cat."

"Probably, but having a machete pressed to your throat gives guilty a whole new meaning."

CHAPTER NINETEEN

After appearing on the morning news to discuss the death of Robert Bridgeman, Cat and Marci found themselves in demand as speakers for political action committees, women's organizations and business groups concerned about the rapidly rising increase in sexual assaults. They were the PBSO representatives to both SART (Sexual Assault Response Team) and the local chapter of RAINN (Rape, Abuse and Incest National Network).

Cat had been approached by the History Channel and the Discovery Channel as both stations were launching new series based on real life survival stories. She was conflicted about participating in either show as she was hesitant to reveal personal details of her life while at the same time believing that the topic of rape needed a broader audience—an audience willing to hear the truth about personal responsibility and a woman's role in protecting herself.

The first time Cat and Marci spoke publicly on rape, they did so before a gathering of sex crime investigators and federal officials at a conference organized by the Police Executive Research Forum in Washington, D.C.

"Good afternoon. My name is Marci Welles. I am a Homicide Detective with the Palm Beach County Sheriff's Office and along with my partner, Detective Jessica Leigh, we are actively involved in changing the way law enforcement and society view the crime of rape. Detective Leigh will speak to you as a survivor of assault in a few minutes but for the moment, I would like to direct your attention to the charts behind me.

Every year the FBI releases the Uniform Crime Report, which we refer to as the UCR. As you know, that report includes statistics on the number of rapes committed during the previous year. Unfortunately, the figures are based on a definition of rape that is 80 years past due for a revision.

Currently, the crime of rape is defined as 'carnal knowledge of a female, forcibly and against her will.' Critics have long protested that the definition is not encompassing enough. One of the areas where it is lacking—the definition does not account for assaults where the victim has been drugged or is inebriated. Equally as important, the definition completely excludes males who had been assaulted. As a result statistics are skewed.

Occasionally, the UCR reports a drop in sexual assaults when there has actually been an increase, and this miscalculation can lead to a potentially dangerous outcome. Anytime a drop in crime statistics is reported, legislators take it as a signal to reduce services and resources devoted to assisting rape victims. Additionally, reduced crime statistics result in less money being allocated on local and state levels toward the capture and prosecution of rapists.

All this is true because society views rape as a sex crime— something which is considered shameful and embarrassing. Rape is neither of those things. It is a violent crime and like all violent crimes, the men and women who survive deserve to have their suffering properly acknowledged by law enforcement and the public.

Until we better educate society… until we remove the stigma of shame that is associated with rape, women and men who are brutalized by this crime will remain shivering in the shadows. That will change if we refuse to remain silent. Those who are determined to bring their attackers to justice are heroes. Do you know how much courage it takes for a victim to face her/his assailant in court? More than most people—even those of us in law enforcement—will ever require in an entire lifetime. These brave survivors are on the front line, fighting within the structure of the law and sending a powerful message to predators that they will not quiver in fear.

Law enforcement should be obligated to define the crime correctly. Society should be obligated to sing the praises of survivors who are determined to see justice done, and we must do that in voices loud enough that rapists know we are coming for them. Until we make victim a word to fear in the heart of every deviant, we will never reduce the incidents of sexual assault.

Whenever someone approaches Jessica or me about how to react when confronted with a rape survivor, we ask them not to hang their heads in pity and whisper 'I'm so sorry.' We suggest they look the survivor in the eyes and say, 'Thank you for having the courage to speak out.' Say, 'You are my hero' and mean it! That is the attitude we all—private citizens and public officials—must adopt and present if we are to make positive change.

Ladies and gentlemen, it is my privilege to introduce my personal hero, my partner, Detective Jessica Leigh."

As Cat rose and took her place on the stage, the applause from the audience washed over her and made her momentarily dizzy. She held on to either side of the lectern and gathered her thoughts.

"Good afternoon. Marci and I are sincerely grateful for the invitation to speak to you today. One thing we have learned during the past year is that there are two words which have the power to clear a building with amazing speed. One, of course, is fire. The other is rape.

With rape, people don't actually exit a room, but they do leave—mentally and emotionally. Sometimes I watch and note how many heads suddenly drop toward their lap when Marci or I begin to speak. A non-existent loose string or button suddenly becomes immensely interesting. I hope that won't happen today but I will be watching and Marci is taking notes.

This afternoon I would like to focus on how law enforcement protocols and societal mindsets affect rape survivors. Gentlemen, I apologize that many of my comments will appear to exclude you. That is not my intention. Men have been and continue to be victimized by the predators among us and, unfortunately, those predators often include the people controlling our legislatures. I am not going to address date rape or pedophilia—two topics with different and distinct sets of circumstances. Today, I am addressing sexual assault in broad terms.

Please know from the outset that I despise the term sexual assault because it perpetuates the myth that rape is about sex. As Marci already stated, it isn't but you already know that. Unfortunately, I must use the term because we haven't yet convinced the powers that be that the term is harmful to our cause. For the record, my preference would be anatomy specific assault."

Cat's voice began to crack and she shuffled her note cards to cover her momentary loss of control. The audience waited patiently for her to continue.

"After a recent appearance on a program that discussed the survivor's role in lessening rape statistics, I had a conversation with a local journalist who emphatically stated that it wasn't the victim's job to de-stigmatize rape. Yes. It is. Who can do it better?

Cultural norms dictate that rape victims' identities be hidden from the public. As a survivor, I continually ask, "Why?" I, or rather we, didn't do anything wrong. We have no reason to be ashamed. Why is it that victims of other violent crimes bask in media attention, but rape survivors are hidden away?

It isn't until we personalize any issue of value that society recognizes its legitimacy. If we don't give rape a name and a face, it becomes a crime that happens to someone else— someone nameless and faceless. It becomes the crime that happens to those women who approach me in stores and in parking lots and, with tears running down their faces, admit that I am the first person they have told that they were assaulted. Some of these crimes happened 40 years ago. These women have never gotten the help they need because someone—a parent, friend, religious leader, an entire community—made them feel that they were responsible."

Again, Cat's voice began to vibrate but this time it was with anger at a system that blamed women for the crimes committed against them. The passion she felt for her topic was evident in the determined look on her face and the way she leaned forward at the podium, as though trying to touch her listeners.

"Consider Rosa Parks. If Ms. Parks hadn't been willing to take a stand on the issue of segregation, the dividing line between the races would extend far beyond the back of the bus. There is a quote by Ms. Parks of which I am especially fond. She said, 'Knowing what needs to be done eliminates fear.'

When it comes to rape, we know what needs to be done. We must eliminate ignorance. We must educate society as to the psychology of the rapist and what women can do to protect themselves. There are people who will try to convince you that rapists can be cured either with behavioral modification, chemical castration and/or religion. They can't. Rapists are born, not made. The only reason it appears these methods work is because rapists get better at hiding their crimes. Most experts agree that once a rapist/always a rapist is the most accurate description. When you are in the midst of an investigation, please remember that the only good rapist is one who is behind bars for life."

The applause that followed Cat's and Marci's speeches was deafening. Leaving the auditorium took over an hour as more than 100 were people lined up to shake their hands. A surprising number of women asked to speak with Cat privately whenever she had time. Her appointment book was already filled with notations to "meet for coffee" so she was well aware of what the topic of conversation would be.

CHAPTER TWENTY

"I know who killed Kincaid." Marci fairly danced a jig around Cat, who was forced to stop mid-yawn as she stumbled off the elevator into the dark before the dawn emptiness of the Homicide Division. It was Friday of one of the longest weeks either woman could remember in a long time and the friends were looking forward to three days of uninterrupted fun and frolic at home.

"So do I but we can't prove it."

"We were wrong. It wasn't Doranda Fitzpatrick, at least, not directly. Follow me." Marci led the way to her desk where she picked up a Xerox copy of a photograph and held it out tauntingly to Cat. "Look familiar?"

"No. This is a driver's license photo. Everyone looks like Frankenstein's monster. It's intentional so that drivers are too embarrassed to get stopped for speeding."

"Imagine longer, more bleached blond hair."

"Sorry… still don't know."

Marci fairly ripped the photo from Cat's fingers. "Damn! Concentrate. Maybe this picture will help. I blew it up 200%. Take another look." She dangled another photo under Cat's nose.

Cat studied the photo through bleary eyes and was just about to hand it back when …

"Holy shit! This is Lieutenant Charles' wife."

"Uh huh. Keep looking."

"She's wearing the earrings."

Marci smiled broadly and took a much deserved bow.

"This is great work, Marci. Whatever made you look at her license?"

"Boredom mostly. The evidence boxes have been sitting in the conference room for weeks and I thought I'd take one more look. I was skimming through our notes from the day we interviewed Lieutenant Charles and thought 'Let me see what the Babe Magnet's new misses looks like.' I accessed the Motor Vehicle data base and there she and the earrings were."

"I guess Lieutenant Charles wasn't exactly truthful when he said there was no bad blood between him and Kincaid."

"Bad blood? When it comes to jealous husbands and cheating wives, there isn't any other kind."

"Call in the warrant. This one is all yours."

When Marci, Cat and two uniformed officers arrived at Ocean Rescue, they found Lieutenant Charles sitting at his desk reading the latest brown paper wrapped issue of Playboy. Someone, most likely Charles, had printed POPULAR MECHANICS in thick black marker on one side of the paper in an unsuccessful effort to fool anyone entering the office unannounced. Despite some quick maneuvers to hide the centerfold held vertically in front of his nose, there was no mistaking the lascivious look on his face.

Although men have been known to drool over issues of Popular Mechanics, in the magazine's 100 plus year history, the only centerfold published was a photo of a web printing press. That edition was released in 1903 and while a beauty in its day, the printing press never caused spittle to drip from anyone's lips.

Lieutenant Charles quickly shoved the magazine in his desk drawer. He couldn't do anything to hide his red cheeks.

"Morning, babe magnet," Marci smiled her words ever so sweetly.

"Detectives. What's going on?"

"Well, for one thing, your wife will no longer need to worry about you flirting with the beach bunnies while at work."

"I never... I don't... What do you mean? Why are you here?"

"Sure you did and do. Isn't that how you met her? Don't bother. We already know the answer."

"The reason we're here is your wife has pierced ears." Cat didn't share Marci's love of dark comedy. Her voice showed not a trace of humor.

"Wh... What?" Lieutenant Charles stuttered in confusion.

"Allow me to explain. Your wife had an affair with Kincaid and you found out about it."

"No. My wife would never do that."

Marci's humor was quickly fading away. "I would suggest you think before you speak. Lying to the police is a crime in itself. It's called obstruction of justice."

"You found the earring I dropped, didn't you? I wondered if you could get DNA from something so small." Charles' shoulders drooped. He sat hunched over in his chair gathering his thoughts. With only a modicum of reluctance and not a bit of prodding, he laid his tortured soul before Marci and Cat.

"I saw a draft of the book and recognized Tracy, my wife, immediately even though her name wasn't used and Doranda had changed her physical description. Then, I saw the photo of Doranda on the back cover. She was wearing the same earrings Tracy refused to take off. Since she wouldn't talk to me, I confronted Doranda, who tried to protect Tracy, but there was no hiding from the truth.

Nate seduced her; he treated her like shit the way he did all the women in his life. He was the fricking devil incarnate, you know. When I confronted him, he laughed at me like it was no big deal."

"So, you killed him."

"It was an accident. Really. I didn't set out to kill him. The most I hoped to do was break that vulture's beak of his. I swear."

"Yeah. Yeah. Tell it to your lawyer." Marci seemed to be enjoying her job more than usual. She snapped handcuffs over Charles' wrists and motioned for the two police officers to lead him away. "Does your wife know that you know?"

"Of course. But she doesn't know about this."

"Well, I hope she likes surprises." Happy to have another case closed, Marci began to strut around like a proud peacock. She did a pretty fair imitation of the bird's head and body bob.

Cat found her antics hilarious. "That was way too easy, Marci. I'm not sure you get the win on this one."

"Yeah. He didn't even try to deny it."

"He actually seems like a decent guy who got caught in something he didn't know how to handle." Cat felt sorry for the Lieutenant. Her dislike for Kincaid and the assault on her person had changed her perspective about crime and crime victims.

Marci understood the empathy in her partners eyes. She commiserated with Cat. "The guilt was probably killing him. Right now, he is probably thinking death would be a welcomed relief."

"He did the wrong thing for the right reason. With knowing what we do about Kincaid, I feel a little bad for him."

"The way you feel sorry for Doranda and all those other women?"

"I suppose. A little bit."

"He'll get a good lawyer and plead involuntary manslaughter. Maybe do a few years. When he gets out, the little wife will be waiting for him all apologetic for falling prey to the big, bad wolf."

"What number do you think she was?"

"Whatever number, her husband is going to pay too high a price."

"Do you think Doranda and the other ladies know about Charles' part in Kincaid's death?"

"I guess we'll just have to ask them. Now that Lieutenant Charles has confessed, there's no reason for them not to talk to us."

"Unless they helped him."

"Why do you have to rain on my parade? Okay. Let's find the former Mrs. Kincaid and see what tale she has to tell."

CHAPTER TWENTY-ONE

Three months later Marci and Cat entered the homicide division's kitchenette to find Damian Mack, Keith Kennedy and Moe Di Lorenzo covered in powdered sugar. Also licking his fingers was Pete Shonto, Di Lorenzo's partner, whose pockets bulged with photos of his identical twin sons.

Over the past few months, Moe had often been heard to complain, "Two of everything. They look exactly alike. Take one picture. None of us would know the difference."

Sgt. Paulie Padrone spoke between chews and swallows as he poured himself a cup of fresh java from the new restaurant grade coffee maker. The pot sat atop a counter that also served as a Lost and Found for an absurdly large number of thermal cups and much-chipped coffee mugs no longer wanted by their owners. The amazing machine offered a choice of regular, decaf, espresso and cappuccino although the idea of any serious law enforcement officer drinking decaf was pure absurdity. In fact, one clever cop had printed a sign and hung it on the wall over the coffee maker with an arrow pointing toward the decaf button.

If it ain't caffeinated, it ain't coffee!

"Morning, Cat. Morning, Marci. Hungry? We've got donuts, croissants and pastries fresh from that French bakery on Clematis Street."

"Hey, Cat. What was it Kincaid always wrote in his seduction letters? Something about Paris." Damian Mack was busy wiping strawberry jelly from his tie. He cursed as the wiping turned into smearing which then became a big red stain smack in the middle on his beige Tommy Hilfiger original.

"'Paris is the most beautiful city in the world. You can't help but fall in love.' Or some such crap." Cat popped a croissant into the microwave.

"Yeah, well, I don't know much about the falling in love part unless he was talking about the food," Moe Di Lorenzo chimed in. "One thing is for sure, coming to work is going to seem like a trip to France until the $25,000 runs out."

Paulie Padrone held up his cup in salute. "Here's to the Casanovas of the world."

"Casanova was Italian," Damian Mack corrected him.

"Who's French?"

"Who cares?" Marci redirected the conversation by holding up the new coffee mugs she had bought for herself and Cat. Each was imprinted with the words *World's Best Detectives* and sported photos of the partners standing side by side wearing deerstalker caps and holding magnifying glasses. Both Cat and Marci had calabash pipes stuck between their teeth.

"Pour me a cup," Marci requested in her best British accent, "… and another for Dr. Watson." Marci turned to give Cat her mug only to be presented with her back exiting the kitchen. "Cat? Hey. Cat. I'm sorry. You can be Sherlock."

Cat kept walking and Marci pursued her. "Where are you going?"

Cat waved a croissant over her shoulder. "I'll be back in a sec."

With the door closed to the office she shared with Marci, Cat picked up the telephone on her desk and dialed. "Morning. I, uh, I wanted to thank you for backing me up in court during the re-trial of the McWalters case. Why did you?"

"Good morning, Detective. You are welcome." G's normal voice was a soothing mix of southern charm and perfect elocution. "I've been wanting to congratulate you on solving the Kincaid case. Both you and Marci fought against my findings—not that I minded. To be honest, I, too, felt the fall wasn't an accident. I just couldn't prove it. You went with your gut and never gave up."

"Marci gets the credit. She made the connection between the earrings and Lieutenant Charles' wife."

"Yes, that was the first real break in the case, but both of you kept digging until you uncovered Doranda Fitzpatrick's role in the murder cover up. It must be true that you read each other's minds. I've never met two detectives so in tune with each other as you and Marci."

"We've been friends a long time. I'd like to be able to say that about you and me one day."

"I don't see why that shouldn't be possible. Tell me. How did you get Ms. Fitzpatrick to admit she used her fire pit to burn the wood Charles smashed into Kincaid's head?"

"It was really just a case of laying out all the pieces of the jigsaw puzzle and showing her how perfectly they fit together. Charles said he called Doranda after reading her book and discovering his wife's affair with Kincaid. Doranda confirmed that they spoke. She said she had never heard anyone so angry.

Knowing how deep her own hatred for Kincaid went, she anticipated that Charles would want to act on his feelings so she went to the beach in the morning, hoping to dissuade him from doing anything stupid. Her intention was to stop him. I've got to give her credit for that.

If you remember, when we interviewed her she said she had gone to Coral Cove to stop her son from confronting his father, but that wasn't true. She had no idea that Jason would go to the park and his presence there was a surprise to her... a surprise that, eventually, became an easy lie with which to cover up her real reason for being there.

She even lied to Jason about being in New York. She never left Jupiter. She never answered her phone either hoping to make her absence more believable. When she saw Jason in the parking lot, she panicked. Then, she heard Kincaid call to Patricia Murphy so she knew that the Lieutenant hadn't arrived as yet. She figured her son had gotten into a battle of words with his father and had lost. She could tell he was angry from the way he was walking.

Anyway, she sat in her car hoping that Ms. Murphy's presence would deter Charles from wreaking revenge on Kincaid. She actually left Coral Cove right after Murphy left thinking the worst was over but some voice in her head told her to go back. By the time she got to the tower, Charles and Kincaid were fighting. Kincaid was taunting Charles and Charles, looking more animal than human, threw the earrings in Kincaid's face and swung the driftwood he had picked up from the beach.

Doranda kept defending Charles saying that he only meant to threaten Kincaid with the wood but the need to defend his wife's honor against some pretty demeaning comments Kincaid was making made him… Well, to use her words, 'Temporary insanity' replaced his normally calm demeanor."

"What did Doranda do?"

"What could she do? She was smart enough not to get between them. She tried yelling from a distance but her efforts were futile. When it was over, the Lieutenant broke down crying and she rushed to comfort him. She found one of the earrings—the other Marci found embedded in the decking. Doranda put the one she found in her pocket intending to dispose of it, which she did. She also took the piece of wood home and turned it into ashes."

"She tampered with a crime scene. What is the prosecutor planning to do?"

"Tampering and withholding evidence are third degree felonies which could have gotten her five years in prison. The D.A made a deal with her in exchange for her testimony against Charles. She won't do any time but she will be on probation for five years. I'll make you a bet her new found notoriety will help push book sales. She's going to be a rich woman.

As for Charles, he'll do very little time as well. With 800 plus women willing to testify on his behalf, it will be impossible for a jury not to feel sympathy. I see a movie in the not too distant future starring artificially beautiful actors who don't resemble the real characters even one tiny bit. 800 Women starring Tom Cruise."

"The nose would be perfectly cast if nothing else."

"Ah, G, you have a mean streak. Good to know."

"If hell hath no fury like one woman scorned, I can only imagine the fury generated by 800 bent-on-revenge females. Good job, Detective."

"Thank you. G, you never answered my question. Why did you back me up in court during the hearing on the McWalters case?"

"I told the truth, Cat. I've never known you to be anything but the utmost professional in the line of duty—thorough to the extreme. The judge may have felt that his lawyers did not fulfill their obligation to mount an effective defense, but the allegation that there had been no meaningful investigation by you was ludicrous.

McWalters was a psychopath. He raped and murdered three women, leaving two of the bodies to decompose in John Prince Park and the other buried under rocks in a drainage canal. Those are the premeditated actions of a madman—a madman who stared into the eyes of his victims as he slowly choked the life out of them.

You got him to confess. I never doubted your methods. I'm not happy the judge offered a plea deal because life in prison without parole just doesn't seem like real justice."

"You're a good man, G. I'm sorry that I let my personal problems get in the way of our relationship."

"You know, Cat, there's a quote I use to guide my actions. 'I shall pass through this world but once. Any good that I can do or any kindness that I can show, let me do it now.'"

"I like that. Who said it?"

"Jerry Lewis."

Cat laughed softly as she hung up the phone. She stared down at her wrist and gently ran her finger over the teal blue ribbon tattoo inscribed "I Survived." The tattoo covered the deepest of the scars caused by the zip ties that had held her captive.

With a new lightness in her step, she picked up the now hard-as-a-rock croissant and returned to the kitchen. The homicide hot line was ringing as she crossed the bullpen.

EPILOGUE

May 2006

The soaking wet body of Janice Handera was found on the evening of May 14th. Nothing about the crime scene hinted that the murder of this unassuming mother of four adult children would be the first in a series of gruesome deaths committed on national holidays. When PBSO Homicide Detectives Jessica "Cat" Leigh and Marcassy "Marci" Welles were called to Mounts Botanical Gardens at 7 pm, the last thing they expected to find was the petite Mrs. Handera wrapped in a banner proclaiming Happy Mother's Day. The nine inch florist's spike through her throat guaranteed that any happiness she felt had been short lived.

County Medical Examiner Mark "G" Geschwer was already at the scene when the partners made their presence known. Their muttered curses echoed in the night as they pushed their way through the heavily-thorned bougainvillea bushes that camouflaged the maintenance area where equipment was stored.

For once, Marci's penchant for suit jackets and heavy rubbed soled shoes even in the heat of summer proved to be a good thing. She was spared having her arms and legs turned into pin cushions although her hands were covered with scratches and there was a close-call gash at the corner of one eye.

Cat, on the other hand, paid a price for choosing to be and look cool while on duty. Her arms had long cat claw-like lacerations which were seeping blood and her calves were covered in raised red welts. Her red silk blouse looked like it had been used by a toreador at a bull fight—and the bull won. At least she wouldn't be throwing away another pair of designer shoes. Having learned many an expensive lesson about the unpredictability of the weather and the condition of crime scenes, she kept well-worn sneakers and sandals in the trunk of the car.

"What have we got, G?" Marci ducked under the last branch of the flesh eating plant guarding the recycling dumpster and made her way to the medical examiner's side.

"Evening, Detectives. This is Janice Handera. She's 61 and until about five hours ago, she was a healthy, happy woman with a passion for all things green."

It was obvious that the medical examiner, a man prone to bad imitations of Jerry Lewis, was deeply touched by this case. Otherwise, his subdued greeting—"Evening, Detectives"— would have been voiced as "Hey! Hey! Detective Ladies" in that whinny nasal that Lewis' *Nutty Professor* character had made famous.

"There's a contusion on the back of her head so my guess right now is that her attacker hit her with something, maybe a rock and, while she was stunned, drove a nine inch florist's spike through her throat with great force. So much force, in fact, that it is protruding from the back of her neck. I'll know more after the autopsy."

"She was alive when he did that?" The anger in Cat's voice was hard to ignore.

"Yes. I believe so. There are no drag marks in the dirt, which should be obvious despite the rain, so how he got her back here is a mystery you will have to solve. I can't imagine he was able to carry her through that thicket of thorns and there is no reason why she would have wandered into this No Trespass area unless she was enticed to do so."

"I'm assuming the storm washed away any traces of contact by her assailant."

"There isn't much to go on. Her hair and clothing are saturated, and the ground is one big mud puddle. I doubt the lab will find anything of use but we'll give it our best shot."

Cat stared down at the victim, deep sorrow in her eyes. She especially hated murders that happened on holidays. The families of the victims were never able to put the horrors of the day behind them. "Was she alone?"

"Husband is sitting in the gazebo at the end of the path. Two officers are with him."

Cat and Marci thanked G and elicited a promise that he would do the autopsy asap. Asking was merely a matter of habit; they already knew that the medical examiner always made their cases a top priority.

The women carefully picked their way back through the bushes and followed the soggy mulched road to the Tranquility Garden—a place where solace was meant to be found among the hollyhocks, liatris, crape myrtle and numerous varieties of wildflowers that were favored by butterflies and hummingbirds. One look at the recent widower's face was confirmation that solace was in short supply.

According to Handera's husband, Ray, he and his wife had planned to spend a leisurely day taking a self-guided tour of the popular tropical paradise in the middle of West Palm Beach. The 14 acre site was home to plants from six continents and offered a wide variety of horticultural learning experiences covering everything from edible landscapes to aquatics and desert climes. Visiting the Gardens on Mother's Day was a 20 year tradition for them as Janice had been an amateur botanist who dreamed of one day discovering a new way to pollinate flowers. An avid environmentalist, she was deeply worried about the dearth of bees able to fulfill Mother Nature's job description.

The time was about 18 minutes past 1:00 pm when Ray and Janice climbed into their car. Ray, a plumber, had just started the engine when he was flagged down by neighbor and friend Martin Montemurro and asked to perform an emergency Heimlich maneuver on the toilet in their master bathroom. Martin and his wife, Maggie, had a three-year-old son, Marty. Ray called them the 3M Company— mother, father and son were inseparable. Martin found the nickname amusing. He readily admitted that Marty, an only child, was the default Chairman of the Board. On this afternoon, Marty had tried to give his favorite stuffed rabbit a swimming lesson in the toilet bowl and "accidentally" flushed. Water was everywhere but retrieving the hysterically crying child's best friend was the biggest priority.

Not wanting his wife to miss a minute of her day, Ray dropped Janice off at the Gardens. The clock in his car glowed 2:00 pm as he pulled out of the parking lot. He remembered because he was trying to estimate how long it would take him to do surgery on the Montemurro's bathroom pipes.

By the time he finished un-stuffing the toilet, showered, changed and arrived back at Mounts, approximately two and a half hours later, Janice was nowhere to be found. At first he had leisurely walked the Gardens, following familiar paths to their favorite places. When over an hour passed without finding her, his movements became more frantic. He repeatedly called her cell phone and send text messages—all ignored and unanswered. Returning to the front office and not finding anyone who had seen his wife, he called the police.

Of course, the husband is always the first suspect on every investigator's list. However, the Montemurros were text book perfect alibis; and if their word hadn't been enough, Bunny, the stuffed rabbit, was spinning wildly in the washing machine when Marci and Cat interviewed the family later that evening. The smell of bleach filled the laundry room.

"Are you okay, Marci?" Cat gently inquired of her best friend while standing in the driveway of the Montemurro's house. "This is your first Mother's Day with Sonora."

"I'm okay, but trust me, when I get home, I'm wrapping that beautiful little girl in my arms and never letting go." Marci and her husband, Ian, had adopted the newborn Sonora Leslie one month earlier and were nervously awaiting the court's official stamp of approval.

A thorough search of the crime scene and of Janice Handera's clothes gave up not even the smallest speck of fiber or hair. After two weeks of repeat interviews with every employee of Mounts Botanical Gardens... after speaking with Janice's children, friends and co-workers at the Rosemary Avenue Publix where she was the bakery manager... after exhaustively searching for every and any possible motive, the only plausible explanation for her death was thrill kill. Her passing was a murder of convenience for a madman who had now left an indelible mark on Palm Beach County on one of the most honored days of the year.

"What's that quote by Arthur Conan Doyle—the one about how hard it is to track certain crimes?" Marci asked. She and Cat were both big fans of Sherlock Holmes.

"The most difficult crime to track is the one which is purposeless."

"Yeah. I think we've got a whole mess of purposeless here."

#

June 2006

Wallace Lanier celebrated his sixtieth birthday on June 17. The party was not attended by his two sons who had never forgiven him for deserting them and their mother while they were still at the rug rat stage of their lives. Not only did Wallace disown them emotionally, he never contributed a dime for their care—not education, health, food or clothing. Wallace never visited or sent gifts for holidays or birthdays. He never cheered them on at Pop Warner football games where both boys excelled on the playing field. As far as Wallace Lanier was concerned, he was childless. As far as his sons were concerned, they had been found under a cabbage leaf and were better off for it.

Needless to say, the boys, now in their thirties, never visited or sent their semen donor a card for Father's Day, which just happened to be June 18 and the day Wallace's body was found buried up to his neck on the pitcher's mound at Roger Dean Stadium. He had been stoned to death with baseballs. His killer had taken the time to mound the blood spattered balls around Wallace's head so that from a distance only a pile of white would be seen. A 4 foot by 8 foot Happy Father's Day banner was draped around and across the pyramid like a boa constrictor crushing its prey.

The grounds keeper, who had arrived at the stadium early in the morning to prepare the field for the afternoon's game between the Cardinals and the Yankees, was sitting in the bleachers in shock when Cat and Marci arrived. A paramedic stood nearby in case he needed medical help. Julio Sanchez could barely speak; his heavily Spanish-accented English now punctuated with pleas of "Dios mio" in the hope that God would remove the memory of Wallace Lanier's staring dead eyes from his mind.

Again, the murder site provided no real clues. If not for his badly battered face and head, Lanier's body showed no signs of abuse. His sneakers, shorts and tee shirt with a popular beer logo on the front and a much-maligned slogan on the back—*The perfect beer for removing 'no' from her vocabulary for the night*—were pristine except for the dirt from his makeshift grave.

Working slowly and methodically in the hope that the ground held some clues, the Crime Scene Investigation Team unburied Lanier. They gathered up all the baseballs and carefully packaged them to take to the lab. All the shovels in the Stadium's work shed were bagged and tagged. Other than the holiday banner and the complete absence of evidence, there was nothing to tie the murders of Janice Handera and Wallace Lanier together.

By the time Lanier's body was found, Cat and Marci had already visited 50 party supply stores in the northern end of Palm Beach County. Each store carried the same banners used by the killer and no store owner had even a vague recollection of who had bought them recently. Add to that the hundreds of web sites where the banners were available and it became obvious that the lead was no lead at all.

"Okay. How did the killer, whoever he is, know that Janice Handera and Wallace Lanier had children? Why did he pick them? What made them special?" Cat was growing more frustrated by the day.

"I don't think whether or not they had children was a consideration and I don't think there was any science to choosing a victim. Most people in their fifties and sixties have children. It was a gamble that paid off. I'm more interested in how he killed them without attracting attention."

Marci was as troubled as Cat by the lack of evidence and eye witnesses to the killings. Whoever was committing these crimes had a well thought out plan.

Cat and Marci were anxious to interview Lanier's sons. Under duress, the men were flying in from their home in the Tri-State area to claim their father's body. Since Wallace had never remarried, the boys were his only living relatives.

Peter Lanier, age 38, and his brother, Paul, age 36, were as different as day and night. Peter was quiet and reserved almost to the point of being mute. Paul was gregarious—loud and quick to laugh albeit sardonically.

When Marci and Cat interviewed the brothers, laughing was pretty much Paul's first reaction to news of his father's death. "That son of a bitch finally got what he deserved. You should have just dug the hole deeper and thrown dirt over his head. He always preferred his beloved baseball to us."

Peter, on the other hand, looked sincerely sorry. "Don't say that, Paul," he admonished. "He's still our father."

"Yours, maybe, but not mine. He never acknowledged us and I have no intention of pretending to be sorry he's dead. There better be an insurance policy. I'm not paying for his funeral."

Like Ray Handera, the apostle brothers were the most likely suspects in their father's death. At least, Paul was high on the list. However, also like Ray Handera, their alibis were text book perfect.

The siblings lived 1,200 miles away in Fort Lee, New Jersey, the city that anchored the east side of the George Washington Bridge. Their wives and co-workers confirmed that the men, who jointly owned an auto mechanics business employing wounded veterans, were hosting a company picnic in Fort Tryon Park in Washington Heights, a suburb of Manhattan and the city that anchored the west side of the GWB, on the day of the murder.

The two boys who had never had a father had become father figures to many deserving young men.

#

July 2006

Marci was in mid-catch of a Frisbee when her phone rang. She ignored it. It was July 4th; family and friends were gathered around the pool and picnic table in her backyard; the mouth watering smells of grilling hamburgers and hot dogs filled the air; and she and Cat had earned a long weekend free of the grisly crimes committed by less than

171

human beings. They were both physically and mentally exhausted from trying to find the missing pieces to the puzzle that had become the Kalendar Killings—so dubbed by a clever journalist who couldn't resist showing off her advanced degree in English literature.

Barbara Thatcher, reporting for the Palm Beach Post, had headlined her most recent story *"The Kalendar Killer strikes again. Is God watching?"*

Not surprisingly, spelling calendar with a "K" had prompted many Letters to the Editor complaining that the paper needed to hire better proof readers. It didn't seem to matter that Thatcher's article had included an explanation that Kalendar was the ecclesiastical way of spelling calendar; few readers even knew what ecclesiastic meant.

When, from the corner of her eye, Marci saw Cat with her cell phone to her ear, she was filled with an impending sense of doom. Her first reaction was to yell, "Don't." Unfortunately, she was a half second too late and Cat was already taking down the address of the next horror awaiting them. A quick change out of bathing suits and shorts and the partners were on their way.

The Mitsubishi dealership on Northlake Boulevard in Lake Park was only a short minute drive from Marci's house. She had high hopes that this holiday crime would not require a barf bag and a Ouija board. Clues may have been in short supply where murder was concerned but the barometer of the macabre was on the rise.

Marci wished aloud that she and Cat would be spared the ordeal of having nothing to go on, which seemed to be the only similarities between the deaths of Janice Handera and Wallace Lanier. "Do we dare hope that this isn't another Kalendar Killing?" She bit the cuticle on her middle finger as she spoke.

"If Sheriff Brickshaw hears you using that term, he's going to make you the next murder I investigate. I can't remember the last time I saw him so angry with a reporter." Cat maneuvered the car around a truck towing a boat so large the Miami Dolphins could have used it for a practice field.

"You have to admit, it is kinda catchy, and I have to agree with Thatcher. God does seem to be missing in action where these murders are concerned. I can't help but feel that whoever is doing this is doing it for fun." Marci sucked on her finger, which had begun to bleed.

"Do you ever think that those bloody stumps you call fingers could contaminate a crime scene?"

"That's why I have stock in Johnson and Johnson." As proof, Marci produced a box of band aids from her pocketbook and wrapped one around her finger. She held the finger up for Cat to see.

Anticipating her best friend's reaction, Cat was already laughing as Marci's middle digit pierced the air.

The partners approached the dealership entrance and found it lit by what seemed like the entire fleet of PBSO green and whites, all flashing red, white and blue in honor of America's independence. A ten foot tall inflatable Uncle Sam waved his hand and nodded his head in the breeze as though acknowledging their arrival.

It wasn't until the uniformed officers protecting the crime scene parted like the Red Sea that Cat and Marci saw the body of PFC Timothy Varde tied to one of Uncle Sam's legs, a bayonet through his right hand which had been placed over his heart. Four Happy July 4th banners held Private Varde securely to the balloon—two were wrapped around his waist and two were wrapped around his neck. A whistle of sound put everyone on notice that air was slowly seeping from the bayonet puncture.

As Marci and Cat watched, PFC Varde's body was carefully lifted from its perch and Uncle Sam sank to the ground, his top hat holding its shape long after the rest of him became unrecognizable. G and his staff reverently laid the Private's body on a stretcher and covered him with a sheet.

There was no need for Marci and Cat to ask G if he had found anything significant on or around the victim. The slight shake of his head was all the confirmation they needed. Plus, the tight set of his mouth made it clear that the medical examiner was having a hard time living up to one of his favorite mottos, "In our darkest moments, humor gives us a reason to go on."

"Damn," Marci whispered to Cat. "This is a nightmare. I don't understand how three murders can be committed in public places and no one sees anything. There has to be a clue… some evidence… something to point us in the right direction."

"Did you notice the bows?"

"Yeah, what of it?"

"Our killer is left handed."

"How do you know?"

"I'm left handed. My bows always look awkward because I make them in the reverse. So did whoever killed Private Varde."

"Well, that's something. Now we only have to investigate ten percent of the population of the world and, since lefties have a 20% higher risk of psychosis and are more prone to anger… "

"How quickly we forget. I just told you I'm left handed."

"I've seen you angry."

"Funny. Trivia question… did you know that there is something called an Ian Knot?"

"Ian. Like my husband?"

"Yeah, but not in his honor or anything. Some English guy named Ian, who was left-handed, got tired of always breaking the right side of his shoe laces. He figured out that right-handed people most often broke the left lace. It has something to do with laces not being symmetrical. Anyway, he discovered that by making a loop in both ends and pulling them through each other it would not only make a symmetrical bow, it would also be faster than the traditional way. Hence, the Ian Knot."

"No wonder I always lose when we play office Jeopardy."

#

August first dawned and Cat and Marci steeled themselves for another bashing in the press. The Palm Beach County Sheriff's Office was taking a beating for not capturing the Kalendar Killer, and Marci and Cat were feeling the heat from their superiors.

Headlines like *"Kreative Kalendar Killers too Klever for Kops"* were intentionally meant to cast aspersions and draw attention to the Sheriff's Office lack of progress in the case. People were no longer nonchalant in their attitude toward crime. They were scared. Even those who normally considered themselves untouchable due to their positions in the social strata had suddenly come to realize that crimes which usually happened to someone else could now happen to them.

"Did you know that today is National Girlfriend's Day?" Marci cast an inquiring glance at Cat as they drove into work together.

"And you're telling me this why?"

"It's a holiday. Not a national holiday but, jeez, we already know that whoever is behind the Kalendar Killings has a dark sense of humor. Do you think he might consider honoring girlfriends a good reason to murder someone?"

"You did a search of the web, didn't you? So did I. I never realized how many ridiculous things are celebrated with named days. Tomorrow is National Mustard Day; then comes Sisters Day, Single Working Women's Day, National Underwear Day and Happiness Happens Day. If we have anything to worry about, it will happen on the eighth. This guy is definitely not into happiness."

"August 13 is International Left-Hander's Day. Maybe he'll kill himself."

"Have you noticed that we always refer to the killer as him?"

"I'm not being sexist. I just don't believe a woman could commit these murders." Marci had the car door open before Cat had fully pulled into their assigned parking space. The partners were scheduled to meet with a witness in a new case and had no time to waste. "At least, I hope no woman could ever commit these murders. Let's go."

As Cat and Marci ran to catch the elevator to the sixth floor Homicide Division, they came upon Detective Pete Shonto, who was shuffling along, a look of misery on his face.

"Rough night in Major Cases, Pete?" Marci gently jabbed the man referred to as Timber around the office. The name was a reference to Shonto's 6'9" frame. He had been drafted by the Lakers right after college but had never really played. Tired of sitting on the bench, he quit the team to enter the police academy.

Pete Shonto did not mind the nickname. In fact, he embraced it and used it to his advantage whenever possible. There was, however, one thing he hated about being so tall. It was the inevitable question, "How's the weather up there?" Anyone daring to ask quickly found out that the weather was stormy.

"No, nothing like that," Shonto responded with a yawn. "Moe Di Lorenzo and I have been putting in long days trying to shut down that drug trafficking ring in the south end of the county. Haven't had any time off in three months so this weekend we decided to take a break. Yesterday, being Sunday, I was looking forward to sleeping late and then just hanging with my wife. Maybe, do a little mattress dancing." Shonto's eyebrows did a little dance of their own. "We're trying to start a family."

"Sounds like a plan." Cat punched the elevator button.

"A good plan until 7 am. That's when some crazy landscaper decided to cut the limbs off our neighbor's oak tree."

Cat and Marci exchanged glances knowing this story was not going to have a happy ending. Marci put her finger on the elevator button and kept it there while waiting for Pete to fill in the details.

"I was annoyed but I wasn't angry. I threw on a pair of shorts and went outside to ask the guy to stop. He couldn't hear me over the chainsaw. I yelled, 'Fella! Fella! Hey, Fella!' He finally looked over and in broken English, he asked, 'Whatta ya want?' I tell him it's seven o'clock and we've got a noise ordinance. Nine am... not before. You know what he said? 'I don't give a fuck 'bout no noise ordinance. I gotta work to do. Get outta here.'"

Even in the retelling, the look on Pete Shonto's face was disbelief. "Can you imagine?"

"What did you do?" Cat wasn't sure she wanted to know.

"I told him I was trying to be nice. That it was my day off and I'd like to sleep. I asked him to do something quiet for a while—like rake leaves or pull weeds."

"Okay."

"He told me 'You rake a the fuckin' leaves.'" Pete's imitation of the landscaper's speech pattern got more pronounced as the story unfolded. "He told me to get ear plugs. Then, he yanked the chain on the saw—my chain, too. I was literally screaming at this point. He gave me the finger and went right on cutting."

"Holy shit. What did you do?" Marci had removed her finger from the elevator button and was nibbling away at her cuticles—a good way to keep from laughing.

"I went in the house, got dressed, grabbed my badge and went back outside. Imagine this..." Pete removed his badge from his pocket, cupped his fingers around it and raised his hand so the badge was level with his face. "I held up the badge like this as I walked over to him. I calmly but authoritatively said, 'Stop now or I'm going to arrest you.' He gave me the finger again."

Pete Shonto re-enacted the scene as it had unfolded the day before. Middle finger protruding stiffly from his tight fist, he imitated the landscaper's response... 'Maybe you din hear me before.'

"I thought I was losing my mind. I started to walk toward him but he turned and ran at me with the chainsaw held over his head. I had no choice but to scramble back to my house. By then, my wife was on the porch screaming in absolute fear."

"You're making this up. Right?" Marci had heard plenty of un-neighborly stories but this one took the cake.

"No joke. I called the local precinct and ten minutes later two patrol cars pulled up. Now, there were three of us. We approached the

177

landscaper, who finally laid the chainsaw on the ground. One of the officers asked him to step away and put his hands behind his back. The guy answered, 'What the fuck for? I told this stronzo I gotta job to do. Just go the fuck away and lemme finish.' I wish I had a camera. The look on those cops' faces was priceless."

"Wait. Wait. What did he call you?"

"Stronzo. It's Italian for asshole," Cat translated for Marci.

"Yeah. That's it. You learn something new every day. Anyway, the second officer, who happened to be Italian and spoke the language, told the guy to refrain from using foul language in front of my wife. Guy could not have cared less. He looked at the cop with utter disdain and said, 'Fuck the senora and fuck you.'"

By now Cat and Marci were laughing so hard they were doubled over, holding their stomachs. The elevator bell rang but they didn't hear it. The doors opened and closed; the elevator departed.

"I'm gonna wet my pants," Marci gasped her words.

"It wasn't funny. It took the three of us to wrestle him to the ground, handcuff him and get him into one of the squad cars. My day was ruined. Never did get back to bed if you know what I mean."

"Are you pressing charges?" Cat asked wiping her eyes.

"Arraignment today at two. Can't wait."

#

When Cat and Marci entered Interrogation Room A, audible whistles of surprise escaped their lips. Mitchell Heighton, age 22, was well over six feet tall. He was thin, had high chiseled cheek bones, almond shaped eyes, full lips and hair extensions that reached to his slender waist.

He wore a fitted designer dress, five inch heels and a cubic zirconia studded choker around a neck that giraffes would envy. His calf muscles gave new meaning to the term "defined" and, when added to the work of art that was his face… well, Leonardo da Vinci was no doubt wishing there was some truth to reincarnation. The Mona Lisa paled by comparison.

Two days earlier, on Sunday, July 30th, Mitchell and two cross-dressing friends, prostitutes by trade, had been meandering along Old Dixie Highway in Riviera Beach when Juan Luis Santos offered them a ride in his truck.

"Mr. Heighton, please tell us what happened on Sunday evening or, rather, Monday morning." Cat was consciously trying not to stare at the young man who carried himself with the poise of a beauty pageant contestant.

"Well, me and Terrence and Darryl were walking on Old Dixie at about 2 am. We were thirsty and wanted to get drinks at the all night grocer just over the bridge on Blue Heron Boulevard before going home. Our feet hurt. I guess we were hobbling a bit."

"You're talking about Terrence LaRocque and Darryl Jefferson, yes?"

"Yeah."

"Had the three of you been doing drugs? Any candy flipping? Had you shared an A-bomb?" Marci, too, was struggling not to stare.

"No, nothing like that. We were just walking, minding our own business. Santos pulled up and asked if we needed a lift. People do that all the time for us so we climbed in and everything was fine for a while. He drove over the bridge and stopped at a gas station."

Standing on opposite sides of the room, Marci and Cat began an expert game of interrogation ping pong.

"Had you been drinking?" Marci took the first shot.

"No."

"Did you or anyone else proposition Mr. Santos while in the car?" Cat volleyed.

"Of course not."

"Did Mr. Santos offer you drugs?

"No."

Did he ask for sex?"

"No. We were just riding… talking."

"So, everything was nicey nice. There was no talk of sex or drugs. No arguing over money or services to be rendered in exchange for the ride." Heighton's appeal was fading fast for Cat who could smell a liar a mile away. "Is that your statement so far?"

"I told you. Mr. Santos seemed like a nice man. We were grateful that he offered to give us a ride."

"What happened when you got to the gas station?"

"We got out. The station had an all night store so we figured we could get a drink and call a friend to pick us up."

"Why didn't you call a friend before accepting Santos' offer?"

"There's no room in those little evening purses we were carrying for cell phones. We knew the cashier in the store would let us use his phone. We'd done it before."

"Ah huh. Then what happened?"

"Well, we got out of the car and Terrence turned to say thank you. That's when Santos pulled out a gun and shot him and Darryl. I was already walking toward the store so I guess I was out of range. Terrence fell to the ground. He wasn't moving.

Darryl was leaning up against a parked car screaming for help. He was bleeding from the stomach. There was a lot of blood. I hate blood. I started yelling and ran to the store. The door was locked and the cashier just stood there staring at me. I tried pounding on the glass, but he wouldn't let me in."

"What happened then?"

"Mr. Santos drove away."

"He didn't get out of car and try to shoot you?"

"No. He left."

Cat loved dissecting a witness' statement. "Okay. Let me get this straight. You were all carrying dainty little evening purses too small for cell phones. None of you had been doing drugs or drinking alcohol. You didn't proposition Santos with offers of sex for money. For no reason whatsoever, Santos shot Terrence LaRocque and Darryl Jefferson after they got out of the car. Santos did not pursue you even though you were a sitting duck with the door to the convenience store locked. Correct?"

"Yes… but it wasn't for no reason. Santos hates people like me and Terrence and Darryl."

"You mean transvestites."

"Yes."

"So this was a hate crime?"

"Yes."

"Are you aware that Mr. Santos claims the three of you threatened to kill him if he didn't give you money."

"He's lying."

"Could be. He said Terrence offered to buy him beer so he got out of the truck."

"He did not get out of the truck. He shot Terrence and Darryl from inside the truck."

"We'll look into that, but Mr. Santos said that he got out of the truck and you grabbed him by the arm. Then, Darryl held a knife to his throat while the three of you demanded money. I'm curious. Where did Darryl keep the knife? Did it fit in his pocketbook?"

"There was no knife."

"Maybe. Santos said he was able to knock the knife out of Darryl's hand and punch you in the face. By the way… that's some bruise on the side of your mouth. Lovely shade of purple. Goes nicely with your dress."

"It's nothing."

"Looks painful to me. Anyway, Mr. Santos claims he got back in his truck and grabbed his gun out of the glove box. Terrence tried to pull him out of the truck and Santos shot him. Then he shot Darryl who was climbing in the passenger door."

"He shot Terrence and Darryl for no good reason. We didn't do nothing to him. Now Terrence is dead and Darryl is in critical condition."

"All right, Mr. Heighton, if you'll be kind enough to give us a few minutes, we'll type up your statement and you can sign it."

"What happens now?"

"We still have the store clerk to interview. Then, it will be up to the State's Attorney how to proceed. Please do not leave the county as we may have further questions."

Fifteen minutes later, Heighton sashayed out of Homicide Division; the eyes of every male in the department following his swaying hips as he headed for the elevator.

"I never get tired of this job," Marci remarked as she checked out her own hips reflected in the window of the interrogation room. She took a few steps imitating Heighton's swagger. "What do ya think? Have I got the moves or what?"

"*What* is both the question and the answer." Cat gave her partner a shove out the door.

At the end of shift, Cat and Marci decided to grab a beer and unwind at O'Shea's on Clematis Street. The pub/restaurant was a favorite after work gathering place for law enforcement and many of the attorneys, clerks and assistants working at the main court house a few blocks away. Although a crowd was beginning to form, Marci and Cat found a table in a corner where they were able to talk without raising their voices.

"So, what did you think of Heighton?" Marci asked licking a bit of foam from her lips.

"His answers or his appearance?"

"Both."

"I think he's lying but that's a safe bet with anyone involved in a crime of this nature. I think Santos is lying, too, so somewhere in the middle lies the truth. I'm anxious to hear what the cashier has to say. As for his looks, I'd trade the devil five years of my life for his legs."

"I hate it when you say things like that. You're talking about dying sooner than already decided by fate. If you met the devil, you'd fight for every second of your life—long, short or stumps for legs aside. Anyway, what have you got to complain about. I'm the one who's feet and inches challenged. It's a good thing Heighton sat down because I was getting a stiff neck from looking at him."

"I don't relish the idea of a trial. It's going to be a media circus."

Just as Marci and Cat were finishing their drinks and about to head home, Detective Moe Di Lorenzo and his partner, Pete Shonto, entered the bar. Shonto stood out like a redwood tree in a forest of bonsai making it easy to spot them in the crowd.

"Pete. Moe. Over here." Cat's voice carried above the music playing on the juke box.

"Good evening, Detectives. How was your day?" Moe Di Lorenzo, dressed in his usual black from head to toe, bowed slightly from the waist.

"Our day was fine," Marci chirped. "We want to hear what happened in court with the less than courtly landscaper."

"Ah, you are going to love this, Ladies. Let me just order us all some beers and I will regale you with a tale like no other you have heard." Shonto waved his long arm over his head and held up four fingers.

"Okay, so according to the cops who took him to the station yesterday, Zocchio— Joseph Zocchio—was fingerprinted and allowed to make his one phone call. No more than thirty minutes passed when his two sons arrived. They approached the sergeant at the desk— Merrill Cohen—and rudely inquired where they could find their father. Cohen informed them that Zocchio was being questioned and that they would be notified when they could see him.

The sons, probably in their early to mid thirties, began to talk to each other in Italian. The older son kept encouraging the younger one to ignore Cohen and just go get their father. He kept saying things like, 'Fuck this guy. Let's get dad.' The idiots convinced each other it was a good idea to defy a police officer in a police station filled with cops. They got up and began to walk toward the squad room. Cohen ordered them to sit down.

They started talking again in Italian and the names they were calling the Sergeant were anything but politically correct. Cohen, much to their surprise, yelled at them, 'Hey, jadrool'—that's cucumber in Italian but they use it to mean something like lazy bum… don't ask me why. Anyway, Cohen says, 'Jadrool, don't be fooled by my last name. My mother is Siciliana.' Am I saying that right? You know… his mother is from Sicily. Doesn't matter. Cohen says, 'I know the language and we don't allow talk like that in here.'"

Marci and Cat were laughing into their beers and a chorus of "Oh, my god" echoed across the table.

"It gets better. The elder son reacted exactly as his father had while at my house. He kept talking in Italian and he kept cursing Cohen. He told his brother, 'Fuck him. He can't stop us. Let's find dad.' Again, they got up and tried to enter the squad room. Cohen had enough. With a nod of his head he summoned two uniformed officers. They handcuffed the boys and put them in the cell with good old papa. Story has it that it was a few hours before the precinct was quiet again but everybody is now a little more conversant in Italian. If nothing else, they know all the curse words."

"If we keep meeting like this, I'm going to have to wear Sonora's diapers."

"Better put on a Depends because the story gets better. I hope they had the cameras running in court today. Moe, tell them, was it a scene from a movie or what?"

"Better than any movie I've ever seen. Today was proof that the adage 'You can't cure stupid' is absolutely true."

"Fill us in."

"Judge John DeSheplo was on the bench. You know he has a reputation for being stern but fair. He also has a wicked sense of humor. Zocchio came into court; his sons were with him. He was dressed in a suit, tie and shirt that was two sizes too big. There was an air of arrogance about him which seems to be the way he approaches everything in life. He was carrying a beat up old brief case like it was the Holy Grail.

We all watched him walk to the front of the courtroom and stand at the defense table. The boys sat behind him. No lawyer. The bailiff announced court in session and Judge DeSheplo took the bench. We all sat down—all of us except Zocchio. DeSheplo told him that he should take a seat behind the railing while we waited for his attorney. Zocchio said, 'No. No. I am defense.'

The Judge wasn't happy about that. He asked Zocchio if he knew how to represent himself and Zocchio nodded his head. 'Yeah. Yeah. I don't need no help.' You could hear the chuckles crisscrossing the room and DeSheplo himself had a hard time keeping his face straight."

Di Lorenzo's shoulders were shaking as he reminisced about his afternoon in court. "The judge told Zocchio to present his case. What happened next… Pete's right, I really do hope the cameras were on."

By this time Cat and Marci were hanging over the table, not wanting to miss one word. Marci had been holding her glass half way to her mouth for the last five minutes and had failed to take a sip.

"Well, what did happen next?"

"Okay. So, Moe and I were sitting in the front row across from Zocchio but behind the railing. Pointing over his shoulder at me, he said, 'That fucking mother fucker…' DeSheplo's gavel came down so hard I thought my eardrums would break. 'I don't allow language like that in my courtroom.'

Zocchio nodded his head and waved his hand as if to say, 'I got it. No big deal.' DeSheplo told him to continue and Zocchio began again, 'Like I was telling you, this fucking mother fucker…'

The Judge… well, he kept hitting his gavel on the desk until it broke. He yelled for the bailiff to remove Zocchio from the courtroom. Zocchio's arms were waving about his head like Medusa's snakes. 'Whatta ya mean I gotta go? Wait. Wait. I gotta tings to say.'"

"Oh my god… this is better than Sunday's story. What did DeSheplo do?" Cat signaled for another round of drinks.

"The Judge is really a classy guy. He told Zocchio, 'For your sake, I strongly suggest you say them to an attorney.' Zocchio was still cursing, as were his sons, as the bailiff led them out of the room. We have anudder court a date in tree weeks. Wanna come wid us?"

#

The remainder of August was taken up with interviews and paperwork on the Santos case. Cat and Marci were still looking for leads on the Kalendar Killer murders but so far they were chasing their tails. The only potentially useful bit of information was G's supposition—based on the angle of the florist's spike in her neck—that Janice Handera's killer was right handed. That information led to the possibility that there were two killers—one left handed (PFC Varde) and one right handed (Janice Handera). Knowing that September and Labor Day were just a few weeks away, Cat's sometimes ulcer began to churn an intense burning in her stomach. Marci's fingers were covered in band aids and the band aids now had teeth marks.

The one bright spot was the afternoon they spent in court watching the final installment of The Tale of the Loudmouthed Landscaper. Moe Di Lorenzo and Pete Shonto were with them.

Joseph Zocchio did not heed Judge DeSheplo's advice. He again acted as his own attorney. Each time Zocchio used foul language, DeSheplo's gavel rang out and a fine was imposed. Each fine caused the landscaper to bellow with rage which only led to more cursing. The gavel banging on the sound block eventually took on a rhythm of its own. Judge DeSheplo seemed to be enjoying himself. By the end of the hearing, fines totaled $1800 and the landscaper was ordered not to return to Pete Shonto's neighborhood. In fact, although not a formal decree, Judge DeSheplo strongly suggested Zocchio never work in Palm Beach County again.

Interestingly, the following Sunday Pete was once again awakened by the sound of a chainsaw. It was 9 am and, when he glanced outside, someone new was cutting the limbs from his neighbor's oak tree. "Some weekends are so boring," Pete told Marci and Cat when their paths crossed a few days later.

#

September 2006

Cat was a Jersey girl by birth but a Florida girl by choice. She loved the ocean and before joining the force had spent many an idle afternoon at Blowing Rocks Preserve on Jupiter Island. The barrier island sanctuary, which is home to endangered plants and animals including rare loggerhead, green and leatherback sea turtles, was a favorite spot to bring visitors from her home state and for the past ten years she had done that many, many times.

Whenever children were a part of the group, Cat loved to point out a section of coral shaped like an alien—misshapen head covered in green algae with two large round eyes and an open mouth that appeared to be howling. The kids loved it. Most adults remarked that it looked like artist Edvard Munch's painting, *The Scream*.

Although South Jersey was known for its beaches, the state offered nothing like Blowing Rocks' Anastasia limestone outcroppings which graced the water's edge and at high tide produced plumes of saltwater shooting 50 feet into the air. Cat enjoyed strolling the boardwalk that ran beside the Indian River Lagoon and visiting the Hawley Education Center with its ever changing natural history and art exhibits.

When late on Labor Day afternoon a call came in that a body had been found hanging from one of the Gumbo Limbo trees in the Preserve's maritime hammock, Cat felt a deep sense of dismay. No longer would she be able to visit this beautiful gift from Mother Nature without seeing the specter of death.

Volunteer extraordinaire, Peter Colangelo, was a godsend to Blowing Rocks. The retired president of a local Electrical Workers Union, he gave freely of his time and expertise by repairing and replacing wires and lighting that had fallen victim to the salt and sea. He was often on site hours before the Preserve opened to the public and long after the other volunteers and employees had gone home. A sudden holiday thunderstorm had produced thousands of lightning strikes, one of which hit a generator causing a complete power outage. Although not on duty, when news of the storm and the blackout was broadcast on television, he headed south from his home in Port St. Lucie.

"There could be a fire," Peter Colangelo told his wife, as he kissed her on the forehead and headed out the door.

Since without lights there was no way to keep the Education Center open, everyone went home early. That left Colangelo to work on the generator by himself and when last seen, he was headed behind the building with a toolbox, flashlight and a spool of wiring in hand. When found by a night watchman, Peter Colangelo was hanging by a 20 foot extra heavy duty extension cord from one of the lower limbs of the tree.

The odd thing was that when the night watchman first saw him, Colangelo appeared to be standing under the tree admiring the setting sun. His body was posed in a upright position—spine straight and feet flat on the ground. His head had been tilted at an angle that seemed natural from a distance. Only on closer inspection were his protruding tongue and bulging eyes confirmation that he had ceased to see the sun or anything else a few hours earlier.

G and his technicians arrived at Blowing Rocks at the exact same moment as Cat and Marci. The big black van stenciled with the seal of Palm Beach County and the words Medical Examiner parked beside the detectives' unmarked car in the lot. After giving instructions to his assistants, G walked with Cat and Marci to the crime scene.

"Detectives, please tell me you have some idea who is committing these murders. I'm losing my faith in mankind and, for me—considering all the deaths I have seen—that is a fate worse than my own demise."

"G, we're just as frustrated as you. Three murders so far... now this one... and no clues other than your right-handed stake stabber and Cat's left-handed bow maker. If you don't find us something more today, we might have to resign. The public is growing furious and the faces at headquarters are anything but friendly." Marci was biting off pieces of skin from her cuticle, a nervous habit which was an irritation to her partner and a health concern to G.

"You have to stop chewing your fingers, Marci. You are going to get an infection and it could be serious."

"I know. I know. I'm trying."

"I've been asking myself how murders can be committed in public places and no one see anything, and I think I know." Cat fell a few paces behind G and Marci; her reluctance to face another murder in one of her favorite places obvious in her slower steps. Marci and G waited for her to catch up.

"Committing a crime in public isn't hard if you know where to do it. Consider the beach. On any given summer day there are hundreds of people sharing the sand and surf, yet, how often do you really notice the people around you. Most sunbathers lie on their stomachs, eyes closed. They are in a half sleep while they catch some rays.

Even if they are awake and sitting upright, the sun beating down on their heads gives everything a fantasy like quality—like a mirage. They might be wearing sunglasses and/or a hat, both of which obstruct the view. Maybe their faces are covered with a towel. Even with only a few grains of grit separating them, the majority of people could not tell you who had lain on the beach towel next to them.

If you kill someone quietly... poison them, jab them with a hypodermic, even stab them... then walk nonchalantly to the water like you're going for a swim, you can disappear into the crowd. It could be hours before someone notices the body. Under questioning, there will be as many different descriptions of who was with the victim as there are people on the beach."

"I see where you are going. Each of our murders has been committed in a place where people mostly ignore each other—like the beach. Mounts Botanical and here at Blowing Rocks… even the stadium… people go to these places to pursue their own interests. But," Marci added, "Wallace Lanier was killed before the ball park even opened."

"I get that. I'm making a generalization. People in these places are not looking at other people. They're looking at plants, the coral reef or the game. The same principle applies to the car dealership. Car shopping is nerve wracking and tedious. People are so focused on getting the best deal for their money, they do not notice what's going on around them.

PFC Varde was killed on July 4th. Most people were home barbequing and waiting for the fireworks to start just like we were. There wasn't much traffic on Northlake Boulevard and anyone who did drive by was anxious to get where they were going. Murdering someone is easy if you choose the right location."

"I have to agree with all of that but why choose these people? What do they have in common? We haven't found any connection between Janice Handera, Wallace Lanier and Private Varde. I don't think we are going to find any connection to our latest victim either if this is another Kalendar Killing."

No sooner had Marci finished speaking than she, Cat and G entered the hammock where Peter Colangelo's body hung like a piñata. Draped over and under one of his shoulders like a Miss America beauty pageant contestant was a banner celebrating Happy Labor Day 2006.

"Well, wonder no more, Marci." Cat's shoulders sunk almost to her knees in despair.

With the help of his assistants, G climbed a ladder and examined the body before cutting Peter Colangelo down from the tree. "He wasn't strangled. His death was caused by blunt force trauma. There's a hole at the back of his skull—the type a hammer would make. Not a lot of blood. Looks like whoever did this was prepared to stem the flow so there was no accumulation on the ground."

Marci walked the crime scene looking for clues. "There's a toolbox hidden in these bushes."

"My techs will take it with us."

"It must have taken a lot of time and effort to position the body that way. The killer had to be strong. This man is no light weight and dead he was even heavier. Getting him to stand up couldn't have been easy."

"I agree," G answered as he examined the neck of the victim. "Your killer is exceptionally strong and probably very athletic. He would have had to tie the noose made from the electric cord and then climb the tree and loop the long ends around the limb. I think he probably leaned the body against the trunk and then slowly moved it— little by little—into place in the middle of the branch. He would have had to climb up and down over and over again.

This staging required lots of patience. Lots of determination, too. Balancing the body to keep it upright… getting the feet and legs in exactly the right position… he must have gotten a lot of perverse pleasure from imagining our reaction."

"If he had to climb up and down, do you think there's a chance he left DNA on the limb or the cord?" Cat's voice was hopeful.

"Maybe. I hate having to do surgery on this beautiful tree but the limb has to go back to the lab for testing." G instructed one of his techs to call the county and request an arborist asap. He didn't dare allow an unskilled laborer to damage either the tree or the crime scene.

"Going by his body temp and the degree of ridigity, I'd say death occurred four to five hours ago. The killer would have had to wait for rigor mortis to set to keep the body up straight. This guy is definitely patient and, most likely, obsessively methodical. And, he's also right handed." G pointed to the extension cord. "Right hand knot."

Sitting in the car in the parking lot of Blowing Rocks after G and his staff had left, Cat and Marci began to go over what they knew so far.

"Let's consider the words of our favorite author. Sir Arthur Conan Doyle said, 'When you have eliminated the impossible, whatever remains, however improbable, must be the truth.' What do we know that seems improbable but could be a fact?" Marci had a notebook on her lap and was prepared to list possibilities.

"Well, these murders were not committed without a lot of advance planning so you would assume that our killers knew each of our victims. From what we've learned so far, they don't. That leaves us with the possibility, as improbable as that seems, that the choice of victims was random—wrong place/wrong time. While it does not seem that the victims were connected to each other, they were connected to the manner in which they were killed.

A woman who was a parent and an environmentalist is stabbed with a florist's spike on Mother's Day in a public garden known for programs providing the best horticultural and botanical information. A deadbeat dad is baseballed to death on Father's Day. Women may love baseball but it is a game synonymous with men so the gender, the day, the sport, even the method all make sense. Another male, a veteran, is bayoneted on July 4th and a male, an electrician, is bludgeoned and hung on Labor Day. Equal rights aside, there does seem to be a connection between the holidays, career paths and the sex of our victims." Cat ticked off her thoughts on her finger tips.

"Men appear to be the main target or it could be that so far the holidays are more male centric."

"Or, maybe, there are just more men walking around alone than women."

"We have been talking about him as though our killer is one person, but now we know that, unless he is ambidextrous, there are two killers—one left handed and one right handed." Marci kept scribbling in the notebook as she spoke.

"We also know that whoever killed Peter Colangelo and Private Varde had to be tall, strong and athletic. Otherwise, they would not have been able to support the bodies in a standing position. Those attributes were not as important with Handera and Lanier."

"Tall, maybe not so much, but strong and athletic… I'd say that strength training of some sort gave our killers an advantage. Maybe, they're body builders running on roid rage."

"That's a possibility, but I think we should focus more on mental muscle than physical muscle. A lot of brainpower went into planning these murders. What would drive these guys to commit such heinous acts?"

"To prove that they can."

"Cat, I think you just hit the nail on the head. We've always thought that Janice Handera's murder was a thrill kill. What if this is a competition of sorts? What if our killers are challenging each other to see who can commit the most innovative crime and get away with it?"

"They're not only challenging each other; they are thumbing their noses at us. They're very confident that we won't be able to catch them. I feel like we're in some sort of murder reality show."

"God, that's absolutely frightening, Cat. I'm getting shivers down my back."

"Murder 101. Where would you go to learn how to do that?"

#

October 2006

From October 1 to October 31, it was impossible to drive the I-95 north or south and not notice the brightly-colored monster themed billboards advertising Halloween specialty stores that sprang up like weeds along Florida's Atlantic coast. Every empty store front in every strip mall in Palm Beach County had one temporary tenant selling cheaply-made costumes at custom-made prices. Along with the usual suspects—Frankenstein, Dracula and Freddy—you could bet money that images of superheroes and celebrity impersonators would grace the lineup. You could also bet money that Cat and Marci were dreading the approaching holiday.

The conversation in the parking lot of Blowing Rocks turned out to be a turning point in the Kalendar Killer murder investigation.

Cat and Marci spent weeks reviewing the curriculums of community colleges, state colleges and universities throughout Florida. Every school offering courses in forensics or police procedure was given special consideration. Nineteen schools including Florida Atlantic University, Florida State, the University of Florida and Miami University offered degrees in criminal justice. Three online universities also offered degrees—Kaplan University, University of Phoenix and Brown Mackie College. Additionally, seventeen of the nineteen including Miami-Dade College, Tallahassee Community College and Florida International University offered Associate of Science degrees in Criminal Justice Technology.

None of the subject matter appeared to challenge students to get away with murder although there were some interesting cases being reviewed that would allow for a creative mind to take hypotheticals to the next level. Disappointed but not discouraged, Cat and Marci decided to expand their search to include online non-degree classes. They were just beginning to make some progress when the Fly-by-Night circus came to town as it did every autumn.

Small traveling circuses like Fly-by-Night usually didn't stay around long—Monday to Friday at the most. They set up, did two shows a day, broke down and were gone before the sun rose on Saturday morning. Although small, these circuses offered a variety of acts to enthrall young and old. There were the usual clowns, acrobats, jugglers and trapeze artists as well as dog and pony shows and an elephant or two. There was also a fortune teller who, for a small price, would grant a customer a peek into the spirit world. Unlike the clowns, acrobats et al, who were only popular while performing, the line outside the fortune teller's tent was never without eager customers patiently waiting their turn.

For some reason, normally sane adults who never read their horoscopes were willing to be tricked by a phony seer with a deck of tarot cards. Maybe it was the hypnotic effect of *The Granddaddy of Circus Marches* which was blasted from loudspeakers from morning to night. The marching tune, composed by Karl King in 1913 and often referred to as *Barnum and Bailey's Favorite*, was guaranteed to get the heart and legs pumping. Maybe it was the temporary suspension of reality—the faux romanticism of life on the road—or the smell of pachyderm poop which clung to odor receptors in the nose for hours and days afterward. Whatever it was, twenty dollars bought dreamers empty promises of fame and fortune with which to replace the teeth rotting candy in their Halloween treat bags.

Madame Dinezade, named for the sister of Scheherazade, the famed Persian queen of *One Thousand and One (Arabian) Nights*, was an expert storyteller and the star of the Fly-by-Night circus. Like her namesake, she was also an expert at reading her crystal ball and saying a whole lot of nothing. However, her nothing was so tempting that patrons came back night after night to learn more of what the future held in store for them.

Whether Madame Dinezade had disappointed one of her repeat customers or whether she had been chosen by the Kalendar Killer as the next holiday murder victim was the bonus question of the day. For Cat, Marci and G the answer became obvious immediately upon arriving at the circus campgrounds in the wee hours of Saturday, October 28. They entered Madame Dinezade's tent and found the fortune teller sitting in a chair, hands placed atop her crystal ball staring off into space. A deck of tarot cards had been thinly rolled and fed down her throat one by one. Two cards, both the High Priestess, had been rolled and placed inside her cheeks causing her lips to turn up in a grotesque smile. Wrapped around her head like a turban was a Happy Halloween banner.

Again, no clues were found at the crime scene and other than the glimmer of hope found on the online education sites, it appeared that tourist season, which officially began November 1, and Thanksgiving—just four weeks away—were going to be less than happy holidays.

Cat and Marci spent the next week gathering personal and criminal background information on Lucy Hahn, age 33, of Portland, Oregon—aka Madame Dinezade. A record of misdemeanors— possession of marijuana, reckless driving, petty theft—committed while still a teenager offered no reason to consider revenge as a motive for her death. The thrill of the kill seemed to be the only connection between the five Kalendar Killer murders.

As the days passed, desperation became the bitter beverage with which the detectives washed down their meals. If Marci said once, she said a hundred times, "Right now, I'd pay a fortune to a fortune teller if I thought she could help us."

G was also feeling pressured and the longer his efforts remained fruitless, the more he began to doubt his abilities. Even with the latest technology at his fingertips, he was unable to find a definitive connection between the victims and their killers.

Never before had he been faced with such abysmal results. Not one to give up easily, he worked all weekend re-running tests and reviewing the results from every imaginable perspective. His persistence paid off. When Cat and Marci arrived at the station on Monday morning, there was an urgent message for them to meet him in the morgue. A quick turnaround took them back to the elevator and a trip to the morgue.

Unlike most morgues which left visitors filled with despair, G's home away from home offered the hope of something better yet to come. The yellow reception room walls were covered with images of great comedians past and present. G's preference was for the old timers—Red Skelton, Henny Youngman, Jerry Lewis, Jack Benny and Bob Hope—but George Carlin, Richard Pryor, Robin Williams, Steve Martin, Eddie Murphy and Chris Rock also were honored. Their faces smiled back at visitors from publicity shots and movie posters which hung on every wall. One could not help but feel their burden lighten albeit slightly.

A hard knock on the double doors that prevented non-staff from entering the autopsy suites gained the detectives entrance. G, sporting a two-day beard and blood shot eyes, was waiting outside his office. Although sleep deprived, there was a look of relief and contentment on his face. "I've got something."

He turned and led Cat and Marci away from the main entrance, talking as they traversed the long corridor leading to the lab. "Needless to say, I was not expecting to find any trace of DNA on the tree. Lady Luck, however, took pity on me. A single skin cell was caught in a hole which was probably the result of a woodpecker searching for food. The bird's pecking left a microscopic rough, raised section on the branch which I did not notice the first time I did my examination.

My guess is that in order to move across the branch without falling, our killer had to slide his hands over the limb time and again. One of those times, the notch left by living relatives of the animated Woody tore away a tiny piece of finger pad. The abrasion was so small, he probably never felt any pain. The wound most likely did not bleed so he probably didn't even notice it."

"Holy shit! Did you run it through our data base?" Marci was hopping with excitement.

"I did. Nothing."

"What? Why the big build up if this is another dead end?"

"Nothing in our data base. Outside of Florida, however…"

"G, the suspense is unbearable. What did you find?"

"Juvenile records going back to 2000 show that a Auric Anderson of California was repeatedly picked up for home invasion but was never formally charged. He was 16 at the time. Records were sealed probably because his father has lots of money. Also probably because he paid off the victims. There's nothing on the books once he became legally an adult but his current address, as listed on his driver's license, is Malibu. He lives in a surfside pad owned by Daddy Warbucks. Here's his photo ID."

"Road trip!" Cat and Marci rushed G and wrapped him in a huge hug.

"It's Monday," Marci mentally calculated how long it would take them to get approval to travel, how long they would be away, and who she could get to handle babysitting while she was gone. "If we leave tomorrow and are back by Friday… I know, wishful thinking, but maybe our hard work is finally paying off."

On a hunch, Cat decided to delve deeper into the online educational technology websites she had been researching before Madame Dinezade's murder. One, in particular, had gotten her attention. Humanities.edu offered a course entitled *Anyone CAN Get Away with Murder*. It was taught by a retired Seattle homicide detective who had gone into the private investigations business after a lengthy, high profile career. A quick search of the net brought up numerous stories of Bryan Boucher's impressive arrest record. There were just as many stories about his expressed dissatisfaction with what he felt was an intentional undermining of police authority by politicians seeking office. Since Seattle and Malibu were practically next door to each other give or take 1,200 miles, a little detour on the way to California could reap big rewards. Cat made a notation to bring an umbrella.

The sun was shining when Southwest Airlines flight number 3670 departed Palm Beach International Airport at 6:00 am on Tuesday, October 31st. It was raining when Cat and Marci arrived at Seattle/Tacoma Airport in Washington State seven hours and fifty minutes later. It rained as they hailed a taxi to the office of Investigative Services, LLC (IS) and it rained during the 20 minute ride to Pike Street in downtown Seattle.

During the three and half hours they met with Bryan Boucher, owner of IS, the rain continued to pound against the ninth floor office windows blocking the view of the Space Needle and the Pike Street Market which, he assured them, was magnificent. It rained while they waited for a cab to take them back to the airport for their 5:00 pm flight to Los Angeles.

The meeting at Investigative Services proved to be immensely informative. Bryan Boucher was a no nonsense, intelligent man who was more than willing to help solve the Kalendar Killer murders even if solving those murders put one or more of his students behind bars for life. In fact, if his class was responsible in any way for the loss of lives… It was obvious to Cat and Marci that the possibility weighed heavily on the investigator's conscience.

After the initial introductions and a presentation of accumulated facts and suppositions were laid out by Cat, the imposing private eye with biceps the size of watermelons explained that he never met the people who registered for his class—now in its fifth year. There were thousands, maybe millions, of registrants worldwide. Only rarely did he know a student by name and in even rarer instances was he able to put that name to a face.

There were no on-site seminars held in stadium-sized lecture halls attended by eager young men and women seeking a career in law enforcement. He had never shaken a hand or chatted over warm cups of Starbuck's latest flavor sensation. All he saw were computer codes and identification numbers generated by a server at Humanities.edu main office in New Delphi, India.

It took but a few minutes of conversation for Cat and Marci to recognize that their new acquaintance/soon-to-be friend was a man passionate about justice. Bryan Boucher despised how easily the law was twisted by the legal profession and that those tactics were upheld by the courts allowing petty criminals and murderers to roam the streets.

He had a huge problem with political correctness especially when it was used as an excuse for crime which then led to the re-victimization of the innocent not once but many times over. He was outspoken in his resentment of the media's constant demonization of the police and the lack of support by the higher ups who valued their own careers over the lives of the rank and file they were charged with protecting.

"I'm sure you know all of this. I'm preaching to the choir." The fire in Boucher's voice and eyes singed the air. The more he talked, the more Cat and Marci understood that his outspokenness while on the force had nothing to do with a lack of respect for his superiors. Boucher's frustration was with the way criminal attorneys bent the rules to favor their clients—mostly lowlifes who had committed atrocious acts of violence against innocent citizens.

"Trust me. There are no defense lawyers on my Christmas card list," he informed his visitors with no hint of a smile.

When Boucher first pitched *Anyone CAN Get Away with Murder*, his intent was to use examples drawn from his own experiences to explain why some criminals were never caught and others gave themselves away before the body of their victim was cold. He had taught in-house seminars to new recruits at the Washington State Police Training Academy for years, and his classes were required training for anyone wanting to join a specialized unit like homicide.

The class at Humanities.edu was geared for people pursuing a career in jurisprudence as he had originally done. He came from a family dedicated to law enforcement. Both his grandfather and father had been homicide detectives. Both had worked the streets of one of the toughest cities in the country—Hoboken, New Jersey—back in the days when tommy guns and Studebakers were more prevalent than street lights.

Boucher's childhood had been filled with stories of how organized crime ran the waterfront during the 1950s and how the longshoremen—stevedores in his grandfather's lingo—who worked the docks were indebted to the hiring bosses for their day's pay. Being chosen in the daily shape-up was how the hard working men were able to keep food on the table for their families. If a longshoreman wanted regular work, he had to pay back to the bosses in the form of bribes and protection money. If he didn't or if he decided to complain too loudly, his voice was silenced—sometimes permanently.

A framed full-color original poster from the Academy Award winning film *On the Waterfront* starring Marlon Brando was proudly displayed on the wall behind Boucher's desk. The poster was surrounded by photographs of his grandfather and father—the two men who had most heavily influenced his life. In explaining the significance of the poster, he told Cat and Marci that his grandfather had worked security on the film. On a bitter cold November morning, a sympathetic Brando had brought his grandfather, a rookie cop still learning the ropes, coffee. Boucher still had the Styrofoam cup which had been passed down for three generations.

The title for *Anyone CAN Get Away with Murder* was an homage of sorts to the eldest Boucher. Pops, Boucher's name for his grandfather, had often talked about ongoing investigations and why or why not the perpetrator would get caught. The formula for getting away with murder, Pops had said, was simple, and Boucher had heard the list so often, he could recite it from memory. "The choice of victim must be totally random. The killer must choose someone he or she has never met in a city far from home. The killer must drive to the destination paying for everything in cash. A common make and model car was best. A fake driver's license was an asset but not a requirement. Upon arriving, stay in flea bag motels, moving often if the visit required more than a few days. Make no personal connections." And last but not least, "Commit the crime in public."

A footnote provided by Boucher, the younger, suggested that adopting a visible and easy to adopt physical disability like a limp, a staggered gait, a stutter or slurred speech would make it less likely the killer would be remembered and connected to the crime. "Developing a well executed affliction could guarantee a murderer a degree of invisibility in a crowd. Research has shown that people will avoid making eye contact or speaking with a disabled individual even if the disability is non-threatening. Depending on the degree of disability, people will cross the street rather than interact with someone who is impaired. And, of course, witnesses won't mention it when being questioned for fear of being labeled politically incorrect."

"Marci and I took a course recently on eye witness testimony. It was fascinating; especially learning how memories are remembered differently each time they are verbalized. There's no video replay. I'm not surprised that a disability would add another level of inaccuracy to a witness' statement."

"Cat and I have often thought that a limp and a stutter could easily be mistaken for the actions of a drunk."

"Pops would have agreed with you. He was never surprised when a murder happened in broad daylight on a busy city street with no witnesses. He was surprised that more murders didn't happen that way. People, according to Pops, were self absorbed. They didn't really see who or what was around them because they were too busy pursuing their own interests. He felt, and I agree, that this is why hit men were so successful. They came; they did what they were hired to do; and they left in true Julius Caesar fashion—Veni, Vedi, Vici. They found their victim; they killed their victim; they got the hell out of town. Plus, career murderers are good actors. They blend in; then disappear like cigarette smoke in the wind."

Using conversations he had heard at the dinner table growing up and his own experiences on the force, Boucher had devised a lesson plan to challenge his students. The course was heavily based on role playing but strictly in the written sense. All students played all parts—criminal, victim, attorney for the defense, prosecutor, judge and jury—in scenarios they devised themselves.

There were numerous "games" going on at one time. A leader was chosen for each game and he or she chose the other participants. Each round lasted two weeks and each game had a winning team chosen by the students. Did some of those students take the game too far? That was a question he was determined to help Cat and Marci answer.

Although Boucher had never met his students face to face, he did know them in a psychological sense, especially those who were accepted into the Inner Sanctum where the game playing was most intense. The Inner Sanctum was a private chat room accessible to only a few extraordinarily gifted students who had proven themselves capable of planning and pulling off challenging murders without getting caught—on paper, of course.

Although no one was encouraged to put their plans into action, it was clear from some of the conversations that certain students were giving the idea serious consideration. There was no trick to uncovering the real identities of the most serious murderers in the making. Their egos were so large that they used their real names and actual photographs of themselves rather than the avatars and pseudonyms like Dick Trace Me, Mike Sledge Hammer, Philip Howlowcanyou Go, and Nancy Drewblood, that were popular in the public forums. The reason they were so blatant was because they felt that the best place to hide was out in the open. No one would believe that murders were being planned in a school chat room. And, no one did until now.

Three students stood out from the rest: Harold Kruge, Mace Maloney and, not surprisingly, Auric Anderson. When Anderson's name and face first popped up on in the chat room, Cat and Marci felt a tightening in their bowels. With Boucher's help, they quickly eliminated all other conversations and set their sights on the movie star handsome young man wearing a Smokey and the Bandit tee shirt imprinted with the image of Hollywood icon Burt Reynolds.

Once the three detectives were able to focus their attention on Auric Anderson, it became obvious that he was more than a cyber buddy to Kruge and Maloney. The three students, who lived thousands of miles apart from each other—Anderson in Malibu, California; Harold Kruge in Niagara Falls, New York; and Mace Maloney in St. Louis, Missouri—were joined by what Marci called the insanity connection. They had devised a code so that other students and moderators would not know the true meaning of their words. Once deciphered, a task which Bryan Boucher relished and proved quite good at, the pride and pleasure they derived from inflicting pain upon other people was chilling.

Their suspicions confirmed, Marci called Captain Jameson and began extradition proceedings for the Kalendar Killers—plural. They still had a lot of investigating to do to tie Kruge, Maloney and Anderson to the murders, but all paths appeared to lead to life in prison without parole or, preferably, lethal injection.

Reading through the email exchanges and instant messages, there was plenty of ambiguous language that, to the uninformed, would seem innocent. To Marci and Cat, however, the correspondence was filled with crime details not released to the media. With each successful murder, the three amigos' conversations took on elements of bravado and one-upmanship. As is always the case, ego loosened the killers' tongues and they took less care in hiding their deeds. Additionally, there was one very damning display of guilt. Someone with a knowledge of photo joining had taken three identically posed individual pictures of Anderson, Kruge and Maloney wearing the same Bandit tee shirt and created an image of the men with their arms around each other's shoulders.

Although Reynolds' appeal was incomprehensible to Cat, Marci understood why men and women of all ages were drawn to the still handsome star of nearly 200 feature films. She was a big fan because, as she explained to Cat, Reynolds represented the everyman. He was an Average Joe in the eyes of the movie going public. His quick wit and self-deprecating sense of humor made him immensely popular.

For those reasons and many more, the Burt Reynolds and Friends Museum, located in Jupiter, Florida was a popular tourist destination housing a treasure trove of Hollywood memorabilia. On a backdrop of scarlet and lit by crystal chandeliers, the walls played host to hundreds of signed photographs and posters of celebrities from the golden age of film and television to the present day. Glass cases displayed the thousands of awards won by Reynolds as well as props from his many famous movies, including Deliverance and Smokey and the Bandit.

Marci knew that the tee shirts Anderson, Kruge and Maloney were wearing in the photos were only available at the museum which was a mere three and a half miles from Blowing Rocks Preserve where Peter Colangelo had met his death under a Gumbo Limbo tree. It was 19 miles from Mounts Botanical Gardens—the site of Janice Handera's last Mother's Day outing; less than five miles from Roger Dean Stadium and Wallace Lanier's baseball bludgeoning; 19 miles from the car dealership in on Northlake Boulevard where PFC Varde had been bayoneted; and 25 miles from the South Florida Fairgrounds where a popular fortune teller had not foreseen the shortness of her own future.

Studying the photograph, Marci voiced her thoughts aloud. "How can three totally insane people be so normal? One minute these guys are planning to commit murder and the next they're quoting lines from movies, talking about cars and sports and girls and, well, normal stuff. The human mind is fascinating and frightening."

The legal path to arresting the Kalendar Killers was a maze of tangled tape which Marci and Cat would have to follow before they could bring Anderson, Kruge and Maloney back to Florida for trial. The Uniform Criminal Extradition Act was in effect in 48 of the 50 states in the country. The only exceptions were South Carolina and Missouri—Mace Maloney's home state. According to the requirements set forth in the UCEA, a state may request surrender of a wanted individual by issuing a valid arrest warrant and an official request from the Governor of said state.

In turn, the state having custody of the wanted person would hold a judicial hearing and, after concluding that all requirements had been met with no resistance by the wanted individual, would issue a waiver of extradition to the state making the demand. Custody of the wanted individual would be taken personally by a law enforcement officer of the requesting state within 30 days.

Knowing that Captain Jameson would move quickly to notify California, New York and Missouri of Florida's intent to prosecute residents of those states made Cat's and Marci's job a little easier but not less time sensitive. The clock was ticking toward Thanksgiving. With the possibility that Missouri courts would oppose extradition of Mace Maloney, a backup plan was being devised.

The umbrella Cat had packed as a defense against Seattle's inclement weather served only one purpose—to keep her head dry while her shoes and pant legs soaked up water from puddles the size of rivers. Thankfully, the two and a half hour trip to LAX allowed time for her slacks to dry. Her shoes were an entirely different matter. The smell of wet feet and shoe leather was unpleasant but it did act as a natural barrier in preventing unwanted conversation with the passenger to her left—a bleary-eyed young man sitting knees to chin in the window seat.

Whether due to the near freezing temperatures in the cabin or an addiction to powdery substances, the suspected doper's nose dripped the entire flight, and he constantly sniffled while rubbing his hand across his red and raw nostrils. Cat spent most of the trip leaning left to get as far away from him as possible. Such a position required Marci to spend most of the trip with Cat pressed up against her shoulder. They both spent a good deal of the time wishing the rain would stop. As if there was an actual dividing line in the sky, crossing into California airspace brought about the immediate cessation of precipitation and the emergence of clear skies.

#

The waters off Malibu were a deep, beautiful sapphire blue the morning Sheri Anderson went into labor. Driving to the hospital with her husband, Carlton, she remarked between contractions, "I hope our baby has eyes just like that."

She got her wish. Auric Anderson had the advantage of being born beautiful and smart. From the moment his perfectly shaped head popped out of the womb, people were awed by his cherubic face, saucers-sized blue eyes fringed with thick black lashes and full head of glimmering golden curls. So brilliant was the color of his hair that his mother named him after Auric Goldfinger, the antagonist from the popular James Bond movie of the same name. Her husband, who had a laugh-at-life sense of humor, agreed because he enjoyed poking fun at cultural icons. Unlike most newborns, there was nary a red mark or squiggly feature to mar young Auric's angelic countenance. Longer than most babies and perfectly proportioned, the doctor declared him a "rare specimen." His parents were beyond ecstatic.

As time passed and the infant grew into a toddler and then into a precocious little boy, he learned to use his good looks to his advantage. Mom and dad had a difficult time saying, "No," or reprimanding their little man for any wrongdoings, especially when his normally upturned lips turned down into a sad frown. If they had been truthful with themselves, they would have admitted having a hard time telling him anything because long before he could talk, his eyes communicated a sense of superior intelligence that intimidated them. Auric would prove to be that odd child who not only thought he was smarter than his parents; he actually was smarter.

By the time he entered grammar school, Auric's mischievous spirit, a point of pride for his mother and father, proved to be less than endearing to his teachers and classmates. However, they, too, found it hard to stay mad once Auric pouted an apologetic face in their direction. His eyes… it was always his eyes that his private school teachers mentioned when talking about young Master Anderson. "There's something about the way he stares at you. I can never tell if there's a devil or an angel looking back at me."

By the time he was 15, Auric Anderson stood over 6'3" and was the epitome of sun-kissed California surfer, but this dude was no dummy. Freshman year of high school was a major turning point for him. Girls—lots and lots and lots of girls—relentlessly pursued him and with his hormones raging, he racked up conquests the way most boys racked a pool table. His adventuresome nature became a desire for daring dos which not only tempted the law but also thumbed a nose at fate.

Strong and athletic, Auric was adept at climbing out his second story bedroom window in pursuit of after curfew activities that would have stunned his in-denial parents. As his father was a highly successful businessman, there was no need for the petty thefts Auric committed, but the thrill these escapades provided was hard to resist especially since, on the few occasions he had been caught, the victims refused to press charges. Auric learned to use his good looks and daddy's money to his advantage. As his prowess grew, it became a mere matter of time before he would move on to bigger and more dangerous activities.

Now 22 and cunning beyond his years, his perfectly chiseled muscles rippled under the tight tee shirts he preferred to wear. His eyes held people in their gaze with a viselike grip. It was impossible to turn away when he was speaking to you. Despite his superior intelligence or, maybe, because of it, Auric often found himself bored with life. High school had never offered him the challenge he craved. Learning came so easily that all he had to do was glance at the cover of a book to know what was inside. Straight A's were a given.

If not for his position as quarterback of the varsity football team—a team he brought to the state championships year after year and won—his homeroom seat would have been empty more times than not. The need to graduate high school came with a secondary incentive. Auric knew daddy would stop supporting him if he didn't go to college.

As the years passed, Auric's name graced attendance rosters in nearly every college in California. He changed majors and minors the way most people changed their underwear, dropping out of school a few weeks into each term. He was at loose ends until he discovered Humanities.edu, an online service that offered courses from educational institutions worldwide at little or no cost. Not that a high tuition would have been a deterrent. Auric's father was willing to pay any amount of money if his son would only choose a career and get a degree.

For Auric, the attraction to Humanities.edu came from a course catalog that offered a wide range of classes. There was also the added benefit of being able to sit at a computer in his bedroom and take classes at times that were convenient for him.

That left plenty of time to pursue his only real interest— danger. Danger was the adrenalin that pumped through Auric Anderson's veins and gave him a reason to live.

It took but a few minutes of perusing the Humanities.edu online curriculum for Auric to find the perfect course—one that appealed directly to his deviant nature—*Anyone CAN Get Away with Murder*. The role playing assignments that were part of the course were especially appealing as were the peer reviews in which students evaluated and offered feedback on each other's work. Here he would be able to demonstrate his superior intelligence while meeting people who shared his passion for outsmarting the law.

#

Cat and Marci were expecting to be met at LAX by Homicide Detective Taxiarchai Petropoulus, their counterpart at the Los Angeles County Sheriff's Department. Not wanting to make a bad first impression, they had practiced saying his name over and over again while enroute from Washington State. They were still hopelessly tongue tied but instantly relieved when they exited the Southwest terminal and saw their greeter with a sign reading, "PBSO – I'm your Taxi."

Taxi Petropoulus had done his homework. As Cat and Marci approached the black sedan with the LASD logo on the door, he stuck out his hand in greeting. "Detective Leigh. Detective Welles. Welcome to Los Angeles."

Once the formalities were over and they were settled in the car for the ride to Malibu, the three homicide detectives shared information. Petropoulus was amazed at what Cat and Marci, with the help of Bryan Boucher, had discovered in the Inner Sanctum. He was not a fan of the world wide web, believing that it was both the best and worst invention in history. However, as Cat and Marci filled him in on details, he grew increasingly "… grateful that Al Gore had invented the internet." A much needed laugh was shared by all.

Thanks to Bryan Boucher's vigilance, the investigators now knew that Auric Anderson was responsible for the deaths of PFC Varde and Peter Colangelo. In his email exchanges with Kruge and Maloney, Anderson shrugged off any praise offered on the successful stabbing of the young soldier. When Kruge and Anderson mentioned "broad day light" and "busy city street" as reasons to gloat, he rebuked them by saying, "If anyone could do it, it was me."

Anderson made it clear that killing Varde had been a simple matter of following the guidelines set forth in Bryan Boucher's course syllabus, a statement that had a life changing effect on the former detective. While PFC Varde's death was not praise worthy in Anderson's opinion, he was proud of what he considered "sheer genius" in staging Peter Colangelo's death at Blowing Rocks. "It took hours to get him to stand up straight…" he wrote to Maloney and Kruge, "… but when I was finished, even I was impressed."

Further research by Boucher revealed that Anderson was ambidextrous and had intentionally tied the bows in Private Varde's July 4th banners with his left hand and then used his right hand to tie the electrical cord noose around Peter Colangelo's throat. Switching hands was a bragging point for him, mostly because he felt his efforts would "confuse those idiots"—meaning law enforcement— and prevent them from connecting one person to two crimes.

#

Harold Kruge had been a creep all of his life. School records showed that he had been a playground bully from the first day of nursery school, biting the other students whenever an opportunity presented itself. In kindergarten, his teachers noted that he seemed to enjoy teasing his classmates until they cried. In first through third grade, his modus operandi was to pull the girls' pigtails and pinch their arms and legs. As he got older, he would trip classmates in the hallway or slam their fingers in their locker doors. With the arrival of puberty, he began whispering dirty little sayings in the ears of unsuspecting girls when no one was looking.

A search of juvenile records showed that the now 25-year-old had been questioned numerous times during his mid teens for being too handsy with the young ladies. Although no charges had ever formally been filed, there were numerous statements from parents refuting his claim that he had "accidentally" touched their daughters breasts and backsides during intramural games. A report filed by a co-ed six years ago, when Harold was 19 and a freshman in a local community college, claimed that he had spiked her drink while she was dancing with his wingman—another 19-year-old—in a nightclub. If not for a very savvy bartender who had been keeping an eye on the two up-to-no-good Lotharios, the co-ed would probably have found herself naked and abused in a back alley hours later.

In the bartender's statement, he told police that when the girl began slurring her words and having trouble standing and walking, he took immediate action. He notified the house manager, who called 911 requesting police and paramedics. Then, he retrieved the girl's phone from her purse and called her emergency contacts—her parents. The bartender explained that it had become standard operating procedure to check smart phones for ICE (in case of emergency) numbers whenever someone was in distress. While waiting for help to arrive, the manager took the now nearly comatose co-ed to his office where he could keep an eye on her. The bartender set out in search of Kruge and his buddy but they had disappeared the minute they realized the bartender was on to them.

Since the co-ed knew Kruge and his friend by name, she made a formal police report the next day after being released from the hospital. Unfortunately, there was no proof that either man had roofied her drink. Even though she pleaded, tears streaming down her cheeks, there was nothing the police could do but release them with a warning. The only punishment Kruge received—when the college learned of the accusations—was expulsion from school. The officer in charge of the investigation had made a notation in the file before closing out the case, "Kruge has a way of twisting every statement so that he appears to be the victim." He ended his report by writing, "We'll be seeing this guy again."

Harold Kruge also took credit for two killings—Wallace Lanier and Madame Dinezade. He wrote glowingly in his emails of how, in the hours after midnight, he had picked the lock on a side gate at the Stadium and waited for someone to walk by. Pretending that the gate was jammed and he could not get it open, he asked Wallace Lanier, a social phobic who preferred to walk in the dark, for help.

Once inside, the rest of his plan went like clockwork. As thanks, he offered to give Lanier a behind the scenes look at the Stadium. Since he had earlier dug the hole on the pitcher's mound, all that was left was to stun Lanier with a baseball bat and bury him up to his neck. Then, he "beamed" Lanier repeatedly with baseballs until the "fear of death was permanently etched on his face."

If malicious laughter could be heard in the written word, Kruger's description of how he had forcibly pried Madame Dinezade's mouth open and stuffed her throat with tarot cards was enough to make Bryan Boucher wish to be deaf. His graphic account of her slow death, including how her lips, skin and nails had gradually turned "a lovely shade of blue" and the written expressions of the sounds she made as she tried desperately to dislodge the cards, were so callous that Boucher began to seriously consider retirement.

#

Mace Maloney was a loner. He preferred locking himself in his room and surfing the net to living in the real world. He wasn't unsociable; on the contrary, he had a winning personality and a smile that could melt a heart made of tungsten. He just preferred his own company. On the rare occasion Mace dated, he chose girls who were low on self-esteem and easy targets for his caustic humor. At 26, he was considered the "old guy" among his few friends who, while the same age, thought him to be a throwback to the caveman mentality. The only time Mace showed any real emotion was when he was using his wits or his fists to pound someone into the ground.

The use of his fists was what had gotten Mace Maloney a police record. A high school history teacher had challenged Mace's views on segregation, civil rights and women's liberation and found himself on the receiving end of a punch. Only the quick reflexes of other students kept the altercation from escalating into a first round TKO with the teacher eating a mouthful of linoleum flooring.

As with Harold Kruge, expulsion was mandatory. The teacher, wanting to avoid further embarrassment, dropped the charges so no further action was taken. A GED certificate served as his diploma; a leather jacket and motorcycle helmet his cap and gown.

When compared to Anderson and Kruge, Mace Maloney had less to crow about. His one and only murder so far was Janice Handera, whom he had stabbed to death with a floral spike. Maloney was quick to tell his peers that his choice of weapon was pre-destined.

While walking to the main entrance of Mounts Botanical Gardens, he had slipped on the spike and nearly fallen to the pavement. Cat and Marci suspected that the weapon had fallen from the landscape dumpster situated at the far end of the parking lot. They had, in fact, searched the dumpster the night Janice Handera died.

From his writings, it was obvious that Mace Maloney was proud of the ease with which he had struck up a conversation with his victim by pretending to be a "nature lover since birth." Standing in the same wildflower garden where her husband sought solace after her death, Janice Handera revealed to him her concern for the bee population. He quickly formulated a lie about finding a huge hive in the trees near the maintenance area and asked if she would like to see it.

"She never questioned why I put on gloves; most likely assuming it was so I wouldn't get cut pushing the bougainvillea branches aside so she could get a better view," Mace reported. "The rest was easy."

Mace's lack of credentials did not seem to bother him. In his emails, he alluded to big plans, which he assured Anderson and Kruge, would leave them "shrivel dicked" with jealousy. All three men had been following the news reports from Florida and gloried in the headlines comparing the Kalendar Killer to Gary Ridgway and Ted Bundy.

#

Needing to talk about something other than the gory details of death, Taxi informed Cat and Marci that the Los Angeles Sheriff's Department had received the expedited extradition papers for Auric Anderson. He further informed them that, due to the vigilance of their 24-hour surveillance teams, they had salvaged an empty energy drink can from a trash barrel and sent it to their lab for DNA testing. Once they had a positive match to the DNA found at Blowing Rocks Preserve, they would proceed with the arrest.

The U.S. Marshall's Service, all necessary paperwork in hand, was ready to move on Harold Kruge. With the evidence supplied by Bryan Boucher positively linking Kruge to Anderson and the Lanier and Dinezade murders, New York State had wasted no time in approving the warrants. Missouri, as expected, was not being cooperative. That inconvenience did not bother Cat and Marci. Their colleagues at the Palm Beach County Sheriff's Office had perfected their backup plan—one that would allow Maloney to arrive in Florida for Thanksgiving dinner with his intended victims.

Three men—different and, yet, alike. What drew them to the anonymous world of internet education and how, out of the thousands of students taking online courses, did they find each other? These were the questions Cat, Marci, Taxi and Bryan Boucher asked each other repeatedly. Boucher was especially troubled by the questions which played over and over again in his head as he decoded the emails being exchanged in the Inner Sanctum. He called Cat and Marci with updates every few hours. During one of those conversations, he shared a memory. He explained how his college Abnormal Psychology professor had said that three elements were necessary for success: passion, clarity of mission and association with like-minded people.

If ever three people shared one mind, it was Auric Anderson, Harold Kruge and Mace Maloney. If ever three people possessed clarity of mission, these men spoke as if with one voice and that voice was filled with passion for the evil they had done and were about to do. Boucher repeated for Cat and Marci a quote which had hung on the wall behind the professor's desk. The quote was attributed to American philosopher Eric Hoffer. "It is by its promise of a sense of power that evil often attracts the weak." So far, Anderson, Kruge and Maloney did not strike him as weak and that, he said, "…scared the crap out of him."

With Missouri unwilling to turn Mace Maloney over to the authorities, Cat and Marci spent hours reviewing the backup plan formulated by their peers back in West Palm Beach. The information had been shared with the Marshall's Service and the Los Angeles County Sheriff's Office. Together, a well-coordinated strategy had been set in place.

In order to successfully arrest Anderson, Maloney and Kruge without one tipping off another, it was essential that all agencies work together. Thanks to Brian Boucher's continued monitoring of emails, the Palm Beach County Sheriff's Office was aware of and prepared for the next assault, which Mace Maloney had planned for Thursday, November 23rd—Thanksgiving Day.

#

November 2006

Unlike the murders of Janice Handera, Wallace Lanier, PFC Varde, Peter Colangelo and Madame Dinezade, the individuals chosen by Mace Maloney for his Thanksgiving Day massacre were not random. Wanting to push the envelope and prove his superiority over Harold Kruge and Auric Anderson, he had chosen a family that he knew but had not seen or spoken with for 23 years. A search of the internet had gotten him the address for Victoria and Douglas Fahey, the parents of James Fahey, his childhood playmate.

The last time three-year-old Mace had seen four-year-old James, was the day the Maloney family moved from Florida to Missouri. Mace, his face pressed against the rear window of his father's Cadillac deVille, remembered James waving to him from the sidewalk in front of his house. James was crying. Mace was not.

Without telling Harold Kruge and Auric Anderson, Mace Maloney had multi-tasked while in Florida for the Mother's Day murder of Janice Handera. A plan already evolving in his mind, he had spend a few extra days finding and following James Fahey. The fact that Fahey still lived in the same house as his parents made Mace's surveillance efforts easy. Once he familiarized himself with James' daily work routine, it had been a snap to arrange an accidental meeting in the coffee shop where James stopped every day on his way to work.

Dressed in a business suit and carrying a briefcase, Mace entered the Starbucks on Clematis Street two minutes after Fahey. He stood patiently behind James on line waiting to place an order. It wasn't until James spoke to the barista that Mace made his move. Feigning just the right amount of shock mixed with a dollop of hesitancy, he tapped James on the shoulder and asked, "James? James Fahey? Is that you? It's me... Mace Maloney."

Instant recognition and surprise showed on James' face as he quickly wrapped Mace in a man hug. "Mace. Holy shit. How great to see you. I can't believe you recognized me. What are you doing in Florida?"

Mace had prepared for this moment. "I'm job searching. Can you believe my interview is tomorrow—the day before Thanksgiving. All flights out are booked so I'm stuck here." Expressing his disappointment at missing Thanksgiving with his family netted Mace his intended outcome—an invitation to dinner with the Fahey clan.

Smiling from ear to ear, James offered, "You're not stuck and you won't be alone. Join us. My parents would love to see you. The whole family will be there."

When Mace was arrested, a bottle of liquid Gamma Hydroxy Butrate (GHB) big enough to knock Asia on its ass was found among his possessions. Wrapped in a dress shirt was a poly carbon dagger, commonly called a Special Ops knife. The weapon was a good choice for a number of reasons. It was made from a super hard plastic resin which made it lightweight and, mostly importantly, the resin made the knife invisible to hand-held and walk-through metal detectors.

In years to come, when law enforcement officials cited examples of cooperation between agencies, the arrests of Auric Anderson, Harold Kruge and Mace Maloney would be the case most often referenced. Before the sun rose on Thanksgiving morning, while Anderson and Kruge were sleeping in their own beds and Maloney was sacked out in a motel on Dixie Highway in West Palm Beach, police officers from the PBC Sheriff's Office, Los Angeles County Sheriff's Office, and the U.S. Marshall's Service pounded on their doors bringing any further dreams of getting away with murder to an end.

The Fahey family—all 17 of them—had been notified of the murder plot and moved to a safe house. Since they had a lot to celebrate, they decided to have Thanksgiving dinner as planned. Turkey burgers and french fries from a nearby sports bar replaced the two 20 pound birds intended for their holiday meal. Once back home, they laughingly admitted to each other that they hadn't missed "the trimmings" one bit. Escaping death had left a most delicious taste in the mouths.

Auric Anderson's father spent most of his Thanksgiving on the phone with high-priced lawyers and even more high priced psychiatrists, hoping to find a way to save his son from the death penalty. Harold Kruge's parents were on an extended vacation and unreachable. Mace Maloney didn't bother to make his one phone call.

"Nobody will care, and what's the point." His comments were directed to the court appointed lawyer who had been assigned to his case. "It's not like I'm going to walk away a free man."

Although Maloney appeared resigned to his fate, getting arrested before he was able to carry out his master plan had left him frustrated. He still needed to prove his superiority over Kruge and Anderson even if only by revealing the details of his foiled attempt at a second murder. He talked to an investigator for hours of how he planned to spike the punch and watch as each member of the family was slowly rendered helpless. Then, while everyone was still conscious but unable to move, he would force them to watch as he slit their throats one after the other.

His plan was to leave James Fahey for last. "I can still see that wimp standing on the curb waving goodbye, tears running down his face. What an ass! I figured to give him something to really cry about."

Upon his arrest, Mace Maloney was taken to the Palm Beach County Sheriff's Office Main Detention Center located at the Sheriff's Headquarters Complex on Gun Club Road in West Palm Beach. Kruge was also incarcerated at the Detention Center once he was returned to Palm Beach County by the U.S. Marshall's Service. Cat and Marci were tasked with getting Auric Anderson back to Florida. They were hesitant about using a commercial airline but had no other option until newspaper headlines across the country announced *Kalendar Killers Kaught! PBC Sheriff's Office puts an end to holiday murders*.

The article detailing the investigation and capture of Auric Anderson, Harold Kruge and Mace Maloney—in particular, the part played by Homicide Detectives Cat Leigh and Marci Welles—so intrigued the nation that offers to fly the detectives and their captive back to Florida by private jet were numerous.

Inside the hanger owned by Rehbein Realty, Cat and Marci bid goodbye to Taxi and expressed the hope that he would visit them in Florida some time soon. With Auric Anderson handcuffed and shackled, they settled in for a very comfortable and very fast non-stop flight to Florida. By the time they landed at Palm Beach International Airport, they had achieved celebrity status. Their egos weren't the least bit pumped.

"We just did our jobs." Marci kept repeating the mantra as she and Cat led Auric Anderson to the waiting patrol car.

"Make sure you look out the window on our way to jail," Cat advised Anderson as she lowered his head into the back seat. "This is the last time you'll see the world without bars in your eyes."

Once all their reports had been filed and the hoopla surrounding the case had died away, Cat and Marci decided to take a much deserved vacation. They wanted a trip to some far away place where they could escape the headlines reading, *"Kapable Kops Kapture Kalendar Killers"* and *"Kops Krimp Kalendar Killers Krime spree."*

"I'm beginning to hate the letter K," Cat moaned as they left the office on their last day of work. "I'm glad we're getting out of town for awhile."

"Me, too. What have you got in mind?"

"I was thinking a trip to the islands."

"I was thinking a place that requires more clothing. If I was single, childless and didn't hyperventilate at the mere thought of wearing a bathing suit, the islands would be a great idea."

"Sorry. I forgot it isn't just about us anymore. What do you suggest?"

"How about Disney World?"

"Disney… the happiest place on earth. Yeah. We could use a little happy right about now."

Cat and Marci were just about out the front door of Police Headquarters when a familiar voice reached them across the lobby. "Ladies. Detective Ladies." Cat and Marci turned and waited for G to catch up to them.

"Congratulations, Detectives. You both did an amazing job on this case." G's normal baritone was filled with pride for his two favorite homicide investigators.

"We couldn't have done it without you, G." There was no doubting the sincerity of Cat's words.

"That's right, G. You found the skin cell on the tree limb. Without that, we might never have solved this case," Marci smiled her appreciation.

"Team work, Ladies. We make a great team. Now, go and have a good vacation. I'll be waiting for you when you get back."

MESSAGE FROM THE AUTHOR

Since my daughter Jessica's kidnapping and rape in 2007, I have been a passionate advocate for victims of sexual assault. Jessica and I have spoken publicly about the need for women to take responsibility for their own safety. It is a message we never tire of spreading.

Much of what I wrote in *Through Thick and Thin* is taken directly from events of July 1st when Jessica escaped death by using her wits and her wiles. My hope is that women will recognize the need for greater precaution in the way they live their lives. We are living in a world of double standards—a world in which women often abdicate responsibility for their own safety to the mistaken notion that their constitutionally guaranteed rights actually guarantee that those rights will be respected.

Shortly after the case against Jessica's attacker was settled in court, I wrote and published her story—*Assault on an Angel, A Rape Survivor's Story,* which you will find at the end of this letter. It was read by the producers of two television shows who felt it was worthy of being featured in an episode. One show was *I Survived* on the History Channel. The other was *Surviving Evil* on Investigation Discovery. Since so many survivors have written to us to say that reading Jessica's story gave them the courage to face their attacker in court, I'm including it in *Through Thick and Thin.*

On October 3, 2013, Jessica appeared on the Katie Couric Show where she discussed the *Surviving Evil* episode. Following the airing of the segment, one viewer wrote that she enjoyed Couric's show because of its usually "light" offerings. She was disturbed by the survival stories presented, and so, had changed the channel.

Changing the channel is what many women are doing when it comes to rape, and it's dangerous. The feminist movement preaches that women can go where they want, do what they want, act as they want and wear what they want—which they can. But they should not do those things without considering the possible outcome.

Almost from infancy, we teach our children about safety by telling them not to talk to or take candy from strangers. We tell them not to cross the street without looking both ways; not to play with matches. As adults we know that water and electricity don't mix. We know not to open our doors to persons unknown. We know not to drive drunk. We know that doing these things can be dangerous and, often, deadly.

If driving drunk is hazardous to our health is not that same inebriated state dangerous when pursuing other aspects of our life? It's not the liquor, per se, that puts us in harm's way. It's the inability to react quickly when the need arises. If a drunk were to approach you on the street, you would be forewarned by his behavior. You could cross the street to avoid contact. Drunk drivers rarely offer an advance warning. Neither do rapists.

Any agenda that preaches "shame on you" to rapists is laughable. To feel shame, a person must have a conscious; he or she must have empathy. Rapists have neither. They are predators, and like all predators, they strike the most vulnerable in their path.

While it is true that what you wear does not, necessarily, make you more appealing to a rapist; what you wear can make it more difficult to escape an attack. Long hair is easy to grab. Five inch heels are not made for running. Drinking to oblivion can be an invitation to assault.

Don't misunderstand. Rape is wrong no matter the circumstances. The victim is never responsible for the attack. Women should have the same freedoms as men… but we don't. It's time to face reality. We are not equal to men when it comes to protecting ourselves. We are vulnerable. We can die if we forget the lessons we learned as children.

We must teach our daughters from a very early age to both respect and protect themselves. If you don't have an extra lock on your door which can be engaged from the inside when you are at home—not a chain lock or some flimsy device that offers a false sense of security—get one today. I'm talking about a second dead bolt only accessible from inside or a flip lock similar to what you would use in a hotel.

No one and nothing can protect you from danger as well as you can do it yourself. Safety cannot be legislated. Mottos and slogans won't save your life. Awareness will.

Rapists don't care about your constitutional rights. Their agenda is self-serving. Think before you act.

Wishing you a long, safe and happy life!

Donna

Note:

Under intense public pressure, in January 2012, the Obama administration finally agreed to a revision to the definition of rape as used by the FBI. That revision will now allow for coverage of assaults formerly omitted and will provide greater leverage for those proposing anti-crime initiatives.

ASSAULT ON AN ANGEL

A Rape Survivor's Story

(copyright: 2009)

"Mommy, help me. I've been raped."

Two years have passed since I heard those words but time hasn't numbed the pain they caused.

Saturday, June 30, 2007 was a perfect day for mother/daughter bonding. My daughter, Jessica, and I have always had a close relationship, and this beautiful Florida morning was the beginning to a day of pampering and shopping. Jessica's apartment at Sanctuary Cove in North Palm Beach, Florida, was within a stone's throw of where her dad and I lived. She picked me up promptly at 10 am, her little sports car with its top down looking more inviting than a stretch limousine.

Off we drove to Starbucks to start our gab fest over hot cups of caramel macchiato—our favorite. Before rushing off to our manicure and pedicure appointments, we chatted for a while at one of the patio tables, an umbrella sheltering us from the already hot sun. Later, sitting side by side at the salon, we continued the conversation that began in the car... talk of budding romance, vacations planned, friends we missed and family members we loved. There was rarely a moment of silence, usually only while we clenched our teeth as our calloused skin was sandpapered away.

Once we were sure that the dreaded polish smudges could be avoided, we slipped into our sandals and drove to the mall. With nothing special in mind, we searched the shops for the perfect outfit for work or play. From store to store, we looked for that ever illusive "What a deal!" blouse or skirt that would turn us from cinder girl to Cinderella.

In the dressing room at Victoria's Secret, we tried on our selections and laughed over their sometimes unflattering effects. Our giggles were so loud the sales staff knocked often to inquire about our insanity. Jess could not resist taking a picture of me in a bathing suit with less than adequate coverage to show her dad when we got home.

By mid-afternoon, our stomachs were joining the conversation so to lunch we went. This was not the day to be weight conscience. Burgers and fries and, of course, diet soda. Again, we laughed over the ridiculousness of choosing Diet Coke over a milk shake. How we enjoyed each bite! Hamburgers are a treat we indulge in only rarely so this lunch was extra special.

After a quick walk through the remaining department stores, Jess suggested we call it a day. We planned to meet again later in the evening for dinner with her dad and then go to a movie. That is exactly what we did. We dined at a new hibachi restaurant and were delighted with the courteous staff and delicious food. On to the theater, and by the end of the evening, Jess and I agreed it had been one of the nicest days we had shared in a long time.

My husband. Mike, did the driving, as husbands are wont to do. By the time we said goodbye to our daughter at the front door of her apartment, it was 11:30 pm. Many not well-stifled yawns were evident on our faces. Mike and I fell asleep almost immediately upon returning home. At 5:30 a.m., my cell phone rang. Imagine, as I know you can, hearing your phone ring in the wee hours of the morning.

Trouble is always your first thought but nothing could have prepared me for the sound of Jessica's voice crying, "Mommy, help me. I've been raped." I swear I heard the air swoosh out of the room. My heart stopped beating and yet it was pounding in my chest. My sleepy mind felt like it had been awakened by a bolt of lightning. I heard myself asking, "Where are you? Are you badly hurt? Have you called the police?" all the while pushing Mike out of bed and motioning for him to hurry and get dressed. Trying to sound calm, I told Jess to "Stay on the line. Don't hang up." She was sobbing into the phone, "Be careful, mommy. He might still be outside. He has a machete!"

As I have already said, Mike and I lived just three minutes from Jess' apartment. Her pleas to "Be careful! Be careful!" followed us and felt like a knife in our chests. As much as I anticipated the worst, nothing could have prepared me for the sight of my daughter's bruised and battered face. To this day, I have trouble verbalizing how I felt. "Dear God," I thought, "the Elephant Man. She looks like the Elephant Man."

Jessica was crouching behind the door to her apartment, shaking uncontrollably, as we entered the foyer. In the darkened space, it was difficult, at first, to see her. With pretend calmness, Mike led her to the sofa and examined her face. A retired doctor, he quickly checked her for injuries and then told me to call the police. I immediately dialed 911 and explained what had happened.

There are no words to express the gratitude we all feel toward the North Palm Beach Police Department officers and paramedics who arrived so quickly. We could not have asked for kinder, gentler, more professional men than these. Our daughter is a strong young woman. As you will learn in this story, she is alive because she remained calm and trusted her instincts.

When interviewed at the police station, she was able to provide the investigating detectives with so much information that formal identification of her attacker was never an issue.

The Attack:

At approximately 2:30 in the morning, Jessica was awakened by the sound of someone outside her door. Her dog, Kneesaa, barked as keys were inserted into the lock. As only Mike and I had an extra set, Jess assumed something had happened to one of us and the other was bearing bad news. Groggy though she was, she sat up in bed waiting for either Mike or me to enter. Within seconds, a dark man was standing at in the bedroom doorway—a machete in his hand. Later, we would learn that he had used a master key, easily accessible at the main office, to let himself in. Jess bolted from the bed but was thrown back, face down, and her hands zip tied behind her back. Although she pretended not to know the identity of her assailant, she immediately recognized him as the maintenance man who had repaired her air conditioner some three weeks earlier.

Telling the next part of the story always fills me with rage for had Mike and I followed our instincts, we might have spared our daughter the trauma that was about to happen. When Jess rented her apartment just five months prior, Mike tagged along when she went to the management office. You could say that he is very protective of his little girl. Being a cautious man, he specifically asked the manager if installing an extra lock was allowed. All we wanted was something that Jess could engage when she was home. "Absolutely not," he was told. "We must have complete access at all times."

Like the law-abiding people we are, we obeyed. Do not, I beg you, do not allow some random person to govern how you protect yourself. In retrospect, I realize how foolish we were to have entrusted our daughter's safety to strangers. With the benefit of hindsight, I know now that, although they threatened, they would never have evicted someone who paid their rent on time and maintained the apartment to perfection.

At the time Jessica's air conditioner was being repaired, she mentioned to Mike and me that she was uncomfortable with the repairman in the apartment. He had done nothing overt; they had not even had a conversation, but something in his demeanor had set off an alarm. Some of her concern may have been the result of the Blue Tooth he wore in his ear while working. Whenever it rang, which was often, it always played a popular rap song filled with angry lyrics. The song would later help to confirm his identification.

When her attacker entered her bedroom, Jessica was sleeping in a tee shirt and a pair of underwear. He rummaged in her dresser until he found a pair of shorts. Then, he forcibly put them on her. Shoving a pillowcase in her mouth, he dragged her, barefoot, her from the apartment, saying he needed money. According to his expressed plans, he was going to take her to an ATM so that she could withdraw cash.

For whatever reason, the attacker chose to drive Jess' sports car. Mostly like, he found it more appealing than his station wagon. As he pushed her into the passenger seat, Jess noticed that one zip tie had become loose. She waited until her attacker was behind the steering wheel, then she spit out the pillowcase and bolted from the car. She ran, screaming across the parking lot. Nobody—not one single person came to her aid, although later we were to learn that people had heard but chose to ignore her screams. At this point, I must implore you, the reader, not to turn a deaf ear should you hear cries of distress. You don't have to get directly involved but a phone call to the police could save a life and you would be a hero.

Bobby Broomfield, III, tackled Jessica into some bushes and dragged her behind one of the maintenance sheds. Jess is 5'10" tall and weighs about 125 pounds. Broomfield was 6'3" and weighed over 250 pounds. She tried her damnedest to fight him, but he laughed at her and taunted her by saying, "You must have taken self-defense. It won't do you any good."

During the struggle, Broomfield's gloved hands pulled at Jess' face, tearing her lips and mouth and causing damage that could only have resulted from a fierce punch. She fought like a tiger but, eventually, he subdued her enough to get the zip ties back on her wrists. This time he made them so tight that they cut into her wrists causing permanent nerve damage.

Rather than try driving Jess' car again, Broomfield now used his own car. On the front console, Jess noticed a Blue Tooth similar to the one the repair man had been wearing when fixing her air conditioner. Later, when Broomfield's cell phone rang, the song playing was the same rap tune.

Despite the fear she was feeling, Jess was aware that under stress, people often point a finger at the wrong person. She wanted to be sure that the man who was holding her captive was, indeed, the maintenance man. The ringing of the cell phone confirmed her suspicions.

After Broomfield strapped Jess into the seat, she noticed what appeared to be a dry cleaning bag on the floor. The sight of it sent shivers down her spine and rightly so. That bag would very shortly cause as much fear as the machete on the seat between them.

Based on Broomfield's quest for money, Jess thought they would now go to the bank. Instead, he took her to a vacant apartment and attempted to gain access with a large ring of keys he took from his pocket. None worked. Back into the car—this time to another vacant apartment near the Intracoastal Waterway. As Broomfield dragged her out of the car, he grabbed the plastic bag and asked tauntingly if she could swim. Jess' heart began to pound.

Due to proximity to the Intracoastal Waterway, Jessica feared Broomfield would throw her into the ocean with the bag over her head. Being a strong swimmer and a dive master, she began to plan her escape. She believed she could bring her legs up through her arms which would free her hands and allow her to rip off the plastic bag. Then, she could kick herself to the surface and, hopefully, to shore. Thinking drowning her was Broomfield's next move, she was shocked when he brought inside the vacant apartment and raped.

When talking to the investigators, Jessica was able to describe to the apartment in detail, including the construction lights set up in what she believed to be the living room. When the apartment was located, the police found her underwear and the plastic bag still in the room.

Once through with her, Broomfield dressed Jessica and again put her into his car. He began to drive aimlessly from town to town, sometimes going back to the apartment complex parking lot, where he would sit quietly in the car before leaving again. At some point, he noticed the damage to Jess' face. The pain from the punch she had taken in the parking lot was bad, but equally disturbing was the loss of feeling in her arms. Jess began to panic and the more upset she became, the more upset Broomfield became. Eventually, he panicked.

From the trunk of his car, he took a wire cutter and attempted to snip the zip ties. When the wire cutter did not work, he tried the blade of a saw, which also did not work. In his haste to cut through the zip ties, he cut Jessica's wrists, leaving blood on her hands and the car seat. When the saw was eventually found after his arrest, it still had traces of Jessica's blood on it. With Jessica's arms becoming numb and nothing he tried working, Broomfield drove to a gas station where he bought scissors. As he got out of the car, he told Jess not to run or he would shoot her.

With the cutting of the zip ties, Broomfield once again appeared calm. He started driving, this time stopping at random banks where he attempted to get money from the ATMs using Jess' bank card. When his requests for cash were denied, he accused her of giving him the wrong pin number. No matter how many times she explained that her account was with Bank of America, he kept stopping at other banks. Each time he stopped, he told her again that he would shoot her if she tried to escape. Jessica never saw a gun, but after what she had already experienced, a gun would have been no surprise.

After exhaustive pleading, Jessica finally convinced Broomfield to drive to a BOA and, there, he was able to get some money from her account. We learned, during the investigation, that not every bank has cameras on their ATM machines. Bank of America was one of them, at least at the location where the robbery took place. Another lesson learned the hard way. Luckily, the other banks where Broomfield stopped had cameras and he was caught on tape.

Eventually, Broomfield and Jessica returned to the complex and her apartment. I should have mentioned earlier that Jess' little dog had bitten Broomfield when he first came into the bedroom. Since he was wearing gloves, her bite was meaningless. However, angry that she had attacked him, he grabbed the dog, wrapped her in a sheet and left the room, machete in hand. All throughout the ordeal, Jess assumed the dog was dead. The only bright spot upon her return to the apartment was seeing Kneesaa quivering under the living room sofa.

Once inside the apartment, Jess, again thinking ahead, offered Broomfield a bottle of beer. During the night's he had talked on and on about himself and his family. He told Jess that his favorite beer was Sam Adams—the same kind she had in the refrigerator. On the pretext of being thirsty, she asked if she could get a drink of water and offered him a bottle. Her reasoning was that if he did drink the beer, his DNA would be on the rim. Unfortunately, he refused, preferring instead to molest her in the kitchen where they stood. When he tired of that, he pushed her back into the bedroom where he raped her twice more.

Details are important. During the course of the night, Broomfield would often bang his head on the steering wheel and state that he had to kill Jessica because she knew who he was. Jessica was adamant that she had not looked at him and did not recognize his voice. When he asked why she did not look at him, she said she did not want to know who he was. It took some time, but she was able to convince him that she truly did not recognize him.

Over the three plus hours they were together, Broomfield grew comfortable talking to Jessica. He told her many, many details about his life—the kinds of details that only a close personal friend would know. He even programmed her cell number into his phone and showed her pictures of his children. Jess learned that he was their sole support.

One minute Broomfield would be convinced that he had to kill Jessica, and the next, he was planning to return the money he had stolen on a weekly basis, leaving $100.00 on her doorstep each Friday. He asked what her plans were for the rest of her day. She told him that she and I were going to the beach, and he asked to join us. Then, again, he would bang his head on the steering wheel and say he had to kill her.

The teeter tooter of life and death plagued Jessica all those hours. She silently prayed, "Please, God, if he is going to kill me, let it be fast. Please, don't make me suffer any more than I already have." Certain that she would die, Jess was begging for mercy.

When Broomfield had finally abused her enough, he insisted that Jess take a shower. He sat on the lid of the toilet, machete in hand, and made sure she washed thoroughly. At a loss for what to do next, he began again to say he needed to kill her. Jess, keeping her wits about her, talked about his children and how much they needed him. "Who," she asked, "will care for them if you kill me and go to jail. They need you."

Broomfield responded that he would go to jail anyway because she would call the police. Again, Jess stayed calm and told him she only wanted the night to be over. She promised she would not call the police or her parents. For whatever reason, Broomfield believed her. He asked, "So, we good?" "Yes," she assured him, "we are good." And he was gone. She locked the door and called me.

The investigation and the trial took two years to complete— two years to relive daily, publicly and privately, the horrors of July 1, 2007. Two years during which emotional scabs would form and be picked away over and over again.

The hours that followed the attack were almost as horrific as the ordeal itself. The verbal reliving of the event to the police officers first on the scene and then the retelling to the detective assigned to the case—each time Jessica repeated her story she felt like she was being raped all over again.

If you think a visit to the gynecologist is embarrassing, try having a rape kit done. Doctors, nurses, victim's advocates… all there for your benefit but none the less invading your privacy.

The female detective assigned to Jessica's case has our undying gratitude. Detective Stephanie Joyce is an amazing woman and the most professional member of any police force I have ever met. From the moment she arrived at the hospital, she took control, protecting Jessica from everyone not directly involved in her care. She was very stern with the emergency room doctor who continually overstepped his responsibilities.

The victim's advocates were and are an incredible group of women. The first one to arrive at the hospital brought clean clothes and underwear, a toothbrush and other necessities to make Jessica comfortable. She remained until relieved by her successor, who stayed with Jessica throughout questioning at police headquarters and during the traumatic face-to-face identification of her attacker.

Two of the three police officers who first responded to the 911 call lived in the same apartment complex as Jessica. One of them lived just five doors away from Jess' unit. These men took the case very personally. As Jessica was certain she knew the identity of her attacker, the officers promised they would have him behind bars before the night was over. They kept their word.

Our criminal justice system moves at a tedious and frustrating pace. Motions and more motions were filed; postponement after postponement became the norm. Our hopes for a speedy trial were constantly being raised and then dashed. Broomfield's family hired a private attorney but he didn't last long. He then went through a series of five public defenders. Each time, the trial date was set back months. Plea deals were offered and rejected, which, on some level, pleased Jessica. She never wanted to allow Broomfield to get off easy. As difficult as it would be to relive that night at a trial in front of a courtroom full of strangers, Jessica was willing to endure it. She wanted other women to know that there is no shame in being raped. "Come forward," she wanted to yell. "Stand proud. Hold your head up!" That is exactly what she did.

The trial, which was supposed to take no more than three days, lasted two weeks. The court system is not a well-oiled machine. Delays are a constant. The outstanding case presented by Barbara Burns, the

Assistant State Attorney, the evidence collected by the crime scene unit and the testimony of the police officers and detectives assigned to the investigation were beyond reproach.

Combined with Broomfield's own condemning statement at his time of arrest, the state's case was more than strong. However, no matter how confident we were, the outcome depended on six strangers who sat and listened, showing no emotion, during the long hours court was in session. Three men and three women—different in every way. What were they thinking?

The final morning of trial was tense for everyone. Jessica's friends and our family had been present every day. Numerous members of the police department, even those not directly assigned to the case, showed their support by their presence in the courtroom. When both sides rested their case, the judge, another amazing woman, released the jury for deliberation. The rest of us went to lunch but no one really ate. We wandered the streets … walking and waiting.

In less than two hours, we were summoned back to court. The jury had reached a verdict. Broomfield had been charged with three counts of sexual battery with a weapon, kidnapping with bodily harm, burglary, robbery with a weapon and larceny. He was convicted of three counts of armed sexual battery, one count of burglary while armed, one count of false imprisonment, one count of robbery and one count of trespass. We felt no sense of victory.

The prosecutor assured us that conviction on just one of the armed sexual battery charges carried a mandatory life sentence. We went home happy that Jessica would be safe from this predator forever. As I wrote earlier, the criminal justice system is not a well-oiled machine. What is the law one day can easily change the next. By the time of sentencing, ninety days later, the mandatory sentence was no longer in effect. Now, we were dependent upon the judge to determine what constituted fair punishment.

As is common at a sentencing hearing, family and friends from both sides are permitted to make a statement, which the judge listens to politely but probably ignores. Having heard all the testimony, I am sure that Judge Smith had already reached a decision before her gavel struck court in session.

Regardless, Jessica and I, the designated speakers, were determined to plead our case. Jessica, knowing she would not be able to control her emotions, wrote the following letter, which she read in court.

Dear Judge Smith:

For as long as I can remember, July has always been one of my favorite months. The fourth was not just a day to celebrate our country's birthday; it was the day our family gathered to celebrate our love and kinship. Red, white and blue signified patriotism and loyalty not blood and bruises. Now, July is the month I celebrate being alive.

Judge Smith, having presided over this case, I know you are well familiar with the facts of my kidnapping and rape at the hands of Bobby Broomfield, III. What I would like to do in this letter is tell you about the changes in my life since the attack.

I no longer live alone. I want to but am terrified that, no matter how many locks are on my door, someone will break in. At 29, I should have my own home—a place to put my feet up at the end of the workday, to entertain friends, to give myself a facial in privacy if that is what I want to do. Instead, I have reverted to being a child, living with my parents, calling my father to meet me in the driveway so I don't have to walk to the front door alone, begging my parents not to stay out too late after dark. Dreading the nightmares that plague my sleep, I have barely closed my eyes for two years. Yes, I could take sleeping pills but then I might become dependent and complicate an already complicated life.

Therapy helps for a few hours, sometimes for a day or so. I have attended sessions once a week since the attack, but when evening comes, I am once again alone and fearing for my life. I want to stop shaking! I want not to be afraid! I want not to crawl out of my skin every time a dog barks or a tree branch hits the window!

Relationships are so difficult. You need trust to even begin the process of dating. I don't trust. I am no longer tolerant of human failings. If a man doesn't meet my expectations—and only a saint could – he doesn't get a second chance. I want a family. My parents would like grandchildren. Neither is going to happen when everyone I meet is found lacking because of my trust issues. I fear never finding anyone who will understand that my tough exterior is a façade—a barrier set up to protect myself. I am incapable of letting it down and allowing someone else in. I don't like who I have become but am unable to change.

Only those closest to me—my mom and dad, my brother, my relatives and friends—know that the happiness on my face each day is part of my makeup. Apply lipstick. Smile. It's hard work to pretend to be carefree but, as kind as most people are, they really don't want to be burdened with my sorrow. As a result, I've never really grieved for the loss of innocence, security, trust and independence. Grieving is weak. I'm afraid to be weak.

For a few days, immediately after Mr. Broomfield was convicted, I began to see a ray of hope. Why? Because I mistakenly believed that some of the charges carried a mandatory life sentence. Now, I know that the length of time he serves rests with you. I don't want to be vindictive, but I do want justice. There will never be a day that I do not remember what happened.

I will always see the machete pressed up against my cheek. I will always feel the zip ties pulled tight around my wrists. I will always taste my blood in my mouth. I will eventually require surgery for my injuries—more scars. I will be a prisoner of these events for the rest of my life. Mr. Broomfield should be a prisoner for just as long.

Judge Smith, I ask you to sentence Bobby Broomfield, III to the maximum allowable under the law. I beg you to send a message to other predators that abuses such as these will not be tolerated in our society. Thank you.

When my turn came, I spoke directly to Judge Smith saying, "When Jessica was attacked, my son asked me how God could allow one of his angels to be hurt so badly. Jessica is as close to an angel on this earth as you will find. She is a sweet, kind, caring young woman with a warm and giving nature. Prior to the attack, she always had a smile on her face and a twinkle in her eyes. Now, the smile is most often replaced by a look of puzzlement and the twinkle, well, it faded, along with her smile, on that Sunday morning. Mr. Broomfield did not just kidnap and rape Jessica. He took a part of her soul. He stole freedom and independence. He stole trust and the dream of happy ever after. Jessica suffered injuries that will eventually require surgery.

There is no surgery to repair the damage to her mental and emotional state.

Just five months prior to the attack, Jessica moved into her apartment—the apartment Mr. Broomfield broke into. She was so excited to have a place of her own—a place to decorate and to entertain friends. Together we shopped for furniture and planned menus. We had so much fun.

Now Jessica lives with her father and me and although we are there all the time, at night she locks her bedroom door not for privacy—for protection. In the morning, it breaks my heart to see the dark circles under her eyes and the haggard look on her face. She has barely slept in two years.

To the court, this case is a sexual assault but to our family it is a homicide. Mr. Broomfield effectively used the machete he carried to take away a part of Jessica's life. She is no longer the daughter we knew and I doubt that time will give her back to us. If Jessica has to suffer pain for the rest of her life, then Mr. Broomfield should have to pay with the rest of his life. He should not be allowed an opportunity to victimize other women.

Emily Bronte wrote, "I have dreamed in my life dreams that have stayed with me ever after and have changed my ideas. They have gone through and through me and altered the color of my mind." Jessica's dreams are nightmares that affect every aspect of her life. They have not only altered her perception. They have changed the very essence of who she is. Judge Smith, my husband and I would like to have our daughter back, and only you can give her to us by guaranteeing that Bobby Broomfield, III will never hurt her or any other woman again."

Perhaps, Judge Smith really did listen. She sentenced Broomfield to life in prison without parole plus 35 years. I wish I could say that justice being served worked a miracle and all the pain and suffering of the past two years went away. That didn't happen, but the healing process has begun. Jessica no longer constantly looks over our shoulder in fear. She has begun to smile real smiles once again. She is dating and beginning to trust.

Jessica's story is filled with women of strong character.

Starting with Jessica, herself, they include Lieutenant Stephanie Joyce of the North Palm Beach Police Department and Liisa Spinello and Deliah Roman, the victim's advocates who befriended and supported her. Randee Speciale, the therapist who saw her through the darkest days, deserves special recognition, as does Barbara Burns, the awe-inspiring Assistant State's Attorney, and the amazing Judge Amy Smith. At her side always were her good friends, Mary Bedwell Bain and Carin Muley. With these women to look up to, how can we not stand tall and proud.

On her wrist, over the deepest scar left by the zip ties, Jessica has a teal blue ribbon tattoo. If you ask her why, she'll tell you, "Since I have to remember what happened for the rest of my life, I want to remember that I survived."

#

Update: In 2011, Jessica married Kevin McKinney in a beautiful ceremony that included her best friend, Mary Bedwell Bain, and Mary's daughter, Samantha. Jessica and Kevin now have a two-year old son, Blake Thomas. He is a beautiful child… a pure joy and gift which none of us take lightly. Today, just as I was editing this portion of the manuscript, Jessica informed me that another baby is on the way… a girl! While there may not be pots of gold at the end of the rainbow, there are definitely miracles being wrought all around us.

The End